PENGUIN BOOKS

THE VISION OF ELENA SILVES

'At the heart of the novel is a love story which has lasted more than twenty years between a young girl of Portuguese extraction and Gabriel, the student grandson of a Chinese indentured labourer. Elena is a devout Catholic, Gabriel a Marxist: it is, as it were, Romeo and Juliet in a modern political setting. They represent the two different strains which promise hope in the bereaved and wasted land . . . the result is an admirably rich and serious novel which appeals both to the intelligence and the aesthetic sense' – Allan Massie in *The Scotsman*

'A meditation on the transcendence of human love over the coercions of church and state . . . which points to the sovereignty of love amid the warring clamour of Catholicism and Communism . . . a quietly compelling achievement' – Anthony Quinn in the *Independent*

'Wily clerics, town loafers, beggars, passionate women revolutionaries, sadistic police . . . Shakespeare's ability to create atmosphere, to swaddle you completely in the stifling world poised between two cultures is unsurpassed' – Mary Hope in the *Financial Times*

'The picture of Peru which one takes away is of a society exhausted by four hundred years of oppression and decline . . . Scrupulous research and a delight in the exotica of jungle culture combine in one of the best books about the continent written by an outsider' – John Melmoth in the *Sunday Times*

D1289636

About the author:

Nicholas Shakespeare was born in 1957 and is the literary editor of the *Daily Telegraph*. The son of a diplomat, he has lived in South America on and off for twenty years, first working as a gaucho and later pursuing Sendero Luminoso guerrillas in the Peruvian Andes. The *Sunday Times* described his Granta article on the Sendero Luminoso and their reclusive leader, Abimael Guzman, as 'an enthralling piece of investigative journalism . . . in the tradition of Graham Greene'. His work for television includes *The Evelyn Waugh Trilogy* (BBC 2), *Cover to Cover* (BBC 2) and *Iquitos* (Channel 4). He is the author of *Londoners*, which has been described by Michael Moorcock as 'one of the best books on London I've read, if not the best contemporary book'.

The Vision of Elena Silves, his first novel, won a Somerset Maugham Award for 1990.

NICHOLAS SHAKESPEARE

THE VISION OF ELENA SILVES

Chinua Asime

December 1994

PENGUIN BOOKS

PENGUIN BOOKS

Published by the Penguin Group
Penguin Books Ltd, 27 Wrights Lane, London w8 5tz, England
Viking Penguin, a division of Penguin Books USA Inc.
375 Hudson Street, New York, New York 10014, USA
Penguin Books Australia Ltd, Ringwood, Victoria, Australia
Penguin Books Canada Ltd, 2801 John Street, Markham, Ontario, Canada l3r 1b4
Penguin Books (NZ) Ltd, 182–190 Wairau Road, Auckland 10, New Zealand

Penguin Books Ltd, Registered Offices: Harmondsworth, Middlesex, England

First published in Great Britain by Collins Harvill 1989
Published in Penguin Books 1990
3 5 7 9 10 8 6 4 2

This is a work of fiction, although the story of Ezequiel is based on my research
into the Shining Path guerrillas of Abimael Guzmán, which culminated in an
article for *Granta* magazine in 1988. For my account of the 1965 insurgency, I
have drawn on Richard Gott's *Guerrilla Movements in Latin America* (Nelson,
1970), and for the San Francisco massacre, on Amnesty International's report,
"'Disappearances', torture and summary executions by government forces after
the prison revolt of June 1986". I am indebted to John Hemming for his chapter
on Messianic movements in *Amazon Frontier* (Macmillan, 1987) and to Karen
Armstrong for her guidance in religious matters. The words of "I'll be seeing
you" are used by permission of Redwood Music Ltd., 14 New Burlington Street,
London w1x 2lr.
I would also like to thank the monks of La Recoleta monastery in Arequipa
where I spent a retreat. I cannot name the priest I would like to thank most
because he lives in the dangerous thick of it all. N.S.

Printed in England by Clays Ltd, St Ives plc

In memory of Bruce Chatwin

I'll be seeing you
In all the old familiar places
That this heart of mine embraces
All day through.
In the small café,
The park across the way,
The children's carousel,
The chestnut trees, the wishing well.
I'll be seeing you
In every lovely summer's day
In everything that's light and gay
I'll always think of you that way.
I'll find you in the morning sun
And when the night is new,
I'll be looking at the moon,
But I'll be seeing you.

(Irving Kahal and Sammy Fain 1938.
Recorded by Frank Sinatra 1961.)

Part One

1983

Chapter 1

IT IS EARLY MORNING in Belén. The jungle is quiet. The sky over the rooftops stretches clear and colourless, except for a red clawmark where the day has pounced.

The air is so fresh you want to inhale it in deep breaths. It smells of copa de oro.

Apart from the tented shape of Sebastián under his black hood and Vásquez washing his barrow by the cathedral steps, the square is empty.

An old man emerges from the corner of Calle Raimondi. He crosses the road to where Sebastián huddles beside a pile of newspapers. Aware of his approach, Sebastián holds up a yellow bucket and rattles it. The percussion of small change is the only sound in the street.

The old man throws in a coin and takes a newspaper from the pavement. He folds it under his arm and shuffles towards the bench under the statue in the middle of the square. In one hand he carries a large canvas bag; in the other a handkerchief. He is about to wipe the surface of the bench when he notices that instead of dew it is covered in blood-red beads. Putting down his bag he reaches out for one. He holds it to the light. He finds himself looking at a dead cattle-fly, half an inch long, the same colour as the sun.

"Colihuachos," he says to himself, throwing it back among the other flies. They lie there as if a string has broken on a necklace. They cover the bench, the ground in front and the flower beds behind.

The old man brushes them off the seat with his handkerchief. He shakes the cloth, replaces it up his sleeve and sits down.

He is Don Leopoldo.

He wears no hat and his face is lined, as if he has walked into a spider's web and forgotten to wipe it away. His love of precise dates and proven facts has earned him a reputation for being a little pedantic. He knows more than is necessarily interesting about the yellow cathedral, its cartridge-shaped windows, its Swiss-made clock; about the origin of the tiles on the old Palace Hotel and about Admiral Grau, the man in whom Peru had once put all her hope, whose bronze whiskers bristle defiantly as if he is still on the deck of the *Huáscar*.

This morning, the flies on the Admiral's head and epaulettes have the appearance of laurel leaves.

Don Leopoldo looks beyond the statue to the metal house opposite, its roof stained with the sun. He can tell anyone who cares to listen – fewer and fewer nowadays – about this house, constructed by Eiffel for the Paris Exhibition of 1896, dismantled for its voyage to another continent altogether, and then transported two thousand miles upriver from Pará to be reassembled, bolt by bolt, for an absentee rubber lord.

The Club de Leones has since moved its premises to a floor above the Banco Industrial, but Don Leopoldo remembers when the members played their poker in Eiffel's folly, drinking bottles of Allsopp's Pale Ale in a hot metal room like an oven.

El Club de los Pájaros Muertos, they called it.

He gazes at Eiffel's house and the buckled pillar into which a car has crashed. It upsets him no one has repaired it. These days he finds it easy to be upset. That's what happens when you are a dead parrot with long memories. Don Leopoldo can remember a time when there was no cathedral and women walked beside the open drains holding geranium-scented handkerchiefs to their noses. He remembers the town in the days when you bought your clothes from Don Ramur – Scotch tweed, alpaca, boaters; when the ice cream you ate in the Booth supermarket came all the way from Liverpool; when the port you drank with Orestes Minero in the Café Nanay was Taylor's finest, shipped from Pinhão.

Now the river is silting up and no boats come from Europe. Now you bought your shirts off the pavement and they had crocodiles on the pockets. Now in the café they hold aerobics classes.

The cobweb tightens on Don Leopoldo's face. They don't even keep photographs of the old town, to remind people it was a town of millionaires and palaces, not of soldiers who have appropriated the

Palace Hotel and let it collapse about them. Instead of picking their noses, they should be restoring the chipped Evora azulejos. They should be repairing the fine ironwork and scrubbing the frescoed ceilings instead of straining their eyes upriver to Ecuador. Besides, who would invade Peru nowadays?

Live for today, forget about yesterday, then show your money with a fanfaronade and wait for the next boom.

As an historian, Don Leopoldo finds this recipe for life unworthy of Peruvians. But to be a Peruvian. What does that signify to the world outside? Nothing.

Don Leopoldo speaks harshly of his countrymen because he loves the land that gave them birth. As a young man he maintained the time had come for Peru to produce her popular historian. A man who could liberate the country from its cosy, obfuscating myths. A man such as Admiral Grau or Lord Cochrane who could ignite the masses like the blue touch paper on a firework. A man who could show them the path they should take by illuminating the path by which they had come.

As a young man he had wished for himself that role.

As an old man he regrets that he prepared himself for it by first writing a *History of the Colonization of Belén*.

At the end of each day since the day of that decision, he has returned to his room and added another manuscript sheet to the disorderly mound by his bed. Don Leopoldo's lucubrations pile up to several thousand pages. These are the pages which every morning, and in no particular order, he stuffs into the mouth of his green bag and carries to the bench.

Often he is influenced by what has been discussed on the bench. Sometimes his companions remind him of things he has quite forgotten. Sometimes they tell him of things he never knew. Always he tries to be on his guard with what they have said. But at night he is not entirely able to shake their voices from his head. Indeed, he sometimes has the uncomfortable impression that what he writes is a mingling of their voices.

Don Leopoldo's *History of the Colonization of Belén* has taken a decade or two more than ideally he would have wished. He convinces himself it is lacking only a final chapter (on the territorial dispute with Ecuador, with a commentary on Gregory XVI's Bull of 2 June 1843 recognizing Peru's right over the diocese of Soreto). Plus an index, of course.

He has given up hope that when complete it will immortalize his name and cause the jungle round about to break out in psalms.

His magnum opus has taken so long because Don Leopoldo finds it easy to be diverted by parallel research. Not a day passes without him making copious notes from some historical journal. By now, even Don Leopoldo considers it unlikely he will survive to embark on the project that would have swept the reader back to the time of the Incas, to a Golden Age when there were no thieves or idle men or adulterous women, when a man who ravished a virgin was buried alive.

Clearer than the outline of Don Leopoldo's thesis is the melancholy which originally informed it (and which he attributes, erroneously, to Portuguese saudade). Although he has with some pride traced his ancestry to a learned quinologist from Ceuta, he feels the blemish of his European blood. It is sad beyond the power of Don Leopoldo's expression to contemplate the arrival of the bearded men from Spain.

After the Age of Gold, the Age of Manure.

What could be expected of a country whose fortunes were built on the violet grey sap of a tree and mountain upon mountain of birdshit?

"No wonder the only people who flourish are terrucos," he murmurs to himself. The only terruco he has time for is Lord Cochrane.

At night, looking into the kerosene lamp, Don Leopoldo can hear the sound of Lord Cochrane muffling his oars on the evening of 5 November 1820. In the flame he hears him creep towards the Spanish flagship *Esmeralda* whose spars are cracks in the darkness. He hears him whisper to his men (the same number, he notes, as had taken Peru three centuries before). "One hour of courage and resolution," he is saying, "is all that is required for you to triumph." The promise stirs them. Don Leopoldo, dressed in white and pike in hand, lifts his tense face to the night where the 44-gun frigate rolls gently in the fog.

But the courageous, resolute men around him don't need an hour. Cochrane and his patriots need only fifteen minutes to board and capture Spain's impregnable flagship (guarded by 27 gunboats and 300 shore guns) and so finally slip cable on the royalists, those pig-farming illiterates who had destroyed a perfect civilization.

Had he wished it, as Don Leopoldo wishes it for him, Lord Cochrane could have been first Admiral of Peru. It is sad that no one else except Grau, sixty years after him, has seized such an opportunity for Peru to be faithful to herself.

The sadness has a cumulative effect on Don Leopoldo. More and more often as he puts on his jacket in the mornings, he wonders if he still has the strength to walk the two blocks to the square. One day the effort will be too much. Who will then wipe the dew from the bench, or the cattle-flies?

This is his favourite hour of the day, when the only voice on the bench is his own, when the square is empty and silent and he can imagine the town as it has been, before it is overcome by the noise of cars and ant-headed motorbikes and buses which, because of the drowsing heat, have no glass in their windows. His eyes water as they move over the buildings – the Bishop's palace, the cathedral, the Zumate pharmacy and Pía Zumate's small hotel on the corner of Raimondi which shares a recessed entrance, always in deep shadow, with the Café Nanay.

His eyes are lingering on the hotel when they catch a movement at a window on the top floor. Don Leopoldo swears he sees a face looking out of the half-open louvres. Before he can make it out, the face has vanished.

"So," he says aloud. "The soft-shoe artist is back."

The movement at the window has ruffled his day-dream. He unfolds his paper. He begins reading.

He has reached *El Oriente*'s leader (on the economic consequences of the current called El Niño) when a second man arrives and sits down next to him. He wears a brown alpaca cardigan and a jipijapa panama that curls at the edges like a leaf. It is made of a straw so fine it can pass through a wedding ring.

This is Don Wenceslau.

He is a thin man with bony shoulders. The creases about his crotch imitate those about his eyes. They are eyes as red as the spirit he buys from Don Vásquez's barrow.

"How many tributaries has the Amazon, Don Leopoldo?"

"Eleven thousand and eighteen."

Don Wenceslau must know each one of them. If he can paddle off on a tangent, he will. He is a story-teller, a lover of red herrings, but they are best caught before lunch when he starts on Vásquez's masato. Until midday, his hangover makes him lucid and he can tell stories even Don Leopoldo listens to with interest. The square is his theatre. As he speaks, he points at things which transform themselves into his narrative. So the yellow copa de oro bushes behind them become the Nanay, the clock in the cathedral tower becomes the moon, the bronze Admiral becomes Christ descending into the Cocha and Vásquez's barrow the house of stone discovered in the jungle, where no stone exists and where chickens nest on an alabaster staircase.

Don Wenceslau sits down heavily. He greets Don Leopoldo. He has a stomachache, he says. He holds his head.

"Never eat cebiche at night, Don Leopoldo, that's my advice." It is not the first time Don Leopoldo has heard it.

"No sign of García?"

"Not yet."

"Probably had a night of it with his whores at the Teletroca." The copa de oro bushes rustle behind them. A man breaks cover.

"Not whores, Wenceslau, princesses," he says. He sits down next to Don Wenceslau, crosses his legs and stretches an arm along the back of the bench. In his face there are the remnants of a good-looking man. The finest feature is a moustache. Its greyness matches the colour of the felt trilby cocked rakishly over his nose. From his breast pocket tumbles a bright red handkerchief.

He is Don García, the singer and a devoted Donizettian. Listening to Donizetti he is almost persuaded to be a Christian. He believes the Italian rescued music from the dissipation into which it sank after that barbarian Rossini – that Marat of melody who would set a laundry list to music – broke the unities. Sometimes, to fill a rare silence, he treats his two companions to an aria from *Lucia di Lammermoor*.

Don García is ever in search of similes to describe life as he sees it – afresh each day – in this square. His temperament gives rise to flights of operatic fancy, such as his belief – though Don Leopoldo assures him repeatedly it is out of the question – that Caruso once sang at the Alhambra in the role of Lord Henry Ashton.

Don García's eyes cannot help prancing over the road to the site of this theatre where on the night of 24 October 1927 the receptionist fell asleep with her cigarette between the pages of Ouspensky's *Tertium Organum* (and where ten years later the celluloid overheated during a showing of *The Rubber Man's Daughter*). On each occasion the place was burnt to a cinder.

Don García does not see the grassed-over stage occupied by three chickens and a derelict bus. He sees the dado mosaic floor, the spangled velvet curtains, the massive backdrops, the castles rising from landscaped gardens. He does not mind that this backdrop was used whatever the work: opera, film, or pantomime. He never minded either when a French company performed *Così fan tutte* and Don Alfonso's beard fell off; nor when in the love scene the chaise longue slid into the orchestra pit and broke the legs of a Swedish cellist (nor when the shoes of the prompter appeared under the curtain). He never minded because he is a man for whom disbelief suspends as easily as that curtain. Which is why he imagines every now and then, when the wind from the river is right, he can hear the opening notes from "Una furtiva làgrima".

Don García is also a picaflor. He likes women. He more than likes them. He adores them. He remembers, before the Alhambra burnt down a second time, when money was in pound sterling and you could get a girl for the price of the handkerchief in his pocket. He spent a lot on handkerchiefs. All men were children of Adam, he used to say then. It was the silk that made the difference.

Now the girls never look at him. But it doesn't prevent him, if a pretty one walks by, from arranging his face to look mysterious, haughty, someone of infinite possibility, when he knows in his heart that all the girl sees is a piece of flotsam on a bench. Or three old men on a bench.

They sit here in the same position every day, the singer, the drinker, the local historian. Three narrators watching over the same scene. No one can hope to cross the square without their knowledge. From the glimpses of those who pass by they concoct whole lives.

"What's this?" says Don Wenceslau, noticing for the first time the dead flies at his feet. He picks one up at the second attempt. He caresses the ruddy wings.

"They're colihuachos," says Don Leopoldo.

Don Wenceslau frowns. "And what is a colihuacho?"

Don Leopoldo tells him.

Don Wenceslau looks closer at the bloodsucking cattle-fly. He imagines its journey from the southern lakes, over the desert and the Andes to the cathedral square in the jungle.

"El Niño?"

Don Leopoldo nods. He passes *El Oriente* to him, his finger on the headlines. "And it's getting worse. The worst in memory, they say." He taps the paper again. "If you can believe it, and I'm not sure I can. Floods on the coast, crocodiles in the sea, plants never before seen springing up in the desert. Worse and worse. Like the terrorists." He pauses. "You hear they've blacked out Piura?"

"Vásquez told me."

"Calling themselves the Shining Path – then leaving everyone in darkness."

"Chimbote, Puno, Tacna," recites Don Wenceslau. "Soon it'll be every department in Peru."

"Not Soreto."

"No, not Soreto. Not yet, anyway."

"You wait," says Don García, from the other end. "I saw Lieutenant Velarde last night. He spoke as if terrucos are behind every carob tree. He said the police and the military have reached the end of their patience. He said they only need one small excuse – and boom."

"Velarde has got to catch them first," says Don Wenceslau whose distaste for men in uniform is well documented on this bench. "And

Velarde never caught anything except a fever."

"They'll catch them," says Don García. "They always catch them."

"I don't know," mutters Don Leopoldo. "There's something about these terrorists . . ." Something which made him frightened for his country.

"They caught the terruco that came from Belén," observes Don García. "They caught Gabriel Rondón Lung."

"Gabriel Rondón Lung." Don Leopoldo tries each word slowly. "The Chino."

Don García nods. "The one in prison in Lima. Remember him? The one who screwed up Velarde's promotion."

"I don't remember the terrorist," says Don Leopoldo.

Don Wenceslau obliges him. His head is clearing. "He was a tall man. But you know what they say. Tall men steal light bulbs."

"I'm well aware of his height, Wenceslau. What I meant is that I never thought he would turn out as he did."

"So good looking," agrees Don García. "Every girl in Belén – their mothers too – he could have had any of them . . ."

"But he didn't, did he?" says Don Wenceslau.

"No, he did not," Don García sighs, overwhelmed suddenly by a sense of waste. "No. He kept his Chinese eyes for Elena Colina Silves."

The name is a spell that sends the three men into silence. They think of that handsome young couple, kissing on the bench opposite, leaning over the Malecón's balustrade to watch the ships sail by, elevated by memory into the envy of Belén.

"I forget what happened to him when she was taken away," says Don Wenceslau. "Didn't he vanish too? Do you have any idea?"

Don García leans forward. His eyes are shining.

"If I had been him," he says, unable at that moment to find a suitable model in Donizetti and thinking instead of Verdi's troubadour, "I would have gone knocking on the doors of every convent and religious institution in Peru until I found her. And that, I imagine, is what he did."

"That's more than 1700 doors," calculates Don Leopoldo. He has never concealed his opinion that the only thing capable of being set to Don García's music is nonsense. "He didn't come back for, let me see, another fifteen years. That's 150 doors a year. Possible, I suppose," he adds in a manner suggesting he thought it wasn't.

Don Wenceslau, who would like to think that melody and speech sometimes belonged together, says: "Isn't it more probable he spent those years with Ezequiel? I read that some of those terrucos spent at least fifteen years training for their revolution."

Don Leopoldo snorts. If only his *History* had taken that time. The time it has taken has given the local historian a contempt for the quotidian. In Don Leopoldo's eyes, men were either books or newspapers. The man next to him was a newspaper. "You oughtn't to believe everything in *El Oriente*," he says.

Don Wenceslau snaps open the first page again. "'El Niño – the worst in living memory'," he reads. "'Record rainfall in Lima. Arequipa and Silar two months now without rain.' You can't imagine it, can you, sitting here?" he says, smelling the inky blooms of the copa de oro and casting his eyes to the untroubled sky. "You can't imagine, at the end of February, that somewhere they've still got El Niño."

Don Leopoldo thinks of the stream known as the Child because it comes at Christmas. He thinks of the hot-headed current crawling every seven years along the coast. He thinks of it elbowing Humboldt's cold drift with all its pescado and pejerrey into the Pacific, beyond the reach of fishermen and guano birds.

"Not even the Christ child caused so much damage," he says.

Don Wenceslau turns to Don Leopoldo. "If you ask me, that's why the terrucos have spared Belén. Our climate. They'd just go off to the Teletroca with García here and that would be that."

Don Leopoldo points to the ground. "So, explain the colihuachos."

Don Wenceslau looks at the dead flies which have tumbled from the sky's belly.

"Ah, the colihuachos. Yes, well." His eyes return to the page. They alight on a paragraph from a correspondent on the coast. "It says here that in their nets men have discovered feathered fish."

"Journalism," says Don Leopoldo.

Chapter 2

THE SIMPLEST WAY to reach Lima's Establecimiento Penal San Francisco is to take one of the crowded collectivo buses from the Inca market. A thirty-five-minute journey along a featureless highway brings you to the northern outskirts of the city. A narrow dirt road, sandwiched between several stalls of avocado pears and sometimes hard to find, leads to San Francisco's entrance.

It is a low prison made from brown brick that merges into the sandhills. During El Niño, the only way for the water to drain was down these hills. The water washed everything in its path – Gloria milk tins, husks of maize, empty bottles of battery fluid – until the detritus of the surrounding shanty-towns slopped against the prison walls and became home to the dogs and buzzards that rooted there day and night, infuriating the guards so much that the towers rang out with the shooting matches they held whenever the Governor took the puddled road into town to be straddled by his mistress.

That Tuesday morning a man joined the friends, relations and lawyers walking up the hill. He was small and square, with brilliantined hair that fell over his ears in dark coils. He walked a pace or two behind the group, looking at his feet and hopping across the rivulets.

One of the avocado women watched him leave the stall where he sheltered from the rain. She called over to a friend. She pointed at the man's receding back, bowed into a dirty leather jacket.

"Palanca," she called. Substitute.

The avocado women knew that in an hour's time when the group came down again, it would not include that man. But in a few minutes they would be passed by another, on his own, who wouldn't be looking at his feet but at the sky, who would start with fright at unexpected sounds.

Sometimes, when the avocado women saw such a man, they liked to shout.

At the main entrance to San Francisco, the man in the leather jacket separated from the others and made his way to a metal door at the side of the prison. He knocked, waited, then knocked again.

The door opened.

Someone emerged, walking in rapid steps down the hill.

He entered.

He walked through a number of green doors, each guarded by a uniformed man on a stool who rose in silence and drew back the bolt. He counted six of these men. Bolt, open, clang. Bolt, open, clang. Bolt, open, clang. Bolt, open, clang. Bolt, open, clang. The last guard wasn't sitting, but scrubbing the concrete floor with a brush. The brush had few bristles and made a scraping sound on the concrete. The concrete was dark with shit, mud and water from the feet of those passing through the sixth door. The man knew once he went through that door, he was on his own.

The only time a guard went through that door was to shoot.

Clang.

The door led into a large open compound. Despite the rain, it was crowded with prisoners. Camarada Edith had described to him the kind of prisoner – pick-pockets from the bull-ring, narco-traffickers from the Huallaga who continued to deal in cocaine paste, murderers, lunatics, innocents.

One or two wore plastic bags over their heads and shoulders. Most did not. They sat with their backs to the brown wall, drenched and glistening, like the animals rooting through the rubbish on the other side. They wore few clothes. The only life came from their eyes, pickled by cocaine or potato-skin alcohol, which licked over him as he stood by the door. He could smell the brutality. It was even stronger than the smells emanating from the soaking pyramids of excrement. These mounds rose from the mud wherever he looked.

He clenched his hands into his jacket pockets. He began walking.

"Two dormitories lead immediately off the recreation ground. You want the one on the right."

As he picked his way through the pools of water to the building, fewer people stood in his path. Those that stared before moving aside were neater dressed and cleaner. Their faces weren't dazed by pasta básica. They were forbidding in a different way.

Walking by, he felt their eyes. They were more uncomfortable than the eyes wanting to violate him by the compound's entrance. Feeling them, he forgot the smells from the drains and the flies rising and falling in a dense bush on the crapheaps and the naked man who lay across the top of one, giggling a hymn.

Suddenly his only thought was to enter the building where there was no one to look at him like that, just a long, empty, high-ceilinged corridor down which he walked towards the men who sat guarding the final door of all, the door into the dormitory.

There were three of these men. They sat on chairs behind a table, reading. The man knew they exerted more power than anyone else in the prison, except those through that door who, like them and like the men staring at him in the compound outside, awaited trial on charges under Decree 046 of "the law against terrorism".

He reached the table.

"I'm the palanca," he said.

Inside the dormitory, about forty young men in their early twenties were arranged on benches, listening to a tall, thin man who stood reading from a book. The light came from a skylight above him. Apart from his voice, the only sound was rain falling on glass.

The palanca moved towards the man in the light. "We know that a revolution is always religious," he heard him say. "The word religion has a new value and it no longer serves only to designate a ritual or a Church."

The palanca found an empty bench. He sat down and looked at the man reading, taking in the first sentence or two. He saw his clean-shaven face, his blond curly hair and the scar on his cheek which darkened when he concentrated. This was Comrade Chino of Belén, one of the first heroes of the revolution, he reminded himself. This was the man who for three years had sent out prisoners to run some of Ezequiel's most effective missions. This was the man who had bribed the guards so he, the palanca, could sit here for a week while someone blew up the electricity pylons in Jauja. Or whipped dogs through Ayacucho with grenades round their necks. Or exploded a donkey in the market at Huanta. Or worse.

Early on he'd offered his services, but while they hadn't laughed, they'd made it clear he was too old a mongrel to teach the tricks they now liked you to learn from the age of six or seven. "To become a Senderista doesn't take months," they said. "It takes many years." But they'd kept his name all the same, which was why one evening a month ago as he was unzipping himself from the overalls he'd bought when he first came to the station as a young boy, he found himself looking at a woman who introduced herself as Camarada Edith. She wanted information, she said. Information that would assist the revolution. And she wanted something else.

"We want you to take someone's place," she said. "Just for a week. We want you to be a palanca."

He thought of the man whose place he was taking, at that moment walking past the avocado women, the man who for a week was carrying his name, his double. Thinking of him, he felt uneasy about someone out there with his name. Dead pylons. Dog bombs. Donkey bombs. He could live with those. But recently he had read of other bombs. Human bombs. Mother bombs. Child bombs. Nor was it just the child bombs. It was the throat-cutting, the head-cutting, the ball-cutting. What if they caught the man who was him slitting a PIP throat, red-handed with the bastard's blood? What then? Then it wouldn't be just a week in San Francisco prison.

Under the skylight, the reader looked up from his book. His oriental eyes fell on those sitting there. "When a tree gives bad fruit, it must be cut down," he said. "We cannot build without first destroying. We cannot have a new birth without blood." He closed the book. "Long live the world revolution."

"Long live the world revolution!" shouted the men on the benches. "Death to the President of the Republic! Long live Presidente Ezequiel!"

When they dispersed, the palanca rose and walked into the light. He kept his eyes on the floor. He saw the man's bare feet. They were watermarked to their ankles in slime from the compound.

"Comrade Chino?" He sensed the man's eyes on him. "I'm the palanca."

"The one from Electro-Peru?"

"Yes."

"From Silar?"

"That's right."

He felt the man before him nod. "Sit down," he said.

They sat on a bench. "The emergency pylons – you've brought details?"

The palanca slapped his leather jacket. "The plans are here." He produced an envelope and handed it over. Without a word, the man placed it between the pages of the book in his lap. Then he said, "What's going on? For two months, all we've heard is rain."

So the palanca told him. He told him about the drought in Silar and Arequipa, where the cattle savannahs had gone without water for nine weeks. He told him about Piura, where the air was usually dry as a cracker. (It had rained night and day for two months, flooding the cotton crops and rotting the cherrywood bed in the house where Admiral Grau had first seen the light of day in June 1834.) He told him about Chimbote, where smell had always meant money and where the harbour's florists stank of pulverized meal from the fish factories. (It was now common to see doorways spilling over with people who had fainted in the odourless air.)

He told him of things he had heard in the electricity station and read about in newspapers. How, germinated by El Niño's strange interaction of water and air, plants were growing along the river banks no botanist had ever seen. How scallops floated on the waves as if boiled in the water. How a burst river had carried a crocodile out to sea where it bobbed for an afternoon among a school of distempered seals.

"In their nets," he said, "men have discovered feathered fish."

And the more he talked without being interrupted, the more confident the palanca became until he found himself able to look into the face of his listener.

"What do they say about us?" said the man eventually.

"They show pictures of Ezequiel with a Devil's tail. They say he drinks the blood of those he executes. They say no one knows where he is. Sometimes they say he's dead."

"No," said the man, turning to the poster on the wall behind him.

The same poster was pasted on the walls of the compound and along the corridor to the dormitory. It showed the handsome face of Ezequiel holding a flag and smiling as he pointed to the sun. The New Dawn. The Dawn which would greet them after the revolution.

"No. He's not dead."

The palanca cleared his throat. "Comrade Chino, I have two messages from Camarada Edith."

The man looked round.

"Well?" he asked.

"One she passes on from Lieutenant Velarde. Something he was overheard saying in a club. She says you might be amused to hear it."

"What does Lieutenant Velarde have to say?"

"He says if you show your face in Belén again, he'll skin it."

"Velarde couldn't skin a carapama. What's the other?"

"She says you've been here three years and not once have you had a palanca. She said she could arrange one for you. She mentioned the name Julio."

Anguish flickered in the blond man's eyes. "How many times does she have to be told I don't want a palanca."

"She knew you'd say that but she said the committee needs to speak to you. There are things you need to be told face to face. She said Ezequiel would wish it."

"Ezequiel would wish it," the man repeated. "Tell me, do you think Ezequiel's wish is a wish, or is it an order?"

The palanca was silent. He was remembering the face of the woman who had come to the electricity station. He was remembering the fear he had felt when she talked, except when she mentioned the name of Comrade Chino.

"Tell me."

"I think it's a wish," the palanca said, and then quickly, "she asked me to tell you they're very pleased with you. She said 'Tell him he's doing a good job'."

"And I'll continue to do a good job – but from here."

"She wants to see you," the palanca repeated.

"No." Comrade Chino shook his head. "It's far too risky."

For a reason he couldn't explain, the palanca found it hard to equate his previous image of Comrade Chino, the revolutionary hero, with the person in front of him. At the electricity station he dealt in every variety of current and short circuit. He prided himself on his ability to detect the same energies at work in people. He looked into the petroleum-coloured eyes of the man on the bench. They didn't conceal passion, he thought. What they concealed was hurt.

Later, the palanca followed the others into the compound. In the rain men were queuing for soup. The liquid was the same colour as the mud they stood in, boiled from the bones of no animal the palanca had ever tasted. It left a flavour in his mouth he couldn't get rid of. Leaving half of it undrunk, he sought out Comrade Chino. He found him lying under a blanket on the floor, reading the same book. He saw the title. *Seven Interpretive Essays on Peruvian Reality* by José Carlos Mariátegui. He sat down beside him. Comrade Chino looked briefly from the pages. The rain fell on the skylight, still the only sound in the dormitory.

The palanca thought again of the man who was him. What was he doing now, this minute? He wouldn't have begun to blow up his pylons, or chase his dogs. He would be releasing other energies. He would be chasing women. He bet he was a one for the women. Whatever this mission, he would have a woman somewhere along the road.

"Don't you miss them here?" The question was cruel. It reflected the taste in his mouth. He felt superior in asking it. It was the only time he had felt superior all day and he felt like this because he knew how much they missed women in San Francisco. They missed them so much that new inmates were taken off and violated by every madman, killer and narco in sight. It wasn't the food or the guards that turned you into dog and buzzard meat. It was cancer of the culo.

"You get used to it," said Comrade Chino.

The palanca inspected the naked pin-ups – torn from *Gente!* – on the wall above his head, beneath a poster of Ezequiel.

"Ever been in love, Comrade Chino?" he asked. He thought of that terrifying woman, Camarada Edith. He thought again of the way she looked when she delivered her message. It wasn't the way you looked when you wanted to discuss Mariátegui.

Comrade Chino put down his book. He stared ahead.

"Yes," he said. "I've been in love."

"What happened?"

"She went away."

"Another man?"

Comrade Chino looked at him. A scar swam into his face, the shadow of a fish on the sand.

"Something like that."

"Where is she now?"

"I don't know."

"Where's she from?"

"The jungle."

"Ah, the jungle," said the palanca, as if that explained everything. He had heard about the jungle, where men were turned into blow-torches and fucked dolphins.

That was where he would go if he was his double, not back to the goat-toothed mountains of Silar.

Chapter 3

ON A MAP, Silar was not far from Arequipa. Yet to arrive there by road meant a two-and-a-half-day journey over three mountain ranges, descending into a bowl fringed on its lower slopes with eucalyptus. Only a dirt track connected the town on the other side with the villages and farmsteads that rose to Sumbay, Crucero Alto and eventually Cabaña.

In completing the journey from Arequipa, the traveller crossed the provincial border into the district of Soreto. The boundary line had been pencilled in Madrid towards the end of the eighteenth century with a geometric caprice that bore no relation to the geography it defined. On noticing he had drawn a shape which at that moment reminded him of a cousin's schnauzer, the cartographer had added a long curved tail.

Silar lay at its end like a flea.

Those two lines drawn one breezy afternoon on a mahogany desk in the Old World committed Silar to Soreto – the capital of which, Belén, lay 1500 miles to the north. In reality the town had never felt itself anything other than Arequipeño.

Like Arequipa, Silar was famous for its convent, its volcano and the houses of the stone whose name it took. These houses – from the high pass they could still give the appearance of a white city – were greyer and shabbier than in the days when, to the chagrin of Arequipeños, at least two Spanish viceroys (and following Independence, a number of criollo generals) repaired there for the summer.

But, partly because of its convent, partly because of its situation off the beaten track, Silar remained an attractive town, prouder than most of its past and keen to maintain, without effort, a reputation for honesty, good schools and hospitality within reason.

That year, however, when the rain-bearing winds refused to cross the Andes, the resources of Silar's population were stretched to their limit.

It took a fortnight for the river to narrow to a slow-moving chocolate thread. One day, the town woke to find it dried completely. The onion fields it had watered turned from green to yellow to a cracked expanse of red soil which the wind blew off in dust devils. Half of the Mayor's cattle turned over in their pastures and died in masks of lime-coloured froth.

Along the river, his mango trees dropped fruit which gave a rattle when kicked. Not even his dogs, their tongues black and swollen, risked panting in the shade beneath in case they were set upon by buzzards drifting down from the mountains like open bibles.

The largest of these mountains was a volcano known as Nakaq. No one in Silar could escape the sight of its red peak. It loomed over every wall. It rose at the end of every street. Wherever you looked it was there. Normally ichu grass covered the slope which dominated the convent, disguising the letters scratched into its surface. El Niño had exposed these letters which now spelled enormously, PRESIDENTE EZEQUIEL.

El Niño, the Child, because it comes at Christmas, had now lasted twelve weeks and four days.

The convent was arranged around a large cloister built from the volcanic rock. The walls of the cloister were tiled, the tiles patterned with blue lilies that glared in the afternoon sun. Their workmanship suggested a European hand. They contrasted with the crude frescoes over the cell doors where the Virgin and Child had been painted in vegetable dyes and rabbit's blood.

A paved cross divided the courtyard into four squares of grass, bordered with the stalks of dead geraniums. A large chicha jar lay on its side in one corner. From another corner grew a stringy cypress which might have been dipped in dust.

In the centre of the courtyard was a goldfish pool, also built of sillar. Two dolphins balanced on a pair of livid green snouts. Their tails supported a sea-shell out of which poked a water pipe. The pipe was dry. El Niño had turned the pool beneath into a grimy pond which had to be skimmed every morning.

It was late afternoon. Inside the cloister, a door opened. A shadow emerged hesitantly into the light. It was the figure of a nun. She took one step up into the cloister, then another, before raising her hand to the sun. Her other hand picked at the habit where some wax had dried. She waited, getting used to the light, the dust, the breathless heat.

The woman's face had the complexion and pallor of the cloister's grey rock. It was without life, except for two piercing blue eyes. They made you realize how beautiful she must have been – possibly still might be under her nun's habit. They were as blue and incandescent as the sky.

She sniffed. Despite the dust there was something in the air. As she stood, trying to work out what it was, a hummingbird swooped past and hovered against the tiled wall. She watched it dash its beak into the glaze. In the drought it had mistaken the tiles for flowers.

She lowered her head and began walking. She kept her eyes on the flagstones. They were covered in the same fine powder that coated the grass, the roof, the surface of the goldfish pool. Her sandals echoed in the cloister, their prints making a rosary in the dust. They did not elaborate the rosary of someone at peace. The nun had completed three circuits of the cloister when she heard a bell. Two shapes moved along the side of the arcade that lay in shadow, then disappeared down the corridor leading to the infirmary. The one who held the bell, the Mother Superior, she recognized immediately. Her surprise in recognizing the other as a man was momentary. In looking up from the flagstones, her eyes were drawn to the mountain which rose above the chapel roof. She saw the words on its slope as she always saw the words, words which gave her the impression of belonging to the volcano – like the wisps which appeared from its cone.

The drought had multiplied these wisps.

They were the reason she stood transfixed.

Nakáq was erupting.

But as she stared, she saw that the clouds bunching the summit were motionless. Suddenly, she realized they weren't clouds of smoke at all, but of the rain she had smelt on the air.

A man scrambled up the sandy slopes from the river. He slipped back twice in his excitement, fell over once and when he reached the road held his sides as he ran.

"Water," he gasped to those who turned, wondering why a man was exerting himself in this heat. "Water," he repeated. A blood-red trickle of water was advancing towards Silar along the river bed.

Twenty minutes later, the four members of the town's band assembled by the river. The guitarist had chicken feathers in his hair. The drummer still wore his key-cutter's apron. Here, to the beat of the drum that bore their name, the Banda Flor Andina began playing.

Father Palacio had followed the Mother Superior through the cloister. She walked a few steps before him, ringing the bell as if she was shaking a bottle to stir its sediment. The bell announced the host in his hands, contained in a silver pyx. When he stepped down from the cloister, into the cell, the contents rattled.

The cell was cool and dark. An old woman lay on a bed under an alcove. She wore a white calico nightshirt buttoned to her throat and a cap on her head. The skin hung from her cheeks like the veil draped untidily over a prie-dieu by the door. Noticing the veil, the Mother Superior removed and folded it.

"Sister, sister," she said, squeezing the black cloth in her hands.

Hearing the quiet reprimand, the woman on the bed opened her eyes.

"I'll leave you, Father," said the Mother Superior. "I'll be outside."

Father Palacio placed his pyx on the floor and drew up a chair. He looked ahead, over the shape of the woman's legs under the blanket, into the aperture. It was designed for protection against tremors. He wondered how well it would resist an earthquake.

"Not long now, Father," said the woman faintly. "El Niño's dried me out."

"Sister, sister," said Father Palacio.

"Drier than the chapel roof."

"I've come to hear your confession."

"Bless me, Father, for I have sinned," came the voice from the bed. Father Palacio closed his eyes. At the end of her confession, she paused. Father Palacio recognized the pause. Usually it meant there was something else.

"There's something else."

Father Palacio turned at an angle to the straw mattress. He waited. The words came out in a rush, each memorized and rehearsed so much that it might have been divorced from its meaning, and Father Palacio had to lean forward and concentrate on what was being said.

The confession related to an incident that had taken place before she left Belén. It involved a young fisherman.

"He was a lovely talker, Father, such a lovely talker." He had told stories in the dark she could remember even now. He had talked her, fifty years before, into spending a night with him in a hotel bedroom.

"I gave myself."

Father Palacio nodded. He was experienced enough to know the length of shadows cast by old sins.

"And you know something, Father," came the voice.

Father Palacio tightened his eyes.

"It was wonderful."

She is dying, he reminded himself, she is dying. She has been shut up in these alcoved walls, like a widow bird. He must relieve her fluttering spirit of unnecessary freight. He opened his eyes. He drew the chair nearer the bed.

"When you made your first confession," he said carefully, closing his eyes again, "you didn't commit a sacrilege?"

"No, no, no, Father. I was sorry. I did have a firm purpose of amendment."

"But?"

"But as the years went by I kept remembering that night with Wenceslau, and the more I remembered the more I felt I had never truly repented. Not truly."

"You should know by now that feelings don't count," said the priest. "One does not have to feel sorry for one's sins. One does not necessarily have to feel that one loves God."

"That's just it," came the voice. "How can I say that I love God if I don't feel I do? What I did was a mortal sin, but, Father" – the voice was a low moan – "I cannot wish it undone."

Father Palacio remained silent.

"I see," he said.

"But, Father, doesn't this make a mockery of my life as a bride of Christ? If here, now, at the last moment, I can't feel sorry. Doesn't that mean my whole life has been a lie? Doesn't it mean I'm destined for hellfire?"

In his mind, Father Palacio saw the old woman lying on the bed as a young novice. He saw her on her knees, day after day, week after week, year after year. He saw her as someone who had not received the consolation she sought, yet all that time she had stayed there, chaste, kneeling, not giving up, despite never having felt the love of God, despite not having seen visions.

He thought of the hotel bedroom in the jungle.

"No," said Father Palacio, "you're not destined for hellfire."

He heard the release caused by his words. He felt the body before him stir under the blanket. From the bed came the voice again. It spoke with strength.

"I want to know, Father, is there love in Heaven?"

Father Palacio opened his eyes. "In Heaven there is neither marriage nor giving in marriage. We'll all be like the Angels of God. Now make the act of contrition."

She began. "My God, I am very sorry that I have sinned against Thee and by the help of Thy grace I will not sin again."

As she spoke, Father Palacio made a sign of the cross and muttered the words of absolution. He reached for the box containing the host. He picked out the round wafer in preparation for the communion.

"Go in peace," he said. "And sin no more."

Father Palacio had sailed from Spain twenty-three years before, when his hair was black and his eyes sparkled like his teeth. He had read Valverde and Zárate on the Conquest, been dismayed by all of the excesses and half expected to find cannibals among his flock.

Instead, the only voracious quality he found was apathy.

He had come with a fistful of good intentions and watched them one by one slip through his fingers. But he had kept his hair, five of his teeth and a smile that raised his eyebrows. Occasionally he thought of Burgos, his domineering sister and his parents' house, but not often.

At the age of seventeen he had entrusted himself to God, who exercising a modicum of infinite wisdom had sent him to Silar and, on this bright afternoon in March, to the convent of Santa Clara.

Father Palacio found the Mother Superior waiting for him outside. She made no mention of the dying sister. He saw no reason to speak of her.

"Father, one more thing," she said, playing with the veil in her hand. "The chapel roof." She explained as they walked.

In the drought, the polilla worm had fattened and flourished. Burrowing into the wood, the tiny bugs had scratched out trails which caught the sun like particles in a sandglass. They had gnawed at four exuberant frames of the Cuzqueño school hanging in the novice room; they had chewed away parts of Saint George's shield on a canvas attributed to Zurbarán; and then, in El Niño's final days, they had set about the chapel's bamboo roof and the leather straps binding its cane.

There were now signs – from the noises that issued whenever Sister Inés pulled the dessus de doublette – that the French organ had become affected.

"I'm no handy-man," said Father Palacio after inspecting the holes and recommending the first thing to enter his head, "but I suggest kerosene." He promised, however, to make enquiries with a neighbour, a journalist who owned a hardware store.

The sun was sinking as they walked across the courtyard. "Father, another thing," said the Mother Superior, pausing by the goldfish pool. "Is it true that you keep a full tank in your car . . . because of the volcano?"

Father Palacio raised his eyebrows without smiling.

"Is that what they say?"

"I wanted to know."

"I do," he said. "But not because of the volcano." It was a habit acquired in the European war when there was rationing. He had not shaken it off. Once or twice he had occasion to be grateful for it. His parish was a large one. There were few pumps between Silar and Crucero Alto and they were usually sucked dry by an army looking for terrorists.

"It's not Nakaq I'm worried about. The whole country is erupting."

"I heard about Chimbote," said the Mother Superior.

Two days before, the telephone exchange in Chimbote had been destroyed by an explosive attached to a chicken.

Thinking about the incident, she giggled.

Father Palacio had not expected this reaction. He stared at the cast-iron coil of dolphins, the lichen-covered spout, the slime on the water of the goldfish pool.

"There's something wrong with those fish," he said.

In the river, the water had become thicker and redder, coloured by the soil from Nakaq. It bloodied the stones and the dogs and the children who rolled in the mud, laughing.

The sounds drew people to the river. Some began dancing, pointing as they danced to the ash clouds suspended above Nakaq which now drifted perceptibly towards Silar, willed on – so it seemed – by the music.

The mountains had swallowed the sun and the band played to the light of candles, made from pig fat, which flashed on the trumpet's dented silver and the gold fangs in the cymbalist's mouth.

He sang a jubilant high-pitched song. Its words could be attributed to the festivals of Corpus Christi, their delivery to the bucket of chicha which had been carried down to the dancers. "It has the power to give twins," the chicha woman told them.

Its power could be seen that evening in the men who made up Flor Andina: the full-throated cymbalist, the guitarist whose hand strummed his catgut at a gallop, the drummer whose instrument rested on a plastic beer crate and the trumpeter whose plaster – covering a hole in the brass – had become stickier and stickier till in a fury he tore it off to give his trumpet a voice of its own.

No one remembered when the music changed, but it must have been after the trumpeter produced a set of quena pipes from his poncho. He jerked his mouth over the reed tubes, as if to clean them.

"'Ojos azules', 'Ojos azules'," shouted the chicha woman. "'Blue eyes', 'Blue eyes'."

The trumpeter turned to the others.

"'Ojos azules'?"

The drum rolled. The cymbalist answered with a clash. The guitarist tightened his strings.

"'Ojos azules', then."

The lights went on in the cloister. The two figures by the pool gave a start. Their conversation had insulated them to the darkness and to the noise from the river which they now heard for the first time.

They stood in the gloom, listening. As they listened, their attention was drawn to the woman still walking through the bright arcade.

"See her, Father?"

"Yes," he said.

"What would you say to the name Elena Silves?"

"No," he said. "Not seriously."

"Indeed."

Father Palacio pushed his spectacles up his nose and looked. In that moment something happened. The nun stopped abruptly. She turned towards the courtyard. She was listening to the music. Illuminated in the overhead light, her face was set in a rictus of agony.

The priest had never seen an expression like it. He moved forward. As he did so, the nun clasped her hands together.

"No, no, not that," she begged. Then louder and louder, "Don't! Please, Lord . . . Please, please, don't!" until in a voice that scattered a confetti of pigeons from the bell tower, she screamed "Gabriel! Gabriel! Gabriel!"

The woman collapsed as Father Palacio reached the cloister. He lifted her by the shoulders. "Take her feet," he told the Mother Superior. Together they carried the nun to a cell. The Mother

Superior went in search of water. Left alone, the priest looked at the unconscious face. Apprised of the identity of Elena Silves, he was surprised by the absence of a sign that any special blessing had been bestowed. While he was contemplating this, he heard through the open door a sound that came from the bowels of the earth, as if the mountains were clapping. It was a sound repeated in the sky as the heavens opened and the rain fell crashing into the cloister.

Muffled by the sound of rain, Father Palacio heard an explosion. Then the lights went out.

On the following Saturday, *El Oriente* carried an item on its centre page under the heading NUN ESCAPES SANTA CLARA.

"There was confusion yesterday over an unconfirmed report that Sister Colina, a nun at the convent of Santa Clara, used the blackout to escape her grounds. Madre Ana de los Ángeles, the Mother Superior, was this morning unavailable for comment. The convent, founded in 1695, is home to 21 nuns of the contemplative order of the Carmelites."

The paragraph was signed in small bold caps, A. W., and followed the report of bomb attacks on power stations in Mollendo, Arequipa and Silar. In an action blacking out these cities, "subversive delinquents" had blown up three Electro-Peru plants and eleven emergency pylons.

Both items were subsidiary to the main news of the week – the rain which had fallen non-stop for thirty-six hours, pitting the cracked fields and terraces and filling the town with the smell of onions.

Chapter 4

THE SUN has turned yellow. It has risen above the roof of the iron house and hangs there like a small ball, not impossibly hot, nor impossibly bright, but a round host that has chased away the breeze which gusted into the square, scattering the red cattle-flies from the shoulders of Admiral Grau and away from the ground beneath the bench.

And still no one has passed the three old men.

Don Leopoldo stirs. He raises a hand to his throat. He scratches its bark.

"The soft-shoe artist is back," he says.

The others lift their eyes to the window on the fourth floor of the Hotel Liberty. It opens into a rectangle of deep shadow where nothing moves. The three men gaze into the shadow.

"A long time isn't it?" asks Don Wenceslau after a while.

"Two years?" suggests Don García.

"Three," says Don Leopoldo.

"What brings him back?"

"Her," says Don García who believes the face they are searching for in the purple darkness is a woman's.

"Her then."

"Perhaps the colihuachos brought her," says Don García.

"La Palometa will be pleased."

Don Wenceslau's remark causes Don García to take up the paper he has been reading. He riffles through it studiously.

"Have we won the lottery?"

"Not yet," says Don Leopoldo.

"Who's the cheat this time?"

"A woman from Iquitos," Don Leopoldo tells him. "A lavandera. She's going to buy a flat in Miami."

"A flat in Miami," says Don Wenceslau. He thinks of how many bottles of masato that would purchase. He shows the whites of his eyes just trying to envisage the quantity. He cannot.

Next to him Don Leopoldo busily converts the property into life-subscriptions to historical quarterlies and shelves of rare books smelling of red Morocco.

Much as Don García would like to give rein to his fantasies, he cannot clear his mind of the person mentioned by Don Wenceslau. As he thinks of her, his eyes catch sight of a small shape flitting down the steps of the Bishop's palace. It carries a suitcase which is placed in the bonnet of a white Volkswagen beetle.

"Bishop Barrantes," says Don García, against the chortle of the car's ignition. "Where's he off to in such a hurry?"

"Must be the airport," thinks Don Wenceslau. "It wouldn't be the zoo."

"I've never seen him look so worried."

"Perhaps someone's told the Archbishop how Barrantes pays for those crosses of his."

The car starts. It accelerates out of the square.

"How does he pay for those crosses?" asks Don García.

"La Palometa told me. She hasn't told you?" says Don Wenceslau, teasing.

"Sometimes, Wenceslau . . ." But Don García doesn't finish. He returns to his paper. "I wonder what's on at the Bolognesi," he mutters.

The question goes unanswered. They all know the answer. They remember the rubber boom when Belén had three cinemas – including the country's very first. They remember the films – such films! – that came direct from Europe. Hardly any films come to Belén now. Don García has lost count of the times he has seen the scratched print of *The Rubber Man's Daughter*.

He finds the advertisement for the Cinema Bolognesi.

"*The Rubber Man's Daughter*," he reads out. "'The happiest and the saddest love story ever told'." He looks up from the page. "Perhaps I'll go tonight."

The thought of the film prolongs their silence. For a minute they forget the afternoons and evenings spent interpreting a soundtrack that, for a different length of time on each occasion, is out of step with the picture. Don Leopoldo even forgets his reservations about the film's historical accuracy. The three of them indulge in another fantasy. They are thinking of Luis Sintra, the hero who wins his girl. They are imagining themselves in his role. The square is an empty stage. There is no one on it to challenge them, except Admiral Grau.

While each man on the bench has enjoyed his own many or infrequent passions, each remembers only the one. For Don Wenceslau it resides in the round face of a pious girl, the youngest daughter of a sugar-boiler, in whose mellifluous arms he spent one night – his first and last – in a room on the third floor of the Hotel Liberty.

For Don García, the picaflor, the man who believes bed is the poor man's opera, it is the face of the hotel's owner, La Palometa, a face he sees every day and in which he does not make out the lines – more than the hennaed hairs on her head – nor the strands of darker hair advancing from her chin and along her lips, but the girl he first set eyes on in the Salón de Belleza, who for more than seventy years has turned up her nose at his advances.

Neither suspects Don Leopoldo of a special love. If he has women, they must be like the demure ladies of Trujillo, knitting their flag for Admiral Grau. Not that they think he has women. They suspect he has only ever taken his shadow to bed.

But he who is silent does not say nothing. Like most men in Belén, Don Leopoldo dreams of someone. The widow of a Portuguese accountant who, crossing the square with an armful of books (and a mad look in her eye that suggested to the seventeen-year-old Leopoldo, as he sat on the bench with a volume of *Os Lusíadas*, that she was intent on throwing them into the river) saw something in his own expression which made her pause and allow a different person into her face, a kind woman with sad, grey eyes who had once tried to teach the children of Funchal history and wondered if he, who balanced Portugal's greatest saga on his knee, would care to relieve her of these volumes.

The seven books she gave him included Espinosa's *People's Dictionary* and *A History of Peru in the Guano Age* by A.J. Duffield. Together with the story she began telling him on that bench, they had fired Don Leopoldo in his chosen profession. They had made him feel his existence was more than that of a swift passing through shadows.

Even today, seventy years on, Don Leopoldo doesn't know what it was that compelled a middle-aged lady to tell a complete stranger half her age the story of her life. He would like to think it was something to do with him, but he suspects otherwise. He suspects she would eventually have told this story – a story she couldn't tell her two children but which she had to tell or her heart would burst through her black dress – to anyone sitting there.

He suspects she would have told it to the grass.

Timing, supposes Don Leopoldo. That was the secret. Nothing else.

"The happiest and the saddest love story ever told," repeats Don Wenceslau. He nods to himself, thinking of the night of his life in the hotel room. "That's the truth. You pay for your happiness. Every moment of it."

Don García agrees. "One of the little things life keeps to herself. Like the fact we can't choose who we love."

"Do you know what the secret of love is?" asks Don Wenceslau.

"Yes," says Don García who thinks he does.

"It's not sex."

"No," says Don García doubtfully.

"It's laughter."

The two of them ponder this. Then Don Leopoldo says: "There's more to life than love, you know."

Don García thinks for another moment.

"No there isn't," he says. "Except music."

"Look!"

The cry is Don Wenceslau's. He is nodding at a woman walking briskly past them towards the river. She has her head in a plain scarf. She walks with her eyes fixed to the ground.

"But that face. I know that face," says Don Wenceslau who has raised his panama. Squinting at the receding figure – the first person of the day to walk by – Don Wenceslau claps his knee.

"It's Elena Silves! The one who saw Our Lady!"

Don García removes his trilby.

"I do believe he's right. Quick, quick, Don Leopoldo, look!"

"But what brings her back?" Don Wenceslau continues. "I thought she was in a convent somewhere in the mountains."

"Fancy." Carefully, Don García screws his hat back on his head. "It must be twenty years at least."

"Eighteen," Don Leopoldo corrects him.

"There must be a problem," says Don Wenceslau.

Don Leopoldo produces a peanut and cracks the shell.

"Without problems there would be no history."

The three men, the pedant, the red herring, the romantic, sit in silence watching the woman until she vanishes down Calle Putumayo. Her appearance has stirred the forgotten years like Pía Zumate tossing her hand through a bowl of dried flowers or Don Leopoldo pressing his nose to the tweed jacket – neatly folded but too small to wear – at the back of his drawer.

"The most beautiful girl in Belén," says Don García eventually. He remembers her black hair and the blue dress that always made him want to run his hands up and down it. He remembers her face, so white it could have been wrought in chalcedony; a face that melted his heart when it smiled "Good morning, Don García. And how are things with Pía Zumate?"

He remembers her eyes.

Those eyes. Where did they come from? There was nothing like those eyes in the entire Amazon basin. Compared with those eyes, Pía Zumate's were raw eggs. They must have come from Europe.

"Her mother was very lovely too," he says. "I never knew the grandmother. Didn't she have something to do with Eiffel?"

"I remember her grandmother," says Don Wenceslau. "Poor little thing. Her husband died in the jungle and she spent the rest of her life in tears."

But Don Leopoldo is not listening. He is thinking of his *History of the Colonization of Belén*. His mind is rummaging through the bag at his feet, searching through a chaos of paper and discord of voices. In his head he is trying to locate the pages his insubordinate pen has written he doesn't know how many years before on the family of the woman who has passed them, the woman called Elena Silves.

Chapter 5

A la Señora Manuela Colina Silves 1884–1943
Estimada y distinguida Amiga mía:

In writing this chronicle of Belén I have experienced something of what it means to be a beggar on a throne of gold (as the historian said of our country). I dedicate it to you in memory of our great friendship and in gratitude to the person who opened my eyes so long ago and by her rare and generous gifts transformed me from a frog beneath a coconut shell, believing no other world to exist, into something altogether princelier – a student in the noble discipline of history.

Believe me to be,
My dear Manuela,
Your faithful friend and servant,
quien besa sus manos,
Leopoldo.

P.S. At first glance, you might naturally feel that Chapter Five – pertaining expressly to the history of your family – should be transposed with Chapter One. Some readers, regarding it as superfluous to the story, might even argue it should be purposely omitted. We who know its truths know otherwise.

Hasta cada rata.

The Silves family, one of the oldest and most distinguished in Belén, did not, as is commonly supposed, settle immediately in the city but in Rapoto, a town on the Curaclo River, two hundred miles east of the provincial capital.

It was on this spot in the August of 1539 that Manco Inca, fleeing from Gonzalo Pizarro, discovered a basket floating towards the Ayaju waterfall. He waded through the reeds and mud and pushed it ashore. Inside, under a finely woven blanket, he found the body of a woman.

She had been dead for three days. Her tongue had been wrenched out, her skin perforated with arrows and her dark legs burnt to two shining stumps.

She had been beautiful once, before her rape, her torture and her sordid death. This Manco knew because he had married her.

The tears he wept for Cura Ocllo, the legend went, formed the thundering river which came to be known as the Curaclo. By the time of Alonso Silves's arrival from Portugal, its thundering days were over and it was a brackish trickle which fed the larger Putumayo.

Elena's grandfather Alonso Silves was a late arrival in the black gold rush. He looked like a pig and sucked his upper lip into his mouth when talking. "God gave me these," he joked of his buck-teeth, "because he didn't want me perfect." It was his only joke. When he tried to be charming to children they cried.

As a child he had dreamed of the strange balls which Columbus had discovered bouncing between the Hawaiians. To the nine-year-old boy, those malleable globes – made of no substance Columbus had seen – were proof that the New World was not a cartographer's joke. One day he would experience it for himself.

It was not enough to finger the waterproof suit once owned by King Carlos which lay in a rumpled black puddle in Coimbra's Museo de Colares. Nor, on the one occasion the curator allowed him, to rub out with the museum's single piece of dry gum a sonnet he had composed in honour of Queen Augusta. Nor even, on the afternoon of his eighteenth birthday, to catch a glimpse of someone directly descended from the man who had done most to promote the milk-giving wood known as the jevea cau-chu.

Francisco D'Oliveira's great-grandson stood on a corner, hailing a woman with a cane. Alonso rushed after him. He wished to convey his admiration for what Francisco had achieved. By the time he reached the corner, his only link with the inventor of the rubber candle (and the bag to hold the urine of incontinents) had vanished in Coimbra's thin afternoon air.

In 1893 Alonso matriculated in mathematics at Coimbra University. He was photographed in a studio against a painted backcloth showing the university library. The expression he wore above his dark robe and rabbit collar was one of someone painfully aware that the real library had been completed from wealth amassed in the New World, not in the Old.

On graduating, Alonso became an accountant, a profession he pursued diligently until at the age of thirty-seven he succumbed to his rubber fever. His "illness" had been exacerbated by the exile of King Manuel and his mother, Queen Augusta, to Twickenham. A staunch royalist who had wept at the assassination of King Carlos, Alonso had no appetite for what life might hold in the new republic.

In the first week of July 1911 he sold his red-tiled house, placed a bunch of comparatively fresh japonica on his parents' grave and for the sum of £18. 12s. 6d. purchased a one-way passage to Manaus on the Booth liner *Ambrose*.

He arrived in Lisbon to find the *Ambrose* delayed a day. He walked to the Moorish fort. He looked out over the straw-coloured Tagus and in the evening he ate a plate of clams and pork in the dining room of the Hotel Borges. In the morning, he took a valedictory stroll through the city. Near the mausoleum to Portugal's kings, he passed a church. On the spur of the moment, he decided to enter, to pray for good fortune in the Amazon – by which he meant the same good fortune being made by ordinary Brazilians, men who could not even write their names.

On entering A Imaculada Conceição, Alonso was surprised to find himself looking down at a large heap of paintings and crucifixes. A caretaker explained the church had been deconsecrated the day before. The objects at Alonso's feet were destined for the market at Sintra.

Alonso was held by one object in particular. Stealing behind him through the Manueline door, the sun struck a painting, slightly larger than life, of the Annunciation. The sight of the Archangel delivering his message to the Virgin had a profound effect on the accountant.

"This is for sale, then?" said Alonso, unembarrassed.

"Of course."

Disregarding the status of the church, Alonso fell on his knees and offered the prayer he had intended all along. That afternoon he boarded the *Ambrose* with a small crucifix made out of Goanese ivory and the painting of the Annunciation—the work, the caretaker assured him, of one of Fra Angelico's pupils.

On the second day Alonso fell in with a couple from Oporto. The husband was a sanitary engineer who had assisted Eiffel on the Douro bridge. He was celebrating retirement with an excursion down the Amazon, accompanied by a severe wife who had a long querulous nose and lips like a dried leaf. When the three of them disembarked at Funchal they were joined on the cobbled wharf by the engineer's daughter.

Her name was Manuela and she was travelling second class by way of punishment. The engineer had always disapproved of his daughter's profession. He believed that in giving a woman an education you were handing a knife to a monkey. The havoc that might be wrought by a female teacher was beyond imagining.

Manuela was twenty-seven and unmarried, but her single status cannot have owed anything to her looks. The young woman Alonso saw on the poop deck must have been as pretty as a duchess. He introduced himself. He learnt she had spent the last four years teaching the infants of Funchal to make angels out of paper doilies. Over the next week he discovered she reserved her deepest passion for the saga of those Portuguese sailors, soldiers and missionaries who had discovered, conquered and converted the world – and then in a blink lost it.

One day he knocked on the door of her cabin and she showed him a suitcase of books. These included an account of Prince Henry's capture of Ceuta, a life of Camões and a popular history of King Sebastián containing evidence that he hadn't died at Alcazarquivir but survived to become, among thirteen other incarnations, a pie-seller in Padua and an intimate of Prester John.

"Sometimes I have dreams he will come again," she said of her sixteenth-century king.

Below deck Alonso told her of his own half-formed dreams. She listened, and by the time the pilot boarded to steer the *Ambrose* into Pará, Alonso had announced their engagement.

Alonso and Manuela were married in Manaus in St John's Church near the floating dock. He bought her a ring from Roberto and Pelosi in Municipal Street and a blue velvet gown with golden loops made in Rue de la Paix. As their wedding gift, Manuela's parents donated a phonograph with a big horn, supplemented by five fado laments, including "Disse-te adeus e morri" (I said farewell and died) and three records of arias from *Lucia di Lammermoor*, with Amelita Galli-Curci as Lucia.

The arias were purchased in the foyer of the opera house where they had taken a box to watch Donizetti's opera performed by Giulia Ragi's Operetta Company. This was not the unqualified success it might have been, due to the indisposition of half the cast, nine of whom had died of yellow fever.

Alonso was deaf to the engineer's complaint that they did this sort of thing much better in Europe. It was his first night at the opera. He watched Lucia's passive role. He heard the celestial wedding hymns before the altar. He felt the earth move in the mad scene when Lucia imagined Edgardo had been restored to her.

That night Alonso sat on the large bed of a room overlooking the river. He stretched out a hand to his wife of twelve hours. "Fur le nozze a lei," he crooned unmelodically through his buckteeth.

The Silveses' honeymoon was marred by Alonso's discovery that he could not afford to be a rubber baron. Nothing had prepared him for the price of land, nor, indeed, the cost of everything else. The hotel bill was four times that of the Borges in Lisbon. He refused to contemplate the expense of Manuela's blue gown.

How deep was his pocket, asked the land agent in Marshal Deodoro street, a Maltese Jew. Alonso thought of the money he had saved and doubled it. The man laughed. He raised his feet to the desk. He advised him to go to Belén.

"Belén?"

"On the border with Peru. Land's cheaper there. You might be lucky. After all it's a lucky name." Seeing Alonso's puzzled expression, he explained.

"Bethlehem. You don't speak Spanish?"

Alonso said he did, of course he did, but it was not something he boasted about.

"You'll be all right then."

Alonso didn't tell the man that whereas in Portuguese he sounded like a poet, in Spanish he sounded like a waiter.

Sucking his lip, he bid farewell to his relieved parents in law – they had decided that Manaus was far enough from Oporto – and pressed on with his bride to the self-styled Pearl of the Peruvian Amazon, a thousand miles upriver.

On the boat, Manuela struggled with an account written five years before by an English evangelist. Belén, she read, lay 2300 miles inland on the northwest boundary of Peru in the heart of the montaña. It was the home of earth's most daring adventurers who cared for neither man nor God and regarded death with strange indifference. "No place on earth is more godforsaken than Belén," Manuela repeated contentedly, not fully understanding.

"Happy, dear?" her husband asked as the boat approached the city.

"Very," she replied, her hand a swan's neck against his mouth.

In the evangelist's day, Belén was producing enough rubber annually to tyre a quarter of a million motor cars. Now, in the autumn of 1911, it exuded a panic palpable even to Alonso. In the space of their journey from Manaus, the price of black gold had fallen from 12s. per pound to 9s.

Alonso reasoned to himself that with demand so low, what better time to invest. Given its constituent material, the trade could only bounce back. He was not to know he had heard the last soprano sing at the Manaus opera house and purchased from the final stock of Madame Bonneterre's dresses.

To the young Silveses, as they stepped off the *Ambrose*'s gangplank, through the cotton bales and into the humid morning, the Amazon valley promised to be the Ophir of Solomon.

They never noticed the man in the grey linen suit, green and white striped tie and badly fitting mauve spats who stood watching them disembark.

That afternoon, at a café on the Plaza de Armas, Alonso entered into conversation with a man in badly fitting mauve spats. He had gelatinous hair and spoke in mellow Castilian tones. He was known locally as El Gordo – for the width of his stories not his waist.

He wanted to leave Belén fast.

What precipitated Orestes Minero's departure was the wind he had received of a report compiled by the British Government into the activities of the Peruvian Amazon Company. Minero was a director of the company, recently floated on the London Stock Exchange. The report described him as "a man of whom no good can be said". It was one of several phrases to which he would take exception. He was after all, not least by dint of his education, a man who had much in common with the compiler of the report, Roger Casement. He had even greeted Casement on his arrival in Belén with the words "How do ye do, sir, I'm an Englishman too."

"Indeed," had been Casement's reply. "How so?"

Three years at Margate College was the reason – the result of his father's posting as a clerk in the Peruvian Embassy. His experiences in a minor English public school had left their mark. Among the atrocities catalogued by Casement and levelled at Minero's door were crimes against the Indian rubber-gatherers "of so horrible a nature that no exaggeration is possible."

At Minero's station on the Yagua, guests reported how dogs would appear at their beds with an arm or a leg between their teeth. On one occasion, peering into a basket of what he thought was fruit, an American traveller unwrapped twenty severed heads and a sackful of ears. "Beasts of the jungle," explained Minero.

"Blow," he once ordered a Bora Indian whose wife had caught his eye, placing a rifle to the man's face. The Indian obeyed. Minero pulled the trigger. The wife became his concubine – one of several – and when, "in the gratification of his animal propensities", he acquired a foul disease, it was her he blamed. In his report, Casement suppressed the account of how she was placed in the stocks and a burning firebrand inserted between her legs. He had chronicled 2,000 similar crimes. He felt he could spare what delicacies of feeling remained to the Edwardian public.

For his part, Minero would rail against what he interpreted as a diabolical defamation. Casement was nothing more than a megalomaniac with a desire for notoriety. Where in his report did it mention the British treatment of Indians in Durban and Ireland? Nowhere was it drawn to the attention of the Anti-Slavery and Aborigines Protection Society that people were dropping dead of hunger in the lanes of Kent.

But all this was in the future. For the moment, Minero's need was to leave the scene as rapidly as possible.

Without informing his fellow directors he despatched his wife to a villa near Mérida, where, with the proceeds of a dishonest sale, he would join her.

Orestes Minero's conversation with Alonso in the Café Nanay resulted in the purchase that week of 430 hectares of "prime plantation" on the left bank of the Putumayo, 270 kilometres from Belén. Sold on behalf of the Peruvian Amazon Company, the Delicias estate was bordered on the east by land belonging to Orestes Minero himself, on the west by the Rio Yagua and on the north and south by open country.

Alonso was pleased to note that the contract was signed in accordance with articles 73 and 79 of the regulations pertaining to "terrenos de montaña".

The ceremony took place in a dingy office off the Plaza Clavero. Drawing up the trouser on his left leg, and unwrapping a bandage from his calf, Alonso released from its folds the gold sovereigns which had become an increasing worry.

"It's three days down stream," El Gordo informed the Portuguese accountant. "Two if you're lucky." Twirling a bunch of keys on a gold chain, he led Alonso back to the map on the wall. The map showed his estate in the shape of a large T.

"It's like paradise."

Alonso was in high spirits after his purchase. He returned to the Palace Hotel to find his wife arguing with the manager. The argument concerned the work of Fra Angelico's pupil.

"He says it's too big for that door."

"Look, señor."

Alonso looked. It was indeed too big for the door. There and then he decided to present the Annunciation to the recently completed cathedral in the Plaza de Armas.

"I'm not sure I liked it anyway," he lied.

Alonso left Manuela in Belén where she was diverted by the discovery of a building by her father's mentor, Eiffel, and houses along the front glazed with the blue and white tiles of Portugal.

Three days later he reached his plantation at Delicias. Instead of paradise, he found a roofless hut in an overgrown clearing. On all sides the jungle reared, its silence broken only by the patter of great drops falling from the trees.

"Green hell," said the boatman. Alonso did not reply. He stared at the unbroken wall of green, his mouth convulsing and threatening to swallow his nose.

It was not what he had expected, but Alonso was no man for jeremiads. For over a year he made a go of it, believing his fortune lay in growing the smooth-barked jevea trees in lines that imitated the plantations of Ceylon and Assam where production already outstripped the Amazon. What Alonso failed to realize was the impossibility of doing the same in a rainforest of parasites. The grey jevea only survived by scattering its seeds. Planted in a line, row on row, it lay exposed to any predator that came along.

He was lamenting the sorry state of his trees when a man climbed up from the river, accompanied by four Indians carrying Winchester .44s. The man introduced himself as an employee of the Peruvian Amazon Company. He wished to know what Señor Silves was doing on company property. Alonso explained the contract he had signed with Orestes Minero twelve months back.

"Minero is nothing but a thief," swore the man. Not only had Minero sold at a reasonable premium, he had done so with a property of which not a single leaf on a single tree belonged to him.

"You are trespassing," the man said. "You have two days to leave."

Alonso knew it was useless to protest. Although Casement's Blue

Book had made everyone consonant with the methods employed by the "civilizing" company, its publication had not effected changes in company policy. Three months before a Colombian grower at Nueva España had been chained to a tree while his wife was dragged onto the porch and raped in front of him.

Alonso could not contemplate the same fate for Manuela, whose body was racked by malaria, whose eyes became glutinous in the sun.

Clenched with shame at his easy deception by Minero, Alonso made for the town of Rapoto, five days upriver.

It was a small settlement of wooden houses. In the middle of the square was a green bust of Admiral Grau. On the edge, a factory. At night the factory's refuse was humped on the roofs and picked clean by vultures. It was forbidden to shoot the vultures. They were about the only thing protected by law.

"This is the back of beyond," whispered Manuela.

"No," said Alonso. "It's further."

They settled in a two-storey house overlooking the square. At night Alonso would sit drinking brandy beneath his ivory crucifix and dreaming of Portugal and the gold library at Coimbra, where he realized he had been so happy.

Despite some muttering of legal action, he did not refer again to his 430 hectares of prime plantation. He reverted, instead, to his old profession. By the light of a kerosene lamp, he kept the accounts of local merchants and innumerate caucheros. Rubber from this area was only subject to the Peruvian Export Duty of 2d. per pound. The duty in Brazil was over 4s. per pound. Many saw the benefit of trading or appearing to trade from the region. Word of Alonso's meticulous, professional eye spread slowly up the Curaclo. Within two years he was clacking the pearly red beads of his abacus over ledger books from plantations half way to Manaus.

He wasn't rich but his stomach for wealth had contracted. He could live more or less as he wanted. Once a year he gave a large picnic in a clearing on the Curaclo to which he invited the factory's manager, Father Felipe, the police chief and two or three of his clients.

Once the Portuguese Vice-Consul attended and spilled wine over his clean white jacket in a patch the shape of Portugal.

Manuela, as beautiful as ever, slipped frailly into the shadows with her lives of Portugal's heroes. She said "Good afternoon" to visitors but considered it indelicate to carry on a conversation. Parsimony required that she wait at table on her husband and his guests. Her own meal she ate with the children afterwards. She had borne two. A daughter, Consuelo, and a year later, in Alonso's fortieth year, a son. He was christened Henriques in memory of Alonso's professor and Portugal's greatest navigator.

A month after Henriques' birth, Manuela was squeezing avocados in the market when Father Felipe touched her arm and told her Europe was at war.

The only person in Rapoto to be affected by this news was Alonso. He felt a middle-aged man now, with a turkey flap of skin about his neck. More than ever he felt a stranger in a strange land. Due to a border dispute between Colombia and Peru, the town he had ended up in, along with its surrounding forest, had since become res nullius. An area the size of Portugal was suddenly ungoverned by any power – not even by the Peruvian Amazon Company.

Yet at home Alonso's own civilization was disintegrating.

In March 1916, Portugal entered the war on the side of Great Britain. That autumn, compounding his sense of apocalypse, Alonso heard of an eight-year-old shepherdess who had been throwing stones down a hill near Fátima when she was visited by the Angel of Peace. A later report described how the Virgin herself had appeared above a small bush, making the sound of a horse-fly in an empty water-pot. The Virgin's repeated warnings of "annihilating nations" affected Alonso in an unexpected way.

One night, in 1917, Alonso listened to Father Felipe's account of bread riots in Lisbon. When the priest had departed, he folded his glasses, lowered the wick of his kerosene lamp and closed his books.

"Botofe bo le iwa. Rubber is death," he announced mysteriously. "But I'm damned if I can't do something with that plantation."

Next morning, while the sun was still peaching the sky, he headed upstream in his best trilby and a long canoe containing his phonograph, five fados and the arias from *Lucia di Lammermoor*.

One of Henriques' first memories was of entering his parents' room to see his mother in a lush blue gown the colour of lapis lazuli. In one hand she held the Goanese crucifix. In the other the matriculation photograph of her husband at which she mumbled incoherently. On her head she wore his hat.

Almost a year after Alonso's disappearance, an embarrassed Indian had been spotted using the trilby as a loincloth, having scooped it off an island in the Curaclo.

Henriques never saw his mother wear coloured clothes again. From cockcrow to sunset, she dressed in black and fidgeted with a rosary made from the beads of Alonso's abacus. People resting from the noon sun on Father Felipe's thick pews knew her as the bicho triste – the sad dung beetle.

Considering his profession, it was surprising how few arrangements Alonso had left for his family. There was no insurance policy and nothing but a few sovereigns in the Banco de Crédito in Belén.

With Consuelo and Henriques, Manuela moved into a two-bedroom house on the outskirts of town. After a month she was forced to seek employment. For 190 soles a week she worked at the local factory which supplied hypochondriacs and beauticians in Europe with medicinal teas, restoratives and oil from palm tree kernels – oil, it was sworn, which would make hair regrow on an old door mat.

Each day after feeding her chickens, she walked the eight hundred yards to the shed where the oil was canned. Here she slipped into a pair of white overalls several sizes too large and sat on a stool with a drumstick. With this she tapped the tins on the conveyor belt to hear if they were full. It was, the manager argued reasonably, an undemanding job which was why they could only pay her 190 soles. Nevertheless, given the temperament of his German machines, it was a job that had to be done.

One day, after eight years, a can of hair oil resounded empty. Manuela abandoned her stool, her drumsticks and her overalls and on reaching home told her teenage daughter she could never return to the factory. Consuelo climbed from her hammock and from then on attended her mother in everything. She washed her clothes, she prepared her meals, she read her the account of King Sebastián's expedition in 1578 to subdue the Saracen. Manuela's only response was to sit blankly kneading her rosary.

Sometimes Consuelo would stumble on her watching meteors from the slope opposite and making strange prophecies. Once she caught her heaving stones into a pattern with bleeding nails. After she had finished, Consuelo led her gently home. Later when she went outside to break a chicken's neck, she saw a line of great uneven letters on the hillside spelling CRISTO VIENE.

Henriques was sixteen when he decided to find out about his father. A river steamer arrived in Rapoto and he overheard its captain mention Delicias to his Indian mate. Henriques was on deck before the boat had nudged the jetty. The captain looked at the thin, tallow-skinned boy and nodded at the Indian. Without a word, he disappeared below. The Indian, who wore rouge and reeked of cane spirit, agreed to take Henriques for the price of 100 soles if he also collected fuel.

Close to, Henriques noticed that one of his eyes was green, the other brown. The rouge disguised the fissures left by verruga fever.

The *Libertad* pushed its way north through air that was black with gnats and heavy with leafmould. Every few hours Henriques leapt ashore to gather wood for the cooking stove. At night, the captain gave him a slab of dried fish and pinched him with a friendly leer between the legs.

All next day they steamed through the tannic waters.

Late the following afternoon, they reached a settlement consisting of several small houses, a larger building which leant against a derelict watchtower and a church with a roof made of flattened kerosene cans.

"Tonight Dos de Mayo," snorted the captain. "Tomorrow, Delicias." They were the only words Henriques heard him speak.

Dos de Mayo was a garrison town. It contained four soldiers who possessed a single uniform between them. Pigs, dogs and chickens ran freely through the rooms.

The captain, his mate and Henriques ate with the soldiers. Afterwards the captain opened a bottle of rum. Towards midnight, one of the soldiers, the one with the uniform, shouted "Let's dance!" Voices and hands were raised in accord. Chairs were scraped to the walls. From behind a Chinese screen rose the sound of a scratched phonograph.

As the *Libertad*'s captain began a grotesque mince with his mate, Henriques realized the wail was familiar. He made his way through the dancers. Behind the screen, he found his body reflected in the horn of his parents' wedding present. From the dark hole in the brass spewed the maddening, wrenching, out-of-time notes of Alonso's favourite fado, "Disse-te adeus e morri".

Of the three records containing highlights from *Lucia di Lammermoor* there was no sign.

The corporal in uniform repented that the padre was the one who really knew the story. But the padre had gone. How terrible that the padre had gone. What he, the corporal, remembered of the story that the padre told him was this: Many years ago, ten perhaps, a man – an unprepossessing fellow, not a jungle type, although he was heading into it – asked the padre if he would look after the phonograph and the collection of warped disks. He would be back later to collect them. That's fine, the padre said. But when he didn't come, the padre gave them to the garrison. It was not the padre's kind of music. And the man, what happened to the man? Who knows? What happens to any man in the jungle? He may have struck lucky and got out, to Paris, Salamanca, Rome. But then, he may not. In his time in this district, he, the corporal, had found, he could count it on his hand, a man eaten by a puma at San Ramón, at Suche a man eaten by the Boras, at Delicias a man eaten by the fishes. And what happened to their bodies? Their bodies?

The padre put their bodies in the cemetery, of course.

When everyone was asleep, Henriques took a lamp and walked to the cemetery. He held the light over the wooden crosses until he came to one that told of an unknown man, found drowned near Delicias.

He put down the lamp and began digging with his machete. Near the surface, he unearthed a large sack. Inside was a piece of cloth and several skeletal remains. Henriques turned over the skull. Seeing the teeth, he had no doubt it belonged to his father.

Alonso's second resting place was a far corner in the cemetery of San Francisco church, beside an adobe wall. Henriques led the mourners. Once or twice on the path to the grave, he slowed down, putting distance between the pall bearers and those who followed. Unable to afford a coffin with a satin lining, he did not want his mother to hear at every step the rattle of her husband's bones.

The arrival in Rapoto of Alonso's remains restored Manuela to calm. She made several visits to the church in which it was observed she not only greeted Father Felipe but remembered the catechism. At home a name came and stayed on her lips.

"Mamá," Henriques said at last, "who is this El Gordo?"

Piecing together the stammered fragments, he learnt for the first time of the fatal transaction which had destroyed his father. Holding his mother's mottled hand, he made a vow.

Orestes Minero had sailed for Europe twenty-three years before. He never thought to return. He was leaving Belén not a moment too soon and with it the sobriquet by which he was known. Several months would pass before his baptismal name rolled easily from his tongue. By then he had met the mole-like financiers with whom he was to invest Alonso's money; men who were to make him into a wealthy, even respectable figure in the clearing houses of Milan, Zurich and Madrid.

He exchanged his spats for English brogues and his grey suit for Donegal tweed, but a bunch of keys still rustled from his hip. As his conscience cleared, so did his past. He founded a scholarship in his name at the University of Mérida and endowed an orphanage in Tordesillas. It was a gesture of gratitude, he explained ruffling the head of his son, Miguel, for his own upbringing at a similar institution in Belén.

Nor was Belén deaf to such activities. In 1934, with the support of both the Departmental Assembly and the Chamber of Commerce, the Mayor extended a warm invitation and the hope that Orestes Minero would accept the honour of Huésped Ilustre de la Ciudad.

In September of that year, Orestes Minero consented.

In December of that year, Henriques arrived in Belén to look for him.

It was fortunate for Henriques that on arriving in Belén he chose to stay at the pension owned and run by Madame Zumate and her three daughters. This large, rollicking woman hailed from Armenia but had forgotten her mother language as she had forgotten the names of her lovers. She had a tongue like a hornet and a heart of gold. It went out to the young man. Yes, she knew El Gordo. She had once spent a night with him. She remembered how he had folded his clothes, down to his socks, on the chair. She remembered his cold white hairless legs which made her toes curl and when she saw his beaming photo in the paper she shook her merry head.

"Por Dios," she said. "So the rat's become a cat."

In those twenty-three years, Orestes Minero had not given a second thought to the bucktoothed Portuguese accountant and the transaction upon which rested his fortune, his reputation and the freedom of his city.

It was a city he had left as an inconspicuous chancer. It was a city to which he returned, with his wife and child, as a modest hero. It was a city, he mused benignly while strolling jacket in hand along Calle Próspero and tipping his hat to the notary Miguel Lache who thought he recognized the face, that he must endow with some enduring monument.

He was thinking along the lines of a bronze statue when he saw the sign of the Hotel Liberty. He wondered if that old whore Zumate remembered him. As he crossed the street to find out, Orestes Minero felt a sudden blow to his right buttock. Spinning clumsily he caught sight of his precious keys spilling to the pavement; then the young man from whose hand peeked the dull tip of a machete.

Orestes Minero never walked in a straight line again. The injury to his hip – Henriques had hacked through the slack flesh to just below the pancreas – ensured that to move forward he would have to sway sideways from one leg to another like one of the square's pigeons. Henriques, he knew, would have struck again had he not in a flash and after all these years seen the father in the son and, falling to the ground, blabbered Alonso's name as the blood puddled about his knees.

Later, in the house in Calle Putumayo where he remained till his death, Orestes Minero returned Alonso's sum, with twenty-three years interest. Henriques would take no more. As his father might have wished, he had squared an account. The sum would keep his mother in comfort and restore some lustre to the family name.

With the money, Henriques bought a large house two streets away from Minero on the corner of Calle Raimondi. Here he installed Manuela and his sister. Then he made for the jungle, to find the trail his father lost.

It was the end of the rainy season and the river still high when Henriques reached Delicias. For a month he cut down the forest. For a month it crept back so quickly that when he left his stick in the ground it grew into a tree. Then it let him be.

Twice he was attacked by a herd of wild pigs, once by a small puma. He learnt to rub his wounds with tobacco juice and live off leaf-cutting ants and dye his face with berries to keep the flies away.

He was not like other caucheros, half-caste rubber men stranded by the slump, who in a single week of riotous living spent the income of a year. He passed their settlements on the way to his distant tributary. They lived in rickety huts near the river, shooting cat-fish from their porches and digging crab ticks from their skin.

Invariably they bore the title Colonel. But their Indian workers knew them by the Bora for Armadillo. Because they only looked back – to the time of the rubber boom. All that remained of the boom were mounds of rusty machinery and a handful of whittled mistresses who wore Aquascutum stockings and drank tepid champagne out of gourds.

Henriques rarely left Delicias. When he did it was to sail with a laden boat for Belén.

He was at his mother's side when she died.

(Manuela's last years had been her happiest. In Belén she had made stimulating new friends with whom she could freely discuss the subjects that had animated her as a young woman. It was even rumoured she might have given her heart to one of them, which was why she died with a smile on her face.

Another interpretation had it that, smelling the creosotic fumes on Henriques' shirt, she was imagining herself again among the smoked hams of her grandmother's store in Oporto.)

He was at his sister's side when she married Diego Guzmán, the Mayor's youngest son. He gave the couple the deeds to the house in Belén and a short, solemn toast. Then before the dancing began he returned to the jungle. "He needs Delicias," Consuelo explained to the groom. "He is making something out of nothing."

Henriques was indeed making something out of nothing. The price of rubber rose again, not to the giddy heights of the boom, but to a level which earned a profit. This he supplemented by growing small-grained Carolina rice and importing cattle. His Indians had never seen cows before. On the day the animals arrived, they painted their faces with red urucum and leapt into the trees.

If Henriques was unusual in the money he was making from the jungle, he was unique for the esteem in which he was held by those who worked for him.

He in his turn understood their melancholy. It was the melancholy of a race that knew it was dying. He nodded when his mayordomo told how he came from a tribe descended from strange birds and how his wife had been created by the God Wako from tobacco smoke. He never put himself in the way of Antipa and Teberos when they asked for a few days leave, though he was well aware of their destination and the Colombian planter they would kill. The man had mutilated three of their cousins. Henriques knew they would eat his tongue for wisdom, his heart for courage and for fertility make their women chew his genitals.

He also shared their resignation. He ascribed theirs to an ability to count to infinity; his to the knowledge he was never made for the jungle. It was a resignation that came upon him at night when he sat still as a bird, listening to the notes that welled from flutes of human bone. These forlorn notes invoked the tree spirits.

They reminded Henriques of his father's fados.

Henriques was thirty-one when he left the jungle. One day he visited Señora Lache's cake-shop in Belén to queue for a rich purple pudding – a luxury he allowed himself after unloading his latex. He reached the counter and was told the last mazamorra morada had gone. Downcast, he made for the door where he met Colina Chorrera. She had heard his question. She had seen the expression on his face. She didn't want the cake, she told him. It was a cousin's birthday. Any cake would do.

They spent the rest of the morning picking at the purple pudding on a bench in the square. That afternoon he attended the birthday party. Ten days later, days which he spent in Belén, he knelt formally on her parents' parquet floor and asked her to marry him. He was sorry to be so forward, he said, but in his family a short courtship was a tradition.

On returning to Delicias, Henriques summoned his Indians and handed each a purse of gold. He told them he was leaving. They assembled on the river bank and wailed as he left, all except Tabaros, the human-flute-player, who took his hand and told him it was good. He had spilled chicha to the spirits and read his fortune in the coca leaves.

Everything was good for Señor Henriques and his beautiful wife-to-be. He did not mention he had foreseen death by water.

Colina Chorrera was the daughter of an unassuming but well-to-do merchant who had ten mills to his Spanish name, including the factory in Rapoto. She was a tall, proud girl with short auburn hair and a chin so round that as a child old men would chuck it and say one day she'd grow up to break hearts. She never did. Like Manuela

Silves, she was more interested in books than boys and though she spoke without a blush to the young men of Belén, it was clear from her mocking laughter what she thought of them.

She was twenty-five when she looked into Henriques' eyes and found there something commensurate with the men created by her authors. Whereas Henriques' mother had been devoted to history, the world as it had been, Colina's passion was for the world as it might be. She smelt of novels. Under her guidance, Henriques developed a taste for Benito Pérez Galdós, Kipling and Hardy (whose work he consumed in bed with a milk punch). Under his instruction, Colina discovered a life outside her parents' library.

Once in the early days after the scissor ants had eaten her best frock, he joked about her lack of worldly ways. Her hands dropped to her hip and her round chin flashed out. "Silves," she said, rolling her dark brows. "And you thought I was a virgin when I married you." Henriques squinted thoughtfully. "No, I didn't," he said. In reply Colina hoisted her red dress above her head and let it drop. They twisted and plunged in the cotton shadows until the sweat on their backs caught the moon.

When they married, Consuelo had offered them back the house in Raimondi. Henriques declined. With his young wife, he went to live near Rapoto. As a wedding gift, Colina's father had given Henriques charge of his canning plant. He needed a reliable manager, one who could adapt to the wind from wherever it blew. The Second World War had ended the demand for restoratives and medicinal teas. Now Europeans wanted barbasco for their insecticides, essence of rosewood for their perfumes, and the liver oil of stingrays for bronchitis. Only the market for the palm tree kernel remained unchanged.

The young Silveses lived comfortably in a roomy house which Colina filled with heliotrope. In January 1948, during the second year of their marriage, she conceived. The baby was a girl with eyes the colour of her grandmother's dress and a mop of dark hair like a door mat.

In one of the last services to be conducted by Father Felipe, she was christened Elena Colina Silves.

Part Two

1986

Chapter 6

THREE YEARS HAD PASSED since the disappearance of Elena Silves and her sighting by the old men in the square.

Shortly before nine in the morning, an hour and a half later than scheduled, the boat from Requena pulled into its berth below the Malecón. Among the last to step from the *Victoria Regia*'s plank was a tall, thin man in his late thirties.

He carried a briefcase, tied with a length of rope through its handle, and was dressed in a brown suit – the jacket more faded than the trousers (suggesting they had not been worn together, and the trousers, which were flared, hardly at all). It was a suit cut to a pattern out of fashion.

The man joined the single file of passengers ascending the steep bank. When he reached the top he turned left along the Malecón until he came into the cathedral square. Hearing the rattle of small change in Sebastián's bucket, he stopped. He looked down at the dark triangular shape of Sebastián beside his newspapers. A brown wrist, like a turtle neck, was the only flesh visible under the black hood. It responded to his presence with another shake of the yellow bucket. The man seemed about to say something, but decided against it. He added several coins, picked up a paper and walked on.

He was making for the Café Nanay when a woman pushed open its glass door and walked straight into him. She apologized, and he apologized in return. As the woman brushed herself down, she could not help noticing he was a good-looking man – one of those blond Indian mulattos which in Brazil they called mameluco. His fair hair – slightly fairer than the moustache he stroked – fell in curls about his collar. His narrow eyes were green and steady. Had he looked in better health he would have been a most attractive man.

"I'm late," she said and hurried out across the square.

He entered the café.

The Nanay was a single room crowded with tables, beer crates and a jukebox. In its day it had been a favourite meeting place for the city's business community who discussed their whisky shipments from Leticia over tall glasses of café con leche. Like most of the objects under discussion, the coffee they drank had usually been winked through the customs.

Behind the jukebox was a staircase. The man had never seen anyone climb it. He imagined the steps led to a room where larger deals were hatched and sealed by those trafficking in everything from cocaine to assassination.

On this day, the café was empty. He ordered a coffee and a sandwich from the boy behind the counter, then sat down at a table overlooking the square.

It was 9.05 by his watch. Though the boat had been late, another 25 minutes remained before his appointment with the Bishop.

The boy walked over with his sandwich and coffee. He thanked him. He looked into the boy's face but he didn't recognize it. He hadn't recognized the face of the woman either. In fact, he wondered just whose face he would recognize in Belén.

After six years he wondered who would recognize him.

Pía Zumate, perhaps. Capitán Velarde. But the policeman wouldn't be on his guard, not now. And Sebastián, to whom he had nearly spoken. Otherwise, he couldn't think of anyone – except Edith.

He swallowed a mouthful of coffee and looked out of the window. In the centre of the square, he saw three old men on a bench. The face of the one on the left was lost under a newspaper. The paper gently rose and fell in time with the old man's breathing. The headline could be read from the table. BRUTAL REVENGE KILLING, it ran. VIOLENCE REACHES SORETO.

He unfolded his copy of *El Oriente*. The headline described the murder of four villagers in Cabaña, a village to the far south of Soreto. The villagers had been accused of co-operating with the armed forces. The executioners had been led by a woman.

"In an unusual departure from their traditional policy of silence, the Shining Path has accepted responsibility for the murders. The action was in retaliation for the massacre of 257 prisoners last week at Lima's San Francisco prison."

In a brief statement Capitán Velarde, Belén's new Deputy Chief of Police, promised his men would not rest until the delinquent murderers had been brought to justice.

The rest of the page was devoted to the prison massacre in Lima of the week before. A spokesman for the military insisted that San Francisco's governor himself had invited the armed forces to quell the mutiny. A novice in the shanty-town above said the gunfire had continued through the night like the popping of grilled maize. A spokesman for the government confirmed that all survivors had been moved to the penitentiary of San Eduardo in the suburb of Monterrico.

There was a blurred photograph of the bombed-out dormitory and beneath, a list of those presumed dead. The man's expression changed only once, when he saw the fifth name on the list.

It was his own.

Gabriel finished his coffee. He rose, took the glass to the counter and asked for another. He checked his pockets for money. There was enough to get through the morning. After that, he would have to rely on Edith.

While the boy reheated the milk, Gabriel made his way to the jukebox in the shadows under the staircase. He looked down through the curved glass dome, searching for a particular record. When he found it, he inserted a coin. There was the sound of crackling, then music.

He returned to his table where he sat, leaning on his briefcase, listening.

Hipólito used to sit here, pounding the table with a purple fist so that the sugar bounced out of its bowl and the coffee had to be mopped up with a tut-tut by Elena. He hadn't thought of Hipólito for a long time. Nor Elena.

Without her he wouldn't be here.

Two weeks, that's all, since Elena's reappearance in the pages of a three-year-old copy of *El Oriente*. The newspaper had been used to wrap a book requested by Gabriel (a banned biography of Mariátegui). Even then, the chances of him seeing the item were slight had he not torn out the centre spread to clean his feet and found himself immobilized by A.W.'s brief account of Sister Colina's escape from the convent of Santa Clara.

Immediately, he did something he had never done in six years. He arranged a palanca. The palanca was his childhood friend and comrade, and the man who had sent the book, Julio Ángel Medina.

Gabriel's face hardened at the memory of Julio as they passed in the guardroom corridor. The corridor was rancid with detergent. Someone had shot away the overhead bulb.

"Thanks, Julio." They touched hands in the dark.

"You know I'd do anything for you, Gabriel."

"You understand, don't you?"

"Yes."

"The chances are hopeless, but I've got to find out."

"Gabriel, I understand."

It was too much for Oliveira, the guard, who didn't want to hear why Chino was taking a palanca all of a sudden and was beginning to regret, despite the wad of notes in his pocket, that he hadn't pressed for an extra packet of Hamilton Lights. He pushed Gabriel in the back, towards the door in the wall.

"Two weeks, Chino. That's all you've got. Then your friend here gets his balls chewed off."

Twenty-four hours later Gabriel was in Arequipa, having slept the night on the bus. In a shop window he saw the moustache he was growing to match the portrait in his documents. He spent the next night on a bench at the station. At six in the morning, he boarded the bus to Silar. Raindrops appeared on the windscreen as it headed out, late, over the Bolognesi bridge.

The road which lifted across the plateau like a rifle barrel began to coil and twist once they reached the first pass, but the rain still gave it the sheen of gun-metal. In the afternoon the bus stopped by a roadside stall selling fruit and bread. The driver advised any passenger who hadn't done so to stock up. This was the last food they'd see for twelve hours. Gabriel bought a loaf of stale bread and six oranges. The stall had been erected where the tarmac ran out.

Because of the weather, the journey to Silar took longer than two and a half days. Gabriel spent most of the time staring blankly through the window from a seat in the back. Once he asked the mother of a little girl when they would get to Silar. She sat against the other window reading a photo-story and chain-smoking. Her daughter's eyes rolled open and looked up at him.

"Further on, after La Falda. I'll tell you." She brushed some ash off her jeans and returned to the story. The girl closed her eyes.

He reread the paper he had bought in Arequipa. On this day in 1610, he learnt, Philip III established the Inquisition in Cartagena. On the same date in 1925, Mao Tse Tung made his historic return to Hunan. It was the actress Cyd Charisse's birthday.

He dozed until the bus entered a town, the first they had come to. The woman seemed prepared for his questioning glance. She smiled and shook her head.

"La Falda," called the driver, looking up into a juddering mirror. "La Falda, La Falda," he repeated.

No one got in or out and the bus lurched off.

They came to Silar in mid-afternoon. He felt the little girl tug at his arm. "Silar," she whispered. In the corner her mother slept. Gabriel was leaving when a soldier pushed past him.

"All out! Come on, all out! And your luggage."

They filed into the Guardia Civil station. No one seemed concerned, except the driver. He looked at the soldiers going through his bus, shaking his head.

Gabriel waited behind a fat man in a cloth cap. As they queued to present documents and open their cases, an officer appeared. He walked down the line. He had brown eyes that never blinked and a mouth he kept shut until he came to Gabriel.

"Name?"

"Julio Ángel Medina."

"Documents."

His eyes remained on Gabriel as he flicked through the forged pages.

"Destination?"

"Here. Silar."

"Ever been to Cabaña, Señor Medina?"

He looked intently at Gabriel.

"Cabaña?"

"That's right. Cabaña."

"No."

"Ever heard of it?"

"No."

"What's a pituco from Lima doing in these parts?"

"I'm writing a story for *Caretas*," Gabriel replied as if his presence in the sierra was a triumph of duty over disdain. "About nuns."

The officer decided to smile. His sister was a nun, God alone knew why. With the Bethlemites. Unhealthy lot. Did he know them? They all had boils on their chins and man's hands and thick glasses. He was sorry for this delay, but. . .

"Capitán, Capitán," interrupted a soldier from behind the low table. He had been searching the mother's bags and now held up her documents.

"No, later dear," she was telling her daughter, nervously lighting a cigarette. She still had rings of sleep round her eyes.

"Momentito," snapped the captain, returning Gabriel's identity card.

Eventually, they were allowed back into the bus, all except the mother and her girl.

No one spoke as they drove into the centre of Silar. No one looked at each other, not even the driver at the mirror. The absence of the two passengers was like the removal of a tongue. When the bus stopped in the Calle Tristan, it disgorged people who wished to go their own way.

Gabriel walked down the street until he found a green Dodge taxi.

"Santa Clara."

The taxi reached the convent in under five minutes. He leant over the seat, counting out change, but his attention was so drawn to the building on the other side of the road that an exasperated driver had to pick the coins from his palm.

For a moment Gabriel stood on the pavement, coming to terms with the place which might have contained Elena for the last twenty years, whose white walls stretched either side of an open gate, thirty feet high, for a block. He crossed the road.

"No es turístico," said a woman selling biscuits at the entrance. Further along a man with a wire brush was scraping away the large red letters which had been sprayed on the wall. VIVA PRESIDENTE EZEQUIEL!

The same name remained indelible on the side of the mountain at the end of the street.

"Please. Can't I look inside?"

The woman hesitated, then wheeled her stand a foot or two along the pavement, allowing room to slip by.

The patio lay in shadow. There was a padlocked door on the right and, beneath a concrete sign with the word Silencio, a wooden tournière. A schoolgirl sat on a bench against the wall, her legs up, reading a book. Her mother, on the bench beside her, delivered a scolding, painting a finger nail as she did so. Neither paid attention to Gabriel.

He revolved the tournière. As it span, he bent to look at the space between the frame and the wall. He revolved it several times, then returned to the entrance where he bought a biscuit in the shape of a star.

Gabriel still had its dry, salty taste in his mouth an hour later when he entered the offices of *El Matutino* in Calle Molgar. The building, sandwiched between a tour company and a bookshop offering mimeograph services, was one of the few two-storeyed houses in Silar. A number of brass plaques encrusting the entrance announced that the ground floor was rented out to a lawyer, a doctor and an oculist.

"I'm looking for someone who might work here," he told the receptionist. "I don't have the name. Just the initials."

The woman smiled when she saw them. "That'll be Arturo."

It was a bad time for Arturo Walker, *El Oriente*'s stringer in Silar. His grey cardigan and once chubby face bore this in their shapelessness. The family business – a chain of three hardware stores – was one step away from the receiver's after an imprudent investment on the Arequipa bourse. His wife, he suspected, following the discovery of four prophylactics in the pocket of her smartest jacket, was conducting an affair with the branch manager of the Banco de Crédito. And his boss had taken off to Argentina on a skiing holiday.

Normally, his boss's absence would have been welcome. When not fulfilling his commitment as *El Oriente*'s correspondent in Silar, Arturo acted as features editor on the local paper, a position he much preferred given the distance and the antipathy (at least on Silar's part) existing between the two cities. Though *El Matutino*'s circulation was tiny compared with Belén's *El Oriente*, Arturo enjoyed greater scope in writing about what interested him. Especially when his editor was away.

For the past two days, however, he had realized his duties this week would consist not in writing anything himself, but in reworking agency copy from Lima.

Most of this concerned the San Francisco massacre.

Even Arturo Walker had to admit it was a story which took precedence over his appreciation of Simón Bolívar's death in exile. That article, provisionally subtitled "Take our bags to the boat, they don't like us anymore", would once again have to wait.

It was at times like these that Arturo Walker – a second-generation Peruvian and the grandson of a Macclesfield carpenter – wished he was not Peruvian at all. But a visit to the British Consulate in Arequipa had confirmed what he feared, that he was stuck with the land of Henry Walker's adoption, rattling like a can on his tail.

He was therefore impatient with the man who walked into his office that afternoon and demanded to know about a dead and irritating story. Had he not announced himself as a journalist from *Caretas*, Arturo Walker would have sent him packing. Not that he seemed particularly well informed. The fellow didn't have a clue about the story which Arturo had just spent a day putting to bed.

"What massacre?"

"You, a journalist, and you haven't heard? Jesus."

Arturo filled him in as he burrowed through the filing cabinet. "According to the government it's all a terrible mistake. Last night the president was televised live in the ruins of the dormitory. You should have heard his voice. 'Either all the culprits go, or I go.' At the moment everything is pure speculation. The culprits, the reason for the mutiny, the names and number of the dead. Ah, here we are."

He produced a sheet of paper from a green folder. Shutting the cabinet with his knee, he held the page at arm's length. For a moment, he did not see the small cutting glued to its centre and underneath the pencilled date, 3 March 1983. Instead he saw the demonic shapes of his three hardware stores, a wife who didn't love him, a brother in Miami who could afford a boat.

Gabriel took the page from him. His face was pale. "That's all?"

"That's all."

"You wrote this?"

"If you can call it writing," shrugged Arturo, who, if he hadn't become an average journalist, was not above believing that his attention to detail and observation of character would have made him a good novelist.

"Why didn't you follow it up?"

A woman entered carrying an electric typewriter. She deposited it on the table. "It works, señor. Only the fuse."

Arturo thanked her, glad of the distraction. "I can't remember," he replied, pressing his fingers on letters that refused to tap. "This happened three years ago, for God's sake."

The explanation remained a long time in the air. Gabriel said nothing. Arturo bit his lip. If the window wasn't shuttered he'd have looked out of it, like his boss had done. More vividly than he cared, he remembered the meaningless shuffle of papers on the desk, the muttered phrases – "highest authority", "know how you feel", "for her own good" – until with a hand on wood came the exasperated shout, "All right, so it's Bishop Barrantes who's made us spike it." That was the turning point, Arturo saw now. He should have stuck his neck out or got out. Gone to the capital, worked for a decent paper where they didn't bend to pressure from corrupt clergymen fifteen hundred miles away in the jungle. A paper like *Caretas*.

"Anyway, how did you find that?" He smacked the page held by Gabriel.

"It's on file."

"They file our stuff in Lima?"

"The most interesting."

Arturo tapped thoughtfully at the obstinate key board. He couldn't conceal his pride.

"I don't suppose there's any harm telling you." With a resounding click and spring of machinery, his index finger found a button that responded to its probing.

"I was with Father Palacio when the Mother Superior rang to say one of her nuns was missing."

Gabriel found Father Palacio over the river, behind the mass table in the Recoleta church.

The congregation was a nun, an Indian girl with a pony tail like a garlic string and a businessman who remained standing for most of the service. "Patrem omnipotentem factorem coeli et terrae visibilium," they chanted as the sun spread its honey on the vault through an onyx window. "Omnium et invisibilium et in unum Dominum."

In his prayers the priest mentioned the dead men in San Francisco. He prayed for their souls and for the souls of those responsible. Gabriel remained seated throughout, his eyes fixed on the communion table and the Virgin towering above him in a haze of blue neon. Then, when the wafer had become Christ and the church had emptied, he walked to the rail.

"Wait for me there," said Father Palacio.

They sat at a table in the communal dining room in a modern building behind the church. On the oilskin cloth a Coca-Cola bottle sprouted four artificial roses. A framed poster of Dali's crucifixion hung on the unpainted wall. Apart from a black piano with a scatter of *Études progressives* on its lid, the room was bare and smelled of cooked guinea-pig from the night before.

Out of his vestments Father Palacio wore a white, tieless shirt, buttoned at the neck.

"Who told you?"

Gabriel told him.

"Of course, of course." Walker had been there. He had found a can of something for the woodworm from his hardware store in Calle Barranco.

"Are you a friend of his wife's?"

"No."

A finger fretted at Father Palacio's lower lip.

"You've been to the convent?"

"This morning. They wouldn't let me in. It was like knocking on a battleship, Father."

"It is," concurred Father Palacio, "highly unusual for a man to be allowed inside."

He filled two mugs from a saucepan, and stirred in spoonfuls of coffee powder which formed lumps in the hot milk.

"Oh dear, this always happens. Do you mind?"

Squashing the blobs in his mug, Father Palacio described the afternoon on which he had been summoned by Madre Ana to hear the general confession of a dying nun, and the moments leading up to the collapse of the sister he discovered was Elena Silves.

"We covered her with a blanket and I went home. Naturally, I was worried, but I made it clear to the Mother Superior she should ring me if she needed to. I cannot say I expected a call. The sisters have their own medic."

He placed his mug on the table and raised his eyes, over the man's shoulder, to the window. It overlooked a small yard containing Father Palicio's pride and joy, a thin puya raimondii which flowered only once every hundred years. He had yet to see its white bud, though he had watered it religiously for twenty of them.

"But she did ring you."

"The following morning. And she was extremely distressed. Sister Colina . . . Elena Silves had been discovered missing."

"Go on."

"To begin with it was feared she had come to and panicked on finding herself in the dark."

He recalled his own return through the blackout, the police whistles, the radios instructing people to cross at street corners, the disembodied flashes of torchlight. He remembered just before he reached home how he stumbled into a couple by a wall. The woman had her hand inside the man's trousers. Seeing the priest, she withdrew it, laughing, burying her face in the man's neck. In that laugh, Father Palacio was confident he recognized Arturo Walker's wife.

"A search was ordered. Finally, when Madre Ana was at her wit's end, the under-prioress came upon a parcel in the laundry room containing Sister Colina's habit. This led to a suspicion something quite different might have happened. The search resumed and at midday they found the rope from the telegraph pole bordering the kitchen yard."

"What did you do?"

"There wasn't much I could do. It was more a matter for Bishop Barrantes in Belén."

"Whom you rang?"

"Whom I rang, and in whose hands it was insisted I leave things."

"And . . .?"

Father Palacio met his eye.

"That was the last I heard."

"She never came back?"

"No," said Father Palacio quietly. "No, she never came back."

"So where is she now?"

"I don't know. If anyone knows anything it's the Bishop – or rather the former Bishop. He was retired last year in circumstances still not entirely clear."

"What's he like?"

"Eucario Barrantes?" The priest contemplated the question.

"There are certain men of God," he said, "who believe the Catholic who is not a revolutionary is living in mortal sin. Eucario Barrantes is not such a man."

"Where do I find him?"

Father Palacio gave an address and the telephone number of a priory in Belén.

"Tell him you want to see his crosses," he added kindly. "He is proud of his collection and might be well disposed to those who share his pride."

"Brrrr," said Gabriel, bringing his elbow down to cause a tremble among the plastic petals. He rose to his feet. His eyes skidded over the bare walls, out into the yard and back into the room.

"I'm sorry."

He lifted his jacket from the back of the chair and picked up his briefcase.

"Sorry," he repeated.

He stopped by the door. He noticed the piano and the scores on its lid, and spread his fingers. He lowered them evenly onto the keys.

"A tuning's long overdue," Father Palacio admitted, responding to the distended chord. "Like that band."

"The band?"

"The band by the river."

"Why," Gabriel asked over his shoulder. "What were they playing?"

"To tell the truth, I'm not very keen on music – that's Father Mariano's piano. But I have a feeling they began with an Ave Maria. Pretty soon after they were onto 'Flor de la cantina' and 'Ojos azules'."

"'Ojos azules'?"

"You know the song. One heard it all the time in the sixties. In fact," said Father Palacio. He tapped his lips. "I remember now. That's what they were playing when she fainted."

In the Café Nanay, the record had come to an end. Gabriel looked at his watch. Another ten minutes. He drained his glass. He drew back his chair from the table. Barrantes was his last hope. After Barrantes, the tarmac ran out.

He rose, inserting another coin in the jukebox. Once more came the sound of crackling as the song he had been listening to began again.

> "Ojos azules no llores,
> No llores ni tengas amores,
> Llorarás cuando me vaya,
> Cuando remedio no haya."

Chapter 7

THERE IS NO BREEZE. In the heat, the gardener pauses under a copa de oro bush. He wipes his forehead, then returns to picking up the yellow leaves flecking the sparse grass.

The square smells of fresh-ground contraband coffee from the Café Nanay. A girl walks into the day from the café's dark recess, holding an ice-cream, and hurries back to work. A dog watches the vanilla dripping from her fingers. It ambles from under a bench and licks the melting drops.

The sound of Sebastián's bucket is joined at the far end of the square by the rattle of a shoe-shine box. The boy rattling the box is hidden by the epaulettes of Admiral Grau. The sun glints on the brave sailor's brow.

Don Wenceslau sighs. In an hour he has hardly seen anyone he knows. He recognizes their faces, not their names. Who has he seen? He spreads a leafy hand to count them.

He has seen Vásquez, with whom he always stops to talk first thing before coming to the bench. He likes to inspect the masato bottles on his barrow, to see there are enough.

And Sebastián, of course. He flattens out a second finger. He squints at the pavement opposite, by the old Club of Dead Parrots, where Sebastián sits in a pyramid of black, holding up his bucket whenever he hears footsteps.

Few know what the face looks like beneath that hood. Don Wenceslau remembers Don Leopoldo thinking he knew. "La Verruga," said Don Leopoldo. "Augustus Zárate referred to it first in 1543 and I believe it is mentioned by Cosme Bueno in *Descripciones Geográficas*." He then repeated in detail Dr Lache's description of the morbid growths, the black swellings, the bleeding warts that characterized the primary stages of the disease.

But Don García disagrees. He does not believe Sebastián suffers from verruga. He believes his disease can only be cured by a dust made from fire-flies.

"He has la uta."

"And what does la uta do?"

"It eats away the face until it is just a hole surrounded by teeth."

Don Wenceslau has never liked to imagine Sebastián's face after that. Instead, he thinks of another face that has passed by them that morning, its nose pointing firmly at the sky – until it notices Don Wenceslau.

"Good morning, Don Wenceslau, and how are you, it's a long time since you entertained us with your amusing stories. . ."

It was the warmth in La Palometa's greeting that caused the man now snoring gently next to him to cover his face with *El Oriente*. But Don García has no grounds for jealousy.

Pía Zumate is called Palometa after a fish with a red fin, because of the henna she still applies to her grey hair in the hope that one day news will come of the Booth liner *Ambrose*'s return to the river, and with it the officer who promised his heart fifty years before, over something he called a pink gin.

Don Wenceslau shivers at the thought of her permanent smile that gives an oval frame to teeth the colour of palm hearts. He has never seen a woman smile like that. It is a smile that has bewitched Don García since he saw it on her young face, seventy years ago, behind the counter of the Salón de Belleza in Juan Próspero, the drug and beauty store now owned by her youngest sister, Dominica.

"She lives in hope," Don García likes to explain. It must be years since anyone has softened her breasts with their touch. Over these years Don García has asked both his companions for their opinion of La Palometa. According to his stomachache Don Wenceslau would reply: "Don García, you know me, you know what I feel, women and melons are hard to know." Or, if after lunch: "There's no such thing as an ugly sweetheart." Or, once, in an unguarded moment: "Why is it as women get older, they look more like men?"

Don García has stopped asking Don Leopoldo, since the time Don Leopoldo replied by saying: "One thing I would say about women. . ."

They had both turned at that, even Don Wenceslau. He never

thought Don Leopoldo believed in anything – except silence and history.

"And. . . what is that?" Don García had asked.

Don Wenceslau cannot help laughing to himself at the memory of Don García's face as Don Leopoldo pronounced.

"A woman with a beard," he had said slowly, "salute at a distance."

Don Wenceslau looks at his hand open with three fingers. Who else has passed this morning? No one, not unless he counts the face at the hotel window. He can't really include a face he doesn't know, though he has grown used to its furtive appearances, one moment pressed to the shutters, the next, away like a hummingbird.

But all this is forgotten as Don Wenceslau sees a shoe-shine boy curl round the base of Admiral Grau. With a whistle, he summons him.

The boy settles at his feet. He opens his box and produces a number of perforated sheets, detaching three of them. Don Wenceslau leans back and extracts a number of coins from his trouser pockets. He counts them out.

"My turn," he tells the boy, with a wink, dropping the money into the box. He folds the three sheets and inserts them in the mouth of the bag at Don Leopoldo's feet.

There are days when it seems the only thing which keeps them going is the prospect of a win on the lottery, but Don Wenceslau wonders what would happen if they did draw the prize and had to turn out that bag to find the tickets. What magnificent wastes would they find among Don Leopoldo's papers, what years of hope, what secrets?

"Now," he says to the boy. "My shoes."

Don Wenceslau always feels important as he lifts his feet onto the wooden stilt, which is why, every day, he indulges in the operation twice. This morning, because of his stomach, he feels in special need of attention.

"No," he says firmly. "That's red and you know it is. I want brown."

He is proud of his shoes. He bought them in a sale from Mr Cazes, the departing British Consul, in 1921. They have leather soles which don't make his feet sweat and long thick laces. Barely decipherable on the place where his heels wriggle are the words Ducker & Son, 12 The Turl, Oxford. For some reason, the boy always tries to polish his Duckers – or Doocares, as Don Wenceslau pronounces them – with a polish the colour of cherry.

"Why do you do that?" he asks in his dyspeptic way.

The boy grins without answering, and scrapes his denim cloth along the scuffed caps. Rouged and browned and blackened from polish, his hands are those of an artist. He taps a sole to indicate he is ready for Don Wenceslau's other foot. Perhaps cherry is cheaper, thinks Don Wenceslau, or brown is in short supply, but the boy never has any trouble in producing the brown tin. It is one of those inexplicable things.

Like the figure in La Palometa's hotel, above the room where he spent the night of his life, where now a sheet hangs out to dry so white he can almost smell it.

He looks at the newspaper sulking beside him. He imagines Don García's eyes closed beneath it, the dreams cavorting under their lids. He looks at Don Leopoldo, who has a fleck of shaving cream in his ear.

"What do you think?" he asks them both.

Don Leopoldo has his eyes shut in the sun. In the lobster glow, he is remembering the shave given him first thing that morning by his barber, and the hair oil applied to his balding head. His face still tingles with the closeness of the blade, sharpened on a strap under the mirror. Don Leopoldo never likes to look at himself in the glass. As his face is squeezed and powdered and sprayed with cold cologne, his eyes fix instead on the deposits of dust on the bumpy wall or the jar of water where the barber dips his comb. That morning his mind had been on a most interesting article he had happened on in the Buenos Aires *Revista*. The article, by Dr López, an historian from Montevideo, argued that the Quechua language was of Pelasgic origin and that the Incas were of Greek descent. A footnote referred to a polemic in another periodical which tendered the thesis that the Incas might have been paper-makers to the

Roman Empire. . .

Aroused by Don Wenceslau, he shakes his head.

"What do I think about what?" he asks with irritation.

"About our friend on the fourth floor."

"Have you seen him?"

"I wanted to know what you thought."

"You know perfectly well what I think."

"You haven't changed your mind?"

Don Leopoldo rubs his eyes as if the soft flesh were dough. No, he has not. In six years, there has been nothing to alter his suspicion that the face belongs to one of the cocaine traffickers who speed the river in gleaming launches.

"I still think he's an Irish peer," says Don Wenceslau, who believes all evils emanated from the land which had given birth to Roger Casement, the insatiable pederast who had blackened the name of Belén.

"That's even more ludicrous than Don García's suggestion," says Don Leopoldo.

At the mention of this name, the newspaper moves. Don García emerges from under the headlines. He seems in a better mood.

"Talking about my Argentine?"

For Don García, the picaflor, there is no other explanation for the soft-shoe shuffle which keeps Pía Zumate awake on the floor below and the American songs which repeat themselves over and over and over again at all times of the day and night, than that their owner is a dancer in exile, an exponent of the Boca's most incautious tangos, a woman locked away by whoever it is that settles the monthly bill and who is only waiting for the appropriate moment to throw open her shutters and let down her coffee-dark hair for Don García to climb.

Don Leopoldo has never made any secret of the fact he considers this interpretation incurably frivolous.

So it is that for want of anything more to say on the subject, the three of them are looking in the direction of the hotel when a light flashes in the entrance lobby as the door of the Café Nanay catches the sun. A man emerges and stands in the brightness of the day. He inspects his watch and makes off down Calle Juan Próspero.

"I am dreaming," says Don Wenceslau. "Tell me I'm dreaming. Surely the bastards. . . "

Don García's reaction is a frightened whisper. "It's not possible. He's a dead man. I've just seen his name in the paper."

Don Leopoldo prefers to believe the evidence of his watery eyes. "Dios," he says, shaking his head.

A noise blares from Juan Próspero. A car drives into the square. "The happiest and the saddest love story ever told. . . " says the loudspeaker on its roof. The square is assailed by information about the day's film at the Cinema Bolognesi. *"The Rubber Man's Daughter*, starring Luis Sintra. . . " The car drives twice round the square and off down Calle Raimondi before anyone speaks again.

It is Don Wenceslau who breaks the silence. He stretches out his feet to inspect their twinkling caps. He wriggles them to catch the sun.

"He must have come back to find her," he says.

Chapter 8

AT 9.30 A.M. Gabriel entered the Franciscan priory in Juan Próspero, four doors down from the Salón de Belleza. It was a small house with ornately grilled windows and a facade of modern tiles. The tiles in the hall were older. They dated back to the rubber boom, when the building belonged to a company manufacturing water-tube boilers.

The hall was in darkness. Gabriel made out the shape of a woman behind the reception desk. She was applying lipstick in the dark. When she saw Gabriel she jumped, put down her compact and touched a switch on the wall. In the light, Gabriel saw clearly the woman's tight white trousers, the overgenerous lips and the bruises on her face where someone may have beaten her. He thought he recognized the woman. He did. They had collided outside the Café Nanay.

"Have you an appointment?"

"Yes. I rang three days ago from Lima."

"Lima?"

"I spoke to someone again yesterday."

"Was it you who rang from Requena?"

"That's right."

She examined the appointments book on her desk. The book was empty except for a name entered in large blue letters.

"Julio Ángel Medina," she reminded herself. "From *Caretas*." She looked up. "You've come to interview His Lordship about his crosses."

"His Lordship?" said Gabriel. "I thought he had retired."

"Yes, but he likes to keep up appearances."

That morning Eucario Barrantes had woken in a great damp patch.

His incontinence had worsened since his enforced retirement and the appointment of a new Bishop to Belén the year before. In his disappointment he consoled himself by accepting most of the invitations he received, from receptions at the Club de Leones to Rotarian dinners at the Hotel Liberty.

In company, with a drink or two, he could forget. Alone in his bed he could not.

It was a disappointment that had taken seed many years before with the vision of Elena Silves; a disappointment fed by his decision to listen to that grison Don Miguel.

It was Don Miguel who had seen the gold at the end of this rainbow.

Poor Bishop. To be struggling through such a no-man's-land.

"A no-man's-land? What're you on about Don Miguel?"

At the bar in the Club de Leones, Don Miguel repeated his phrase, adding a sad smile.

A no-man's-land between the Church's decision on whether to turn the site into an official shrine, and the Church's ability to recoup something from the pilgrims visiting the site.

"There must be thousands, no?" said Don Miguel, urging him to think about it. It was well known the Bishop was in two minds. He should continue to indulge this doubt. The sooner he decided against Elena Silves, the less money Don Miguel could guarantee the offertory.

"And you ought to believe her, Bishop. After all," said Don Miguel, "look at me. I'm the living proof."

The Bishop had looked at him and thought about it. In fact he had thought about nothing else for weeks. The thought of Don Miguel's bribe occupied him as he poured the wine at Mass, it occupied him as he drank it at midday, it occupied him as he passed it from his tormented body in the evening. It was on his mind when he asked Elena's aunt for the umpteenth time about her father's ivory cross from Goa. Nor did it budge a fraction when she told him, Yes, she would sell it, it had brought no luck, and then named a price so ludicrous he was left with no option but to agree that Don Miguel was indeed a living proof and the sooner a diocesan commission was appointed to investigate the vision of Elena Silves the better.

But Bishop Barrantes only knew the fullest flower of his disappointment after Elena Silves' escape from the convent of Santa Clara.

His failure to discover her whereabouts had been greeted in Lima and in Rome with a monstrous frown. They were already tired and suspicious of Barrantes. They were aware it had taken seven years to authenticate the apparition at Fátima. But after eighteen years of prevarication, they smelled a jungle rat. Elena Silves' escape offered the chance to locate it.

The Papal Nuncio was ordered to conduct a discreet investigation. In a despatch to the Curia in Rome, also circulated to the Cardinal Archbishop in Lima, he summarized the results.

Of the twelve members appointed by Barrantes, only seven had found time to discharge their duties. In eighteen years, these members had submitted thirty-seven pages. The Nuncio's gravest charge concerned the Bishop's obsessive devotion to the cross. There was no way, he wrote, that Bishop Barrantes' celebrated collection of crucifixes could have been financed from the stipend due to an Apostolic Vicariate.

Bishop Barrantes was never to know the exact reason for his premature retirement. Not knowing it, he misattributed it, and misattributing it, he felt a certain biliousness towards the world at large and the person he believed responsible.

His reception of Gabriel that morning was tempered by the expectation that a favourable profile in the weekly journal *Caretas* – not a periodical he regularly saw, but one whose influence he didn't deny – would give as much pleasure to his former parishioners as it would discomfort certain quarters in Lima. It was a matter for regret, he saw now, that his attitude towards the press had been one of supercilious avoidance.

The receptionist knocked twice on a door in the hall. When there was no answer, she stood aside for Gabriel to pass.

"Wait in here."

The room was unlit and decorated with the less memorable gifts donated to the Bishop in the course of his episcopal duties.

A bowl from officers serving with the Customs and Excise in Belén, por su valiosa colaboración; a corner cabinet of coins and medals; a silver-plated beer mat from the municipality of Piura, his first diocese, etched with a message of eterno agradecimiento por sus bendiciones, and, on a table in the middle of the black marble floor, a plate with the words Coca-Cola, donated by Belén's small but prosperous Chinese community and containing a cigarette stub.

Gabriel was looking at a framed photograph of the Pope when the Bishop entered. He walked like a parrot with clipped wings, with a stooping back.

When he shook hands, the gesture was more a clasp than a greeting.

When he spoke his breath smelled slightly of mint.

"Did you see His Holiness in Lima?"

Gabriel shook his head. "I was on another assignment."

"A wonderful occasion," said the Bishop, settling into a wooden chair from which his feet hardly touched the ground. "He insisted on flying to Peru despite the threats on his life. A truly impressive person. Now," he said rubbing his hands, "what can I do for you, young man?"

Gabriel opened a notebook. His editor had sent him to find a colour story. Something to interest Caretas's readers. They had been gorged on terrorists. Someone in Lima had mentioned the Bishop's collection of crosses.

"It sounded ideal."

From the depths of his chair, the Bishop swelled visibly. "Quite right too. You Limeños only notice us when the food is spoiling in your freezer. At least these terrorists are forcing people to realize we exist. . . but perhaps you'd better not write that." On reflection, he did not wish the readers of Caretas, still less the members of the Club de Leones, to think they were dealing with a liberation theologian.

"Not that there will be many terrorists left after that business in San Francisco, eh?" The Bishop laughed. "What do you think about that? I suppose you're one of those pressing for an enquiry. If you ask me, it was a massacre waiting to happen."

"I take it your collection is photogenic?"

"Does a fish swim? It's a collection without parallel. Come."

The bishop slipped from his chair and ferreted in his back pocket for a bunch of keys. The first door he unlocked opened into a dining room. On the wall, suspended from a nail through the trigger guard, was an old-fashioned rifle. It stretched at an angle beneath the skull of a small deer.

"My greatest sin," explained the Bishop enthusiastically.

"Once a year Capitán Velarde invites me to shoot with him in the Putumayo. Once a year only, because I'm so bad."

He unlocked the door into the next room and pressed a bank of switches.

"There," he said. "My inner sanctum."

The grey interior was a forest of crucifixes. On all sides, Christ twisted in metal, wooden and ivory agony.

"What did I tell you? A collection without parallel."

He picked up an effigy and blew gently on Christ's head. A nebula of dust rose from the yellow thorns.

"Sixteenth-century elephant's tusk from Goa. Commissioned for the King of Portugal's private chapel." Gently, he handed it over.

For the best part of an hour, the Bishop rotated about the room.

"That's Izearda with a Z," he would say, urging Gabriel to make another entry in his notebook.

Or, "That was a gift from the Marquis of Leiria, a wonderful man, but you had better not put that. The family might not. . . "

Or, "Thieves have only once broken in. All they stole were a pair of my slippers and an eiderdown."

As he scribbled these things down, Gabriel became aware of other items in the room. Behind one crucifixion, an onyx ashtray in the shape of a revolver; behind another, a miniature electric fan with green blades; behind another a ceramic vessel from the Chimu dynasty. When he looked at the walls, he also discovered unlikely objects among the pendulant rosaries; a calendar with a bare-breasted girl, a plastic parrot on a wire perch ("It makes no mess," joked the Bishop) and, in brass surrounds, a number of photographs revealing the Bishop as a younger man. In each he was found to be standing beside someone famous or embracing someone famous until, in a prominent portrait on its own, he appeared to have reached that state himself.

"Come," said the Bishop when they had moved full circle, "I want to show you something very special." He arrived before a large safe.

There was another catechism of keys and the cast-iron door swung open. The Bishop began piling its contents into his arms. When he turned about, he was holding about thirty flat green boxes. These he kept in position with his chin.

"The other room."

Reinstalled in his chair, the Bishop began opening the lids, removing the tissue paper and scooping up the objects that lay in the cotton wool bed. Each was a small cross; each he held up to the light and fondled before passing over. Black pearl, glass, ruby, gold, emerald from Lisbon, Murano, Salamanca, Trujillo. Thirty-five to a box – the boxes specially made in Seville, but he had run out of them – over seventy boxes, almost three thousand crosses and thirty years in amassing. The statistics sent their speaker into ecstasy.

He removed another lid. "Ah," he said, "my favourite. My absolute favourite. Late sixteenth century, commissioned by the Viceroy for his second wife. A silver and ruby Lord of Miracles."

Gabriel held the minute cross in his hand. "Beautiful," he agreed. "Exquisite."

He raised it to the light. "Your Lordship, do you believe in miracles?"

"Oh, yes." The Bishop's eyes seized on another example of Spanish craftsmanship.

"What about visions?"

The Bishop deposited the last of his boxes on the marble floor and sank his head back in the chair. He looked at Gabriel, scratching the hairy back of a hand.

"You're referring to this man in Chile everyone's talking about. All I can say is I've heard the cassettes – they're in my office if you want to hear them. I must confess, I'm not yet convinced."

"Not him especially. In general."

The Bishop caressed one of the chins that concealed the white rectangle of his calling. "I believe they are possible. But the Church has to be very prudent." He formed a circle with his thumb and index finger through which he pretended to peer.

"There must be checking and double checking and doctors' reports before one can trouble Rome."

"What about Elena Silves?" said Gabriel.

The Bishop coughed. His hand wriggled into a pocket from which he produced a handkerchief. He blew a dry nose.

"In the case of Elena Silves, I would say, yes, up to a point the Church was satisfied. My own opinion is that the phenomena, though curious, were not very impressive." His face arranged itself according to his notion of a worldly grin. "Perhaps we have been spoiled by television and Hollywood. The Holy Mother is going to have to advance a little if she wishes to make a competitive appearance in today's world. But the case of Elena Silves was an exceptional case. It can be of no interest to a sophisticated Limeño.

"Now, let me tell you more about myself. My upbringing in Piura. My modest achievements in Belén. My monograph on Jean Gerson which, incidentally, the Spanish publishers intend for next year. And we must discuss arrangements for a photographer. When do you think your article will appear?"

Gabriel looked at the Christ in his palm.

"I'll be honest. I had intended originally to write about Elena Silves."

The Bishop frowned.

"Elena Silves?"

"I want to talk to her."

"But... that's impossible. She's in a closed order. She has been for almost twenty years."

"I know. I've been there."

"You've been there? Where?"

"Santa Clara."

"And?"

"They wouldn't let me in."

"Out of the question. Besides," said the Bishop quickly, "from what I hear, they're all extremely ugly. A handsome chap like you would have them abandoning their vocation before you could peel a grape."

Gabriel smiled weakly. When he smiled his scar became another laugh line.

"She was Sister Colina, wasn't she? She was the nun who escaped."

"Why are you so interested? Why? The whole structure of our society is collapsing and what are you doing? Chasing nuns."

"Elena Silves is my cousin."

There was a silence. The Bishop was goitrous. He tried rising from his chair. He waved at the box lids. "You mean, this. . . all this was an excuse."

"No," said Gabriel. "I'm here to write a feature on you. But since I was here, I had to ask. You're the only person who can tell me where she is. The family has not heard a word. They don't even know if she returned to Santa Clara."

The Bishop calmed himself.

"No, she's not at Santa Clara."

"Where is she?"

"I have no idea. The matter has been out of my control for some time. In the interim I have heard nothing, I have read nothing. I can't help you."

Gabriel knocked his forehead in frustration. "Don't you think it odd that a woman who was twice blessed with a vision of the Virgin Mary, to the apparent satisfaction of the Church, should suddenly vanish after eighteen years and that no one is the slightest bit interested – least of all the Church?"

"Young man," said the Bishop, weighing his words as coldly as a money-lender, "you misrepresent something you know nothing about. Whether or not the Church is satisfied, it is concerned about your cousin. Exceedingly so. But the matter, as I said, is out of my hands."

He began replacing the lids. "If you wish to pursue your investigation, I suggest you make contact either with the Cardinal Archbishop – or the chief of the Policía de Investigaciones."

"For God's sake, why the PIP?"

"This is speculative, certainly not for publication in *Caretas*," said the Bishop. He relieved Gabriel of his cross. "It is thought that your cousin escaped to look for somebody."

"Who?"

The Bishop returned a sheet of tissue paper to the box in his lap. When the lid did not fit, he removed the paper and screwed it angrily into a ball.

"His photograph was discovered among her belongings. Someone she was involved with before the appearance of Our Holy Mother."

"But why the police?" Gabriel repeated, with less conviction. The Bishop put down his box and inspected his ringed fingers – the fingers he would lick when Gabriel had gone, that would search through five issues of his secretary's *Caretas* for the by-line of Julio Ángel Medina; the fingers he would jab at the intercom and tap on the blotter while he waited for the call to go through to Capitán Velarde, the city's new Deputy Chief of Police; the fingers that now formed a gothic vault as he gave his answer to Gabriel.

"It transpires she may have escaped Santa Clara to look for a well-known terrorist."

Chapter 9

"WHAT I HAVE TO TELL YOU about Gabriel's grandfather is not first hand. There is no one alive who met his grandfather. I discovered the following from his father, the mechanic, a courteous man who used to service my motorbike in the days when I could ride one. He seemed pleased at my calculation that the Lungs were almost definitely the fourth Chinese family to settle in Belén.

"In 1872 Achin Man Lung came from Hiempen to work on the railroads. In a contract celebrated at Macao, the twenty-one-year-old coolie placed himself at the orders of the American industrialist, Henry Meiggs. For a term of eight years, he pledged to serve as agricultural labourer, gardener, shepherd, house servant and general workman.

"The following week he boarded the *Lady Charlotte*.

"We may judge from Felix Cipriano C. Zegarra's perfectly serviceable work, *La Condición Jurídica de los Extranjeros en el Perú* (Santiago, 1872) that the journey to Peru was a terrible one. Over seven hundred coolies had joined the *Lady Charlotte* at Macao. Only two hundred and ninety-two of them survived.

"According to the English captain – a metal-hearted sailor who boasted that everything he knew about the sea could be learnt on the Mersey estuary – Johnny Chinaman was not a particularly sturdy race.

"At Callao, the harbour for Lima, the captain ordered his decks to be scrubbed with lime chloride and the vomit to be washed from the survivors. When they were clean, he gave them each a pair of wide calico trousers, a trunk the size of a tea chest and a cane hat.

"'Models of health and sound of limb,' was how the Mersey sailor described his cargo, his mouth widened by a passion for cigars and curses.

"Achin Man Lung did not live up to the advertisement. Dysentery had scooped him away. His eyes were lifeless tadpoles, his mouth a trembling slit. Meiggs' representative squeezed his biceps and spun him like a top.

"'$350, no more.'

"Achin worked on the Meiggs railroad, then on the coast at Pabellón de Pica. He lived in a cave – its rafters made from the ribs of whales – and cleared four tons of guano every day in a tin barrow with a loose wheel. When scurvy made him useless, he was sold to a hacienda at Upaca where his galled ankles prevented him from joining a mutiny. At the age of thirty, because of his experience on the Lima to Jauja railway, he was recruited by the Peruvian Amazon Company. They were planning a narrow-gauge track from their warehouse to the river bank. They wanted cheap, experienced labour.

"It came no cheaper than Achin Man Lung.

"His papers were examined and returned to him by the interpreter. There was one problem. They had an Achin.

"'Call him Pancrasio,' said the agent. He looked out of the window at the line of Chinese coiling like a pony tail around the outhouse.

"'We've got a Pancrasio,' said the interpreter.

"'What about Pedro?'

"'No, sir.'

"'Then call him Pedro. No, wait, I've a better idea.' The agent walked to a shelf. He removed from it a large book. It was Radcliffe Crocker's *Diseases of the Skin – their description, pathology, diagnosis and treatment*.

"'Let's call him Prurigo.'

"So Prurigo Man Lung – those in the queue after him bore names like Tylosis, Tonsurans and Unguentum – was entered into the company ledger. Age 30. Stature – medium. Colour – yellowy white. Forehead – high. Eyes – small. Mouth – wide. Particular marks – a finger missing from his right hand, run over by a guano barrow.

"Prurigo who had been Achin settled by the Moronacocha lake on the outskirts of Belén where he married a loquacious Bora Indian and dropped dead one day without a whisper. The fire had died within him when he walked onto the *Lady Charlotte*, but it reignited in his children and in their children who kept his contract in his tea chest and vowed never to be so subservient . . ."

In his thirty-nine years, Gabriel Rondón Lung had only been subservient to one man. The man whose handsome face looked out from posters on the walls of houses and churches and town halls of every town in the land.

The man who called himself Presidente Ezequiel.

One could no more hope to live without the presence of Ezequiel than one might hope to eat one's food without swallowing dust, or sleep in the jungle without scratching for fleas or look up to the red, volcanic slopes of Nakaq without seeing his name.

The man was everywhere.

Gabriel left the priory and walked down Juan Próspero towards the contraband market. He walked slowly, his briefcase knocking against his legs. His interview with Barrantes had left him in a state of despair. After two weeks, the knowledge of Elena's disappearance was something he couldn't absorb, something unbearable. All of a sudden he wanted sleep. He screwed his eyes tight and opened them again. No. He mustn't. He looked at his watch. 11.35. He had an assignation. To keep himself awake, he changed his pace.

Like a cauchero mistress, Belén still clung to her shawl of tiled palaces and broken-toothed colonnades. They lay in tatters under a clear sky. The rubber days were over, but she continued to deck herself in the proceeds of the jungle. After rubber, oil; after oil, cocaine.

"Whatever applies to other parts of the country," he had told Hipólito, who only half listened as he gave another spin to the balding tennis ball on his finger, "doesn't apply here. Belén is an island in the jungle. People are happy with their lot. There's no need for revolution. There is no desire for it."

"We must try all the same," Hipólito said.

"Why?"

"Because, like you, I cannot stomach the fact that I am a middleman in my own country. Because I believe something can be done about it." He threw up the ball and caught it. "It's not going to be easy, that's all. Catch."

When Gabriel reached Sargento Lores he turned left into the crowded stalls. Under the blue plastic canopies, he saw the commodities he had known as a child. They came from the far corners of the world. Coffee from Brazil, creamery butter from Dublin, aftershave from Paris, gin from London.

Gin from London . . . Hadn't this been the spot where he had met Elena's aunt, her basket clinking with green bottles? Here on this very corner, probably by this same stall, he had asked her the question which he had been asking himself every minute for the last two weeks, the question that had lain dormant for twenty-one years.

"Where's Elena?"

The memory of it engulfed him as strongly as the crowd. No, he thought. His assignation would have to wait. He needed first to sleep.

It was an hour since Barrantes' call.

Capitán Velarde, Belén's newly appointed Deputy Chief of Police, looked at the telephone on his desk. The mouthpiece in his old machine had broken and this grey replacement, smelling of chicken flesh and the colour of putty, was all the exchange could offer. At least it didn't smell of mint, he thought, thinking of Barrantes' breath.

That morning the former Bishop had expended a lot of it telling Velarde about a man who clearly wasn't who he claimed to be.

"Who did he claim to be?"

"A journalist from *Caretas*. Julio Ángel Medina. But my secretary's rung their office and they've nobody with that name. The point is, this man's in town looking for Elena Silves."

"Elena Silves?"

"He says he's her cousin. I only realized afterwards she never had a cousin. The thought crossed my mind it might be Gabriel Lung but, of course, he's dead."

"So far as we know," said Velarde, who, as soon as he heard the name, felt a nasty contraction in his throat as if he had just bitten deep into a hot pepper.

But that first name. Julio Ángel Medina. That was also a name which meant something.

"By the way, Capitán, since I've got you, what about Elena Silves? Any leads?"

"Father Barrantes," said Velarde deliberately, "Elena Silves is the least of my worries. Recalcitrant nuns are your problem, not mine. At present I have a massacre on my hands."

But, an hour later, Capitán Velarde was opening a slim file on Julio Ángel Medina, dated 1965, which linked him with the names of Gabriel Rondón Lung, Edith Pusanga, Bonifacio Medina and a dead man called Hipólito Mercedes. Once more Velarde looked at his phone. "Emergencia 05" he noticed in the centre of the dial. Who the fuck does a policeman dial in emergency?

Take your pick, he thought. The army, the navy, the air force. Or perhaps if it was refinement you were after, army intelligence, navy intelligence, air force intelligence. It didn't much matter. They were all piss poor and none of them talked to the others anyway.

Then again, he could dial his own crack regiment, the Sinchis, those bastards who came in from Satipo with knives in their boots and coke up their nose and thought they were God, except they shitted on God too most of them. They were as bad as Sendero. And Sendero were bad. Bad, bad, bad, he said rapping the desk with his Ray-Bans.

He must buy a new pair next time he went to Lima. The fucking things were too small. They fell off whenever he lost his temper.

An electric fan swivelled on the floor by his feet, ruffling his trouser legs. He would have liked another day to nail Barrantes' reporter. Nail him so the shithead sang like Aunt Angelica's canaries and he could hold his head up in the Club de Leones and say See you mother fuckers, you can't get the better of the Guardia Civil – not a good Guardia Civil.

He would have liked an extra day because it was that terruco friend of Hipólito Mercedes who had fucked up his promotion six years ago. But what if "the man from *Caretas*" was one of those responsible for the murder at Cabaña? If that was the case, then professional pride didn't come into it. It didn't matter who caught him, so long as he was caught and after what the village storekeeper told him, the sooner the better.

Cabaña. He'd never heard of Cabaña till the previous day. He'd had to take off his sunglasses and peer at the map until he gave up and told the storekeeper to point it out, which he did with a trembling finger that covered the whole of a village he'd never heard of because, of course, it was over a thousand miles south of Belén. That was one of the troubles with the jungle. It went on forever.

"But, Señor Capitán . . . it's in the desert." The storekeeper had hardly been able to get his words out standing there by the desk, his hands bunching the hat he held against his crotch as he begged for protection.

He smelled of cane spirit and fear. They had been after him as well, señor, but he had been above the village when they came. He had been unloading cement bags into the schoolhouse.

It was his wife who saw everything, saw them order everyone into the square, saw them line up four men under the goalpost, the alcalde, the postmaster, the magistrate and his cousin who kept the keys to the graveyard.

"And me, señor, then they asked for me."

But they couldn't find him and his wife said nothing, just watched with clattering teeth as they read out something about the People's War and Mao and Mariátegui and jerked their heads back like chickens.

It was a woman who slit their throats so the blood spurted into the bucket she held up to their necks. She was old for one of them, about forty, señor, and she daubed the walls of the church and the door of the school with their blood.

LONG LIVE PRESIDENTE EZEQUIEL AND THE NEW DEMOCRACY! she wrote. This I saw with my own eyes, señor, he had said pointing to two bloodshot orbs that couldn't stay still for a second. And I saw the bodies, he stammered. They were lying on the priest's floor in a dark purple pool like the dye used by the women for wool. They looked twisted and wrong. Then he saw why.

The feet and the heads of the four men had been hacked off and crudely sewn back on.

"The wrong way, señor," came the storekeeper's whisper.

The phrase had haunted Capitán Velarde ever since. As a policeman, he could be next in line. He had found himself looking over the desk at the man's feet poking from rubber tyre sandals and speculating what difference it would make. You could watch yourself shitting, he supposed, but girls would be a problem.

"Corporal," he ordered. "Take this man to your grandmother. Give him the usual allowance — and I mean him, not you, or whoever you spent it on at Señora Zumate's. Yes, I know about last time. But we're going to need him again."

Eighteen hours after he had dismissed the storekeeper, promising him three months' protection, Capitán Velarde's mind was still stained with an image. He saw the dead men, all four of them — their heads like that so they couldn't see their murderers, their feet so they couldn't follow.

No, he couldn't afford to fuck up this time. He lifted his phone. Bracing himself against the smell, he spoke into the mouthpiece.

"Get me head office in Lima. No. I don't care if it takes an hour."

Chapter 10

IT WAS NIGHT when Gabriel emerged along the street known as Venecia. He had slept in a derelict hut on the rice flats. He had slept for eight hours. Now he walked quickly.

The stale light of a lamp stretched his shadow across the mud path and up against the wooden houses. The street was deserted but for a dog that howled like a cock. A television set cast coloured shadows on a clinkered ceiling. In the distance a boat droned. Two kilometres from the cathedral square of Belén, this was a district of fishermen and smugglers and the river's most foetid smells.

Short of the waterfront he turned right and after a hundred yards came to a narrow passage leading to the river. Its entrance was lit by a paraffin lamp. Along one side was a counter lined with bottles. Gabriel knew them to contain aphrodisiacs for men about to enjoy the canoieras – girls who plied the water in flat-bottomed canoes. A man leant against the counter. He was telling the serving-woman that his name was Babilonia. He worked as a cleaner in the Hotel Liberty. He was waiting for the rain to stop.

"It has stopped," said the shrivelled woman retrieving his glass. Her husband who brewed the chuchuasi to raise Babilonia's dead lay on a hammock, snoring.

Gabriel walked to the water's edge. He whistled. From across the river came a cry, then nothing. He heard the sound of splashing. Presently a ferryman emerged from the dark, kneeling at the front of his canoe.

They slid into the night. Gabriel heard the lap of couples making love on either side as they crossed the river.

"Busy tonight?" he asked.

"Busy enough," said the other without turning. His shirt was undone. His knees poked from rolled-up trousers. He dipped his heart-shaped paddle in the water. "But now everyone goes to the Teletroca."

"The Teletroca?"

"Señora Zumate's place near the airport. Only the old ones stay."

"Old chickens make better soup," said Gabriel. The man gave an appreciative cackle and lay his paddle flat.

From where they landed, it was a five-minute walk to the house on San José. The front door was locked. A wire of light shone through a shutter. Gabriel ignored the door. He continued to a fence of corrugated iron. Locating the place where two sheets met, he prised them apart. He stepped into a small courtyard overlooked by an open window.

"Edith," he called softly. He tapped the shutters. Silence. Nothing moved in the room. The floor creaked. It creaked again. A figure edged into the light.

"Hello, Edith," he said, stepping from behind the shutter. The woman looked at him, the gun in her hands pointing straight at his chest. Despite heavy make-up, her face was blank, like the space on a wall where a portrait had hung. She moved forward one step, then another until the pistol pressed against Gabriel's temple. She pushed it into his forehead so that he was forced to move back.

"Gabriel?" Her hands began shaking. She rested the gun on the sill.

"Gabriel?" she said again. "Thank God." And she reached out to embrace him, holding his head tight and kissing and kissing the spot where she had made a cold red circle.

"You've grown a moustache. Different colour, but it suits you," she said, the life returning to her face.

Gabriel looked at her. The features had set in furrows, but it was the face of a still attractive woman.

She sat beside him on a wooden bench in the front room. She squeezed his hand. "I thought you were dead," she went on. "When I heard, I went out for a long walk. I found myself kneeling in church and praying. I was almost glad you were dead. It meant I didn't have to hope."

"Edith," said Gabriel.

"No, don't," she let out. "I know why you're here. It's not because of me." She raised a hand. "Don't even pretend. It's because of her, isn't it? Isn't it?"

"Edith, later," said Gabriel. "What about you? What have you been doing?"

"You caught me doing my washing." She wiped her eyes, attempting to laugh. "Then I heard the chickens and I thought one of those PIP bastards had come for me."

"An operation?"

"Back yesterday."

"Where?"

"Don't let's talk about it." She put a hand to his moustache. "But how dare you survive. How dare you?"

"I went back, Edith. I got into San Eduardo. That's where they've moved the survivors. I saw Rolando."

"I want you to tell me," she said, running her thumb over and over and over the bristles. "Everything. But first I'll get some coffee. You could do with it, couldn't you?"

She squeezed his hand. He returned the pressure. When she returned with the coffee, she found his hand again.

"Now tell me," she said.

So blowing into his cup, Gabriel told how, on his return from Silar, he had visited San Eduardo.

Like San Francisco, the prison had its market women in the road below. He bought a sack of avocados from them. The guards weren't interested in the sack. They just wanted to put a rubber stamp on his forearm.

"New security measures."

Gabriel sat in a booth. On the other side a man drew up a chair.

"Are you mad?" came the hiss through the mesh.

"Hello, Rolando."

"But they think you're dead."

"Then it makes things easier."

Rolando looked down at the formica table. His hands started fluttering. He dug his fingers in his arms to stop them. He was trembling badly.

"Rolando."

"It was terrible," he whispered. "They've all gone, Chino. Fanor, Gregorio, Flores, Néstor. . ." He produced a cigarette from his trousers. The trousers were pulled up to the knee. They revealed a network of moon-coloured blisters on his calves.

He tore off the filter and lit the cigarette.

"Start from the beginning."

"You'd gone when we had the order. It came from Ezequiel himself."

"From Ezequiel?" Gabriel leant forward.

"Néstor took it. He told us the President was hosting an International Socialist Conference. Four hundred journalists had come from all over the world. A perfect time to act." Two trails of smoke descended from his nostrils. He tried to laugh, but he coughed.

"The signal came at daybreak. We gathered in the dormitory. Néstor had fixed guns. On the stroke of six we shouted that a prisoner was ill. Oliveira was the guard. He suspected nothing. He was in the corridor at the time. He walked towards us whistling. Remember how he whistled? When he opened the dormitory door we dragged him inside. It was easy as breathing.

"The Governor turned up. He took away our list of demands. He was furious. He said he might be able to do something about the garbage dumps. He might even be able to help over the food allowance. But did we think anyone would listen to our other requests? He marched off locking the door into the yard.

"We waited all morning. Then on the radio we heard the government had gone into emergency meeting. A statement was read out. It said the President couldn't tolerate the conversion of prisons into a territory beyond the state. It also mentioned a Peace Commission was talking to us. It was the first we knew of it. We'd seen no Peace Commission. We'd seen nothing for eight hours. And why? Because when the Governor locked the outer door, we couldn't hear a thing. Apparently some arsehole was blowing himself blue through a megaphone, calling on us to surrender. It was all on Channel 7. Our failure to respond was taken to be a refusal. In fact, it was because we couldn't fucking well hear. I suppose we would have surrendered by mid-afternoon. By then it was too late. They'd called in the army."

The man threw his stub to the floor. He twisted a heel and lit another cigarette. He didn't remove the filter.

"We heard the helicopter bringing the General. That was at five. Then half an hour later they fired a bazooka at the outer door. It didn't make much of an impact. Some of us took shelter in the small bathroom. Oliveira was shitting himself, telling us it was all over, the military had taken the prison. The next explosion made a hole in the wall. That's when Néstor decided to surrender. He walked over to the figures who were crawling through. There were four or five of them. They wore black uniforms and ski masks round their eyes.

"He said something to them. They shot him in the stomach. More followed behind. They grabbed anyone they could and forced them through the hole. We were pushed into the patio and made to lie down with our hands on our heads. The General was strutting round with a megaphone. I heard him shouting 'Anyone who looks round will be shot.' I heard people say 'Douse them with petrol.' Someone else mentioned an order that none of us should remain alive. Someone else said 'Just do it, eliminate them.' They began to yank us by the hair, demanding our names.

"Your palanca, Julio, was next to me. He shouted he was a journalist. He always wrote good things about the police in the newspapers. He was taken away. Then it was my turn.

"They dragged me to the baths behind the dormitory. They made me strip naked. When they'd got five of us, they took us out and they shot us. I was hit four times, twice in the shoulder, twice in the feet.

"They dug a trench. They threw me in it with the others. They must have dynamited the second floor some time after that. I was buried for two days. I crawled out of the rubble on Friday. By then none of the dormitory was standing. They had blown it all up, the whole bloody thing," he said.

"They wrapped me in a blanket and took me to the hospital. I was told my life had been religiously spared. 'Not even your relatives think you are alive,' they said."

He snorted. Gabriel continued to say nothing. The room became loud with the sound of whispers from other booths. In one a woman giggled. Hearing her, Rolando clawed the mesh.

"Christ, I could do with a woman."

A bell rang. The guard by the door straightened his cap.

Time was up, he shouted. He advanced along the booths, banging each with his rifle butt.

"Come on, you cholos, out, out, out," he said, shaking Gabriel's shoulder.

"What about your woman. Did you find her?" But Gabriel couldn't bring himself to tell Edith that.

"Bastards," said Edith.

"I took him some paltas."

"Fucking, fucking bastards."

"Rolando said Ezequiel was having an emergency meeting. He said you would know the details."

Her face revolved until it stared into his.

"So here I am. Where's the meeting?" he asked.

In a sudden gesture, she took both his hands in hers. He held her to him and shook.

"To bed," she said, removing the cup from his hand. "We can discuss what needs to be discussed in the morning."

They went into another room. It had a couch, a chair and a large cupboard. A number of photographs were pinned to the side of the cupboard. Gabriel looked at them as he unbuttoned his shirt. "Is that me? I don't believe it." A younger man leant at an angle against a bar with a raised glass. It was the bar of the Café Nanay.

"When did you take that?"

Edith turned out the light in the passage. She fetched a glass of water which she put on the floor by the bed. "Don't you remember? No, I suppose you don't," she said, raising her shirt over her head. She wore nothing beneath. "Just before you went to prison."

Gabriel kicked his shoes to the floor. He took off his trousers. Edith stood waiting for him. She heard him remove his underpants, then his watch which made a hard sound on the chair. She knew when he approached he would turn her away from him. She felt his searching hardness against her back like a blind man's hand. She thought, "He doesn't want to see my face." She bent forward onto the creaking couch. She reached back between her thin legs to help him. She heard the slap of flesh accelerating against flesh until the moment he came.

"You're the only one, Edith," he whispered above her.

"Apart from Elena," she choked.

"Apart from Elena."

Gabriel woke early. He lay looking at his younger self on the wardrobe. He heard Edith wake beside him. He felt her hand spider down his stomach. When he asked about Ezequiel, she released him from her grip.

"How is he?"

"The same."

"Where is he?"

"I can't tell you. Not yet. But safe."

"Satipo?"

"Gabriel."

"Piura?"

"Gabriel, don't."

"So now the orders come from you?"

"You've been away."

She withdrew her hand and turned her back to him.

He chose his words carefully. "It's up to you to decide whether I attend the meeting?"

"If you like."

"Don't then."

Eventually she said, "You know what that means."

Gabriel slipped from the bed.

"It's a risk I have to take."

"It's against our code, Gabriel." She spoke to the wall. "To put a personal matter before duty. It's against everything we've been fighting for."

Gabriel pulled on his trousers.

"This concerns something that happened before either of us knew about codes. And you know it. I have to find her, Edith."

She turned over. She lay on her back, her hands held to her mouth, the tips of three fingers between her teeth. She bit hard on the painted nails.

"Don't you feel anything, Gabriel? Anything at all? How many have we lost? Two hundred? Three hundred? People you've lived with night and day for seven years, some you've been working with since we went to Ayacucho. But you're not thirsting for vengeance. Vengeance is the last thing on your mind. Your mind is full of a girl you last saw more than twenty years ago."

"Vengeance is a dish that can be eaten cold, Edith."

"But how can you not feel anything, at this moment of all moments?"

"What did you feel when they arrested me at Requena?"

"Gabriel, no...no..." She twisted, looking up at him from the bed. She couldn't see his face. A muscle prodded the inside of his back.

"Where were you and Bonifacio? Where were my dear comrades who had sworn to defend each other to the death?"

Edith didn't speak. She saw the *Victoria Regia* make its approach to the jetty. She saw the line of policemen, blowing on their hands because the morning was cold. She saw the panic erupt on Bonifacio's face, his flight to the engine room, his arm round the boy's neck, the boy's eyes, the boy's finger pointing at the hole smelling of grease and sawdust and rotting bark where they kept the fuel. She heard the sounds above as the *Victoria Regia* berthed. She realized it was too late to return on deck and protect Gabriel, who sat beneath a blanket nursing his torn cheek, frightened and suffocated.

"No, Edith," said Gabriel. "I don't want to betray the revolution. I just want to forget it for a while."

He walked into the other room. Through the window came the sound of men and women loading their market stalls. He opened the shutter a fraction. He saw black fish and cabbages and the hairless heads of howler monkeys. Across the street a woman swatted flies off a row of chicken parts. Another rolled cigarettes, pasting the papers with yucca gum.

On the tin roof opposite, a vulture arranged a black shawl of feathers, then heaved into the air. The river glared beyond. It flowed into a grey horizon, a frayed green belt of trees.

My home town, thought Gabriel.

When they tortured him, he'd erased it from his mind. In the bath, with the hood on his head, he had drowned his memories. When they came to use the electric wire – Verónica, they called it – he was a man who had never been to Belén.

Not that, strung upside down, he was unaware of Verónica's touch on his gums, his nipples, his foreskin, of cigarette jabs up and down his stomach, of lights shone into his face by men with tender voices and eyes bright with cocaine. But he occupied the torn skin of a man ignorant of anything that could help them.

"In Argentina," said the officer in charge, "we would have thrown him from a plane."

In Peru, they had sent him to San Francisco prison, to join his comrades.

Once you've been tortured, you're always tortured. That's what he'd heard. His suppression of himself had lasted until the moment he read Arturo Walker's article. Now, back in Belén, he wanted only to remember. Only by remembering would he piece together the man who had loved Elena.

He found an open bottle of Inca Kola on a shelf beside the basin. He swilled a mouthful round his dry tongue. The sickly green liquid was flat but out of habit he burped. Stretching his arms, he walked about the room until he came to a shelf of books. He recognized several as his own.

He passed a finger over the spines. To his father's annoyance, his handsome face had been buried in these pages all day. "One deed creates more propaganda than a thousand leaflets," the mechanic used to bark, twisting Gabriel's ear with a paraffined hand. "Now off those steps. I need two bottles of beer from Don Tonsurans."

By the time he was twelve he had read Schiller, Conrad and Bakunin. He knew *Los Tiranos* by heart, and Fanon's *Wretched of the Earth*. He believed he understood what Buonarroti meant when he said no means are criminal which are employed to obtain a sacred end.

He was fifteen before he came upon the blue and white covers of José Carlos Mariátegui, the founder of Peru's Communist Party. He removed the volume from the shelf. These seven essays on Peruvian Reality – written in the 1920s – had affected him most of all. Mariátegui's belligerent vision of a socialist future, dependant on the Indian, was a vision that matched his own. He looked at the confident scribbles of his adolescent pen. He reread the message they underlined.

Colonial rule was a cruel irrelevance. What mattered was restoring the empire that existed before the Conquest; a classless empire invoked by Mariátegui as Tawantinsuyo, the land of the four winds, in which the earth goddess Pacha Mama would be her golden self again.

"The strength of revolutionaries does not lie in their philosophy," wrote Mariátegui in one double-ringed passage. "It is in their faith, their passion, their will. Theirs is a religious, mystical and spiritual strength." And at the age of fifteen Gabriel had felt imbued with it. What Mariátegui had preached from his sofa, he, Gabriel Rondón Lung, would one day put into practice.

At fifteen he had been unaware of Marx's dictum that men about to make a revolution pretend they are restoring a vanished past. Would he have acted differently, he wondered? He replaced the book. He couldn't answer. Things had not turned out as he had foreseen. Certainly not as Hipólito had foreseen.

"Do you still think of Hipólito?" he asked the woman washing her face in the basin.

She glanced at him. The water dripped from her cheeks. It formed a patch on her shirt. "Stupid question."

"Well?"

"Sometimes," she said through the towel. "I try not to. It doesn't help anything."

"Would we be reading his poems today?"

"I don't know. Who cares about writers? I'm going out to get some food. You shouldn't be seen in the street."

The door slammed.

"Hipólito," he said aloud, invoking his friend, the impetuous revolutionary. He saw his morose chubby face, the face of a mediocre poet worried that South American literature was flowering rather well without him. He saw the large animated features which might have suited a character in a cartoon, but in the flesh looked ugly.

He looked down the street to the river where his friend had died. Where that tug is, he thought. That was near enough the spot where he had gone under, his head cracked like a coconut by

Don Miguel's third shot.

How many years? Twenty? Twenty-one? They were off to join the guerrilla leader Federico Fuente. Five students from San Agustín College, who would sail down to Requena and cross into the valleys. Five teenagers who would take power, inspire the masses and destroy the bourgeois regime.

The tug disappeared upriver. Watching its wake rub against each bank, Gabriel forced himself back. If he was to reconstitute himself, he would have to confront that day in May which had determined his future. His future and Elena's.

The boat had been late, which was why the five of them had booked into a hotel. After signing their names and professions – Hipólito put "astronaut" – they had walked to a bar in Plaza Clavero. That was when the police arrived. It wasn't the astronaut which had alerted them. It was Don Miguel, strutting past with his tart, in his embroidered lace shirt with its little silver ends screwed to the collar and a face that would have silenced a howler monkey.

He must have heard something in the customs house. He was still working the river then. He didn't yet have his mayoral ambitions. He didn't need them. For the right sum, you could smuggle anything past Don Miguel. The contents of the contraband market. The hold of a Booth liner. Even the boat. But you couldn't rock Don Miguel's cosy number. And that's what they would have done by sailing to join Fuente, and Don Miguel knew it. He knew the guns and the gelignite and the detonating fuse they carried in their canvas sacks had all passed under his Roman nose and he knew the police would find that out.

So before they did, he told them.

Hipólito had laughed when Corporal Velarde asked for his documents. "I'm the man in the moon," he replied, putting down his glass and running outside. Gabriel followed, shouting for the others to scatter.

The two of them had dashed to the river, into the canoe of an old woman who sold porridge and stewed turtle from two large tins in the stern. The canoe possessed only one paddle. Hipólito had steered them into the river by the time the police arrived on the waterfront. There were civilians among them, encouraged by Don

Miguel's rumours of a terrorist group armed to the teeth with machine-guns. They all had shot-guns, except Don Miguel who had a long hunting rifle which he started to fire. With his first shot he knocked the paddle from Hipólito's hand. Round and round the canoe had spun, dizzying the two on board so they had fallen to the bottom in a wet heap, washed by the warm liquid from the punctured tins.

"Stop shooting," Hipólito had cried, standing up and waving his arms. "Stop, stop, stop," he had cried, struggling to shake his T-shirt like a white flag. A bullet reddened his stomach and he toppled out of Gabriel's reach into the river, clinging with his fingers to the side. "Man in . . ." he whispered. That was before the shot from the shore which exploded his skull.

Gabriel threw himself over the other side. He swam deep, with a full breath, and pulled himself under until his lungs tore at him to come up for the air which he finally drew in with huge gulps in the shadow of a boat.

He could see it now from the window. The floating church of the Seventh Day Adventists.

"Hipólito." Once more he walked to the shelf. Edith must have it. Sure enough, among the books he had loosened, he found the slim volume printed on Hipólito's press.

The Indignant Savage: Poems by Hipólito Mercedes.

He turned the flyleaf. The very first poem he came to was "The Amazon Dolphin", dedicated to G.R.L. and E.C.S.

"It's a sort of love poem. Inspired by Aragón – but you can sing it to the tune of 'Ojos azules'."

Chapter 11

"NO ONE KNOWS where the problem lies. Everything was planned by an English engineer, an amateur plumber called Horney. In laying out his unique system of pipes, he made only one oversight.

"He forgot to leave a blueprint. . ."

To Don Wenceslau and Don García, staring out of the Café Nanay at the waterlogged square, it seems they have heard Don Leopoldo give the same explanation on every wet day there has ever been.

This was a day in January 1965, during one of the intense but intermittent downpours which made Belén heavy with jungle smells and because of a fault in the drainage system turned its roads into sudden rivers – and its squares into lakes.

On this day Gabriel and Hipólito stood in the entrance to the university canteen.

It was Hipólito who first alerted Gabriel to the girl from the house on Calle Raimondi. The two boys were in their last year at San Agustín College, in the next street. At Hipólito's request they had attended a pedestrian lecture by a member of the city's fledgling Communist Party. Neither wished to comment on it.

"It's stopped," said Hipólito. "Let's go."

He set off, expecting Gabriel to follow.

"There's a girl I want you to meet."

Gabriel came after on tip-toe, his trousers raised so they wouldn't get wet, his shoes getting damper and damper.

"Her eyes are bluer than. . . the cobalt sky," rhapsodized the poet. "God knows what she's doing working for Don Miguel."

The offices of Eden Expeditions were housed on the ground floor of Orestes Minero's old house in Calle Putumayo. On his death – he lived to be seventy-six, surviving his gouty wife by ten years – Orestes' son Miguel had inherited the building. He moved upstairs and converted the ground floor billiard room into a tourist company. Through Eden Expeditions he hoped to open up the jungle to elderly Americans and Europeans.

Hipólito led the way into the downstairs room. There was a map of the country on the right-hand wall, below it a row of empty chairs. The room was divided by a frosted-glass panel and dominated by a desk. Gabriel's view of the girl behind this desk was obscured by a large, furious woman in a taffeta dress. In late middle age Ruth Etty had come from the Welsh hills to see if life was any better in the town where her late and only brother had spent twenty years working as resident manager for the Booth Lines. It wasn't. There was no water in her hotel, despite the fact it faced a river which every day poured more water into the Atlantic than the eight great rivers of Asia. There were no seats to Lima for another two days. And this girl hardly spoke English. How Clarence had lasted so long, she didn't know.

"Tell your elusive boss I've got to see him tomorrow. Tell him. . . tell him I'm a friend of the ambassador," she said before steaming out like one of her brother's boats.

Catching sight of Hipólito, the girl behind the desk had laughed.

"I didn't understand a word. Did you?" She stood to allow him to kiss her cheek.

"Elena," said the poet. "My greatest friend, Gabriel Rondón Lung. Gabriel, la señorita Elena Colina Silves."

What were his first thoughts? She was young – about seventeen. She wore her black hair in a loose pony tail. She had large blue eyes without any trace of coquetry and a finely angled nose. She was dressed in a pair of olive shorts, which he remembered thinking had been ironed wrong because they had two pleats. Something about her, though he couldn't put his finger on it, suggested a girl with a mind of her own. The one surprising thing was that Hipólito had never mentioned Elena Silves was white.

But then perhaps he had and he hadn't listened.

"Gabriel Rondón Lung." She spoke his name aloud. Pronounced in her mouth, each syllable a separate note, he became important.

"I can't stay long," she said, walking with them to the Café Nanay. She explained that Don Miguel had employed her because she could read English. He wanted a Spanish guide-book translated by the end of the month. He said there was nothing in English for the whole department. She was finding it an effort. She laughed. "You saw how well I did then." And lifting her face to Gabriel's and running a hand slowly down her arm: "Did anyone ever tell you you looked like Luis Sintra?"

"Why does she live with her aunt in that large green house on the corner of Raimondi? I'll tell you why," Don Leopoldo says. "She's an orphan. Her parents drowned in a freak storm near Rapoto when she was six."

(Henriques was taking his sick wife to Belén. In his impatience, he set off in a narrow launch belonging to the factory instead of waiting for the larger river boat. The wind had blown against the current. Colina never noticed the water tumbling hungrily over the stern, or Henriques reaching out for her, or the river cover them.)

"She also has a very fine voice," says Don García. "Quite a lot of men come to church to hear it, I tell you. That half-witted poet, he's always there on Tuesday evenings, two rows in front of me, his tongue hanging out like a water dog."

But it was plain to everyone that Elena didn't reciprocate Hipólito's feelings. He seemed not to mind. She was an excuse for him to take the lid off his pen and write verses in honour of her hair, her mouth, her lips, her eyes.

Whether she read these outpourings, Gabriel never knew. Those Gabriel read were banal and derivative. They included the poem dedicated to him and to Elena, written after Hipólito discovered what was going on.

But in a way, Hipólito had promoted that too. "The guide-book Elena's doing for Don Miguel. You wouldn't have a look, would you?"

Gabriel's knowledge of English was well-known. He had taught himself since he was fifteen. The texts he wished to read were banned in Spanish and available only in American editions smuggled from Leticia.

One evening he offered his services.

"Hipólito's put you up to it, hasn't he?"

"No, he hasn't."

She handed over her exercise book.

"I don't believe you. Look, you're blushing."

Gabriel took it to read on the Malecón. He sat on the balustrade, kicking his feet between its teeth. At his back a steep bank crumbled into a tongue of vivid green rice fields. According to Hipólito, they were the colour of a poisonous snake that had shed its skin.

"Belén," he read, "still retains the charms of the past which have prevailed throughout the last two centuries, constituting a most valuable cultural patrimony."

There followed a brief resumé of the town's history to the present day. "The Peruvian Amazon now lives in the apogee of tourist possibilities. New urbanizations are emerging in almost all the surrounding suburbs, making Belén a city of sudden contrasts and beautiful combinations. Yet Peru's tropical gateway city and door to the mysterious Amazon still pulses with the raw energy of a frontier outpost. The jungle here is a benevolent wilderness. The many Indian tribes of the Amazon are perfectly adapted to their environment, successfully leading their lives long before 'civilization' came. . ."

The last pages dealt with the town's ancient buildings. These included the cathedral, completed in 1911, with its famous Annunciation. "This painting, believed to be the monstrance of one of Fra Angelico's pupils, is of appalling beauty. But it must be protected from the greed of mankind and the action of time."

Gabriel told Elena he would work on the text. "It's pretty bad, isn't it?" she said in a hushed voice. Gabriel agreed. With her thumb she indicated that the shape through the frosted glass was Don Miguel.

"You can't have something of appalling beauty," Gabriel said, not lowering his voice.

"Can't you?" She seemed disappointed.

Later, walking her home, Gabriel said, "The plea for that painting. Was it your idea?"

"A bit. The original didn't mention what an awful state it's in. Have you seen it? It's really beautiful."

When Gabriel didn't reply – he hadn't seen it – she added it was also a matter of loyalty. The painting had been donated by her grandfather.

"Poor deluded man," she said, then told him about Alonso, the bucktoothed accountant from Coimbra – which was when Gabriel warmed to her.

Outside Edith's house, someone knocked.

"Edith!"

The voice was a man's. He rattled the front door. When nothing happened, he moved to the window. He gave a loud whistle.

Gabriel waited against the wall until the man walked away. He waited a few minutes more. From where he stood, he noticed a paraffin stove under the basin. He filled a kettle with water and lit the blackened gauze.

Sitting at the table, he reopened Hipólito's book. He found the poem again. He read it unseeing. He knew it by heart. Instead of the images on the page, he began to remember the boy and the girl who inspired them.

One day he took her to the zoo at Quistacocha. The zoo lay ten miles west of the city along a red track which petered out into the trees. The track was the only road that led from Belén. Rich young men, like Don Miguel's son, used it to race the cars they imported from Brazil.

On the bus, Elena told Gabriel how Don Miguel had shown his translation to an American priest. The priest had approved it.

"Your translation," said Gabriel.

"No, yours. I had nothing to do with it."

"Why do you work for him?"

It was well known that her father had been instrumental in bringing down the Minero family. But some parts of the jungle cover tracks quicker than others. Perhaps Don Miguel had a superstition about the power of Henriques. Perhaps he couldn't find anyone else. To Elena the matter was simple.

"To qualify as a guide with the Escuela Nacional de Turismo, I need a diploma. And he needs me."

"A crook like that?"

"He's ill."

"Every pig has its Martinmas," said Gabriel. "He's the most corrupt man in Belén. He stinks from the head down."

"He's got cancer of the pancreas, Gabriel. Dr Lache has found a tumour the size of a fist."

Gabriel decided to talk about the diploma.

"What else do you need to know?"

"Everything," she sighed. "Hotel prices, the times of boats and flights, what films are on, where to rent motorbikes and cars, the best discos. . ."

"Which are the best discos?"

"The Surcusal in Próspero. The Dalmacia in Nauta."

"Let's go tonight," said Gabriel, trying to recover some ground.

She shook her head. "I can't. Not tonight."

"Why not?"

"I'm doing something else."

Gabriel was too proud to ask what. Instead he said, "You enjoy learning this?"

"Of course – and Gabriel, don't sulk." She quoted: "'Tourism has had the biggest economic and social impact on our century'."

"Where does it say that?"

"Here, in my guide-book." From her bag she produced a thin pamphlet. She showed Gabriel the sentence. It was underlined in yellow crayon on a page headed "What is tourism?"

Gabriel read the answer.

"It's free.

"It creates work.

"It makes one understand the true history and geography of our marvellous land.

"It is important for men and women to be able to change their lives and abandon their traditional place of work."

The aspirations of the Peruvian tourist board were similar to those of Mariátegui, thought Gabriel. He returned the book.

"Face it, Gabriel, you're an out-of-touch intellectual. Come on, move, we're here."

Quistacocha was named after a legend that a local Indian tribe had seen Christ descending into the lake, or cocha. Other legends were painted on a wall leading down to the lake. Yacuruna, the green-skinned river god which never closed its eyes and lived under water with those it had captured. Sachamama, the mother of the mountains, an enormous yellow serpent with little ears. The Tunchi or devil, which took the shape of a man and on dark nights announced its presence with the whisper: "Fin... fin... fin."

The waters of Sachachorro.

Gabriel pointed. "You know their story?"

"Once you've drunk them you never leave Belén," replied Elena. "They rise below that Benedictine hostel in town, beside the large rubbish tip."

"You'll pass," he replied.

"What about this?" she said of a painting half-hidden by leaves. She brushed them back to show a silhouetted river boat. Its lights blazed, its funnel trailed a wreath of grey smoke, its paddles propelled it forward into the inky dusk.

"The phantom river boat," they both read. "On the night of the full moon, this mysterious shape can be seen sailing down river while its passengers indulge in orgies and bacchanals."

"Where do we board?" asked Gabriel, but Elena was serious.

"My father believed it. He told my aunt he once travelled as a passenger on something similar. One of the men had different coloured eyes."

Gabriel thought better than to contradict her. "Perhaps it was the Tunchi?"

They walked until they came to a fork in the path. One side led down to the warm lagoon – part of a paiche breeding project – and a stretch of sand where two people were punching a volleyball. The other led into the trees.

Elena reached for Gabriel's hand. She pulled him over a rickety bridge to a raised cage. It lay in a clearing in the subaqueous light of the forest. Around the cage, the shadows cast a broken net which caught the sun, diffracting it into a shoal of fishes.

"Look," she pointed. "Isn't he wonderful?"

A jaguar lay panting on its side across the length of the new cage.

Its eyes were shut. Its heart beat rapidly under a white chest. Every now and then an ear twitched against the flies. They flew up from the chicken claws and the dried slugs of faeces on the floor.

As Gabriel took in the creature, he noticed a couple seated on a bench under the trees. From where he stood they also seemed framed by the cage. The jaguar heard the giggles of the girl as the man tried to kiss her. It opened its round black eyes. The giggles grew louder. The jaguar licked its paws. It rubbed its neck against the mesh. It grabbed its own legs for something to play with.

The dress slipped further from the shoulder.

The animal closed its eyes. It screwed up its face as if it were weeping.

The scene affected Gabriel. He felt like the jaguar, a creature condemned to live imprisoned within his own habitat. Yet looking at the bench, he felt a different stirring.

"Turn round," said Elena. "I want to take a photograph. And, Gabriel," she said, stamping her feet, "smile."

He tried a smile. He heard the camera click. "No, stay there." She wound on and clicked again. "Just making sure."

"Now you." Gabriel reached for the camera.

But she backed away, refusing. She hated being photographed – and they had an argument which resulted, finally, in Elena allowing herself to be taken standing stiffly against the cage with her eyes closed, like the jaguar.

It was on a bench in the cathedral square that he began telling Elena of his admiration for Castro and of how it was possible for a handful of people to cause a whole system to come crashing down with a single push.

"Would you want that?" she asked.

He hesitated before answering.

"I don't know."

What he did know made him rise every morning with a hard knot in his stomach as bitter as a lime. The bitterness related to his father.

Gabriel's father was a man who had spoken with fire in his eyes about love and women, but he had never been in love except with

Gabriel's mother, and probably only after she had died.

Gabriel never knew his mother, who came from a family of fishermen from a village near Leticia. She had died in giving birth to him. But ten years after her death he suddenly realized that people had been whispering all along how his parents' relationship was really one between brother and sister.

Nor, though they shared a house, did he know much about the woman his father married a year before his own death. All Gabriel knew was her unhappiness. Each morning he saw her rocking in the shadows, adjusting the red velvet cushion at her back and worrying a mole on her cheek as she remembered every injustice that had ever happened to her in more detail than Funes the Memorious.

She never responded beyond a curt nod of her small head and a stretching of her legs, when Gabriel urged her to cheer up for God's sake, everybody loses their husband some time or other. She understood that, but what she could not understand was how fate could deal the mechanic she had married so late in life a hand that matched his father's, the Chinese coolie from Hiempen.

Prurigo's trunk lay by her chair covered in cream muslin and supporting an out-of-focus portrait, framed in tin, of his lean face – as well as an oval photograph of Gabriel's father on a motorbike (outside the garage from where he returned every night with hands as black as saw blades).

She continued to curse the day on which Gabriel's father had set off to give Don Miguel once and for all a piece of his proud mind.

"That's it, that's it, that's it," he said on receiving the compulsory purchase order which Don Miguel had served on him in order to make the garage, his life's work, a showroom for, he could hardly bring himself to say it, outboard engines. Who knows how many blind eyes must have been turned for Don Miguel to win the concession. Gabriel's father couldn't have counted if he had a 100 fingers. But he knew it was not right, and that's what he went to tell Don Miguel in his wedding tie and jacket, leaving his motorbike in its usual place under the open window.

They found his body next day in the lake at Moronacocha, his head bump bump bumping against a Petro-Peru container, his face mother of pearl in the oil, his lungs full of mud, cold spit and grape-skins. Corporal Velarde could offer no solution, but that he had slipped and hit his head.

Don Miguel said this unfortunate incident had taken place before the intended meeting. The last time he had set eyes on the mechanic was a fortnight before when he was adjusting a piston to his son's Chevrolet. He had yet to receive a bill, but nothing would please him more than to forward an amount he could be confident would cover it.

To the young Gabriel immersed in Mariátegui, the death of his father was a blow that put into painful relief all the things he had read about in his small back room where each night he heard his step-mother tossing and turning and waking in her raving sleep with a curse for each man, woman and child she had ever known or was likely to meet.

"There doesn't seem to be a peaceful way for this country," he told Elena. No amount of legal reform was going to change the system. Three per cent of the population owned eighty-three per cent of the land. In Puno, there was one doctor for 98,000 people. About fifty per cent of all children were dying before the age of five – and it was getting worse.

"But when you Spanish arrived we had one of the most sophisticated empires on earth."

"My family came from Portugal," she reproached him. "Yours from China. And these statistics are as absurd as. . . as saying that the human body is seventy-five per cent water, or whatever they tell us at school."

"You know what I mean."

"What about Hipólito? Does he agree?"

"Hipólito's a poet."

He was not going to tell her about Hipólito. Hipólito wanted the revolution to begin tomorrow. Hipólito quoted Che Guevara in time with his tennis ball. "It is not always necessary (thud) to wait until all conditions for revolution exist (thud), the revolutionary foco can create them (thud)." Their arguments rang out in the shed by the river where Hipólito had installed a press. Arguments about the need for real organization, about the necessity to have the masses on their side, about the inevitability of violence. Arguments familiar to every student revolutionary from Vienna and Paris to Guatemala City. Arguments that raged as Hipólito ran off his poems and Gabriel stacked them in neat piles ready for distribution to the editors who would consider Hipólito Mercedes' unsolicited offering but he must understand that journalism was a hard and unrewarding profession and they could give no firm date as to when publication might be.

"Is he a good poet?" Elena asked.

"That's not the point."

"What is the point?"

"The point is how can we sit here knowing that after four hundred years of colonial rule, the lot of the average Peruvian hasn't improved one bit? He has no rights. He has only obligations. If I make a complaint, it's regarded by Don Miguel as insubordination. If I organize a petition, it's looked on as a rebellion. And you know why the average Peruvian has no rights?" he asked. "I'll tell you why. Because he's illiterate. And he's illiterate because he speaks Quechua. Yet there's not a single school in the whole land which can teach him to read and write in his native tongue. Don't you think that's disgusting? Don't you think that's really disgusting?"

"Do you speak Quechua?" Elena asked innocently. Then spotting Hipólito on the corner of Próspero she jumped up and waved.

"My saviour," she greeted the poet. "Just in time to stop my indoctrination. Now will you both walk me to my aunt's. I forgot to tell you, she's taking me to Lima. You won't be seeing me for a fortnight. When I return, I promise, promise to visit you both in prison."

"Gabriel, what have you been saying?" said Hipólito later.

"Nothing, nothing."

"And it was you who told me to be so careful."

Chapter 12

GABRIEL HAD KNOWN ELENA for three months when she flew to Lima with her aunt Consuelo. In the week that followed he experienced a violent change in his feelings towards her. One day he woke knowing something had happened. He rose from his bed and realized what it was. He was in love.

The day was no different from any other except he felt out of breath at not being with her and the sore shape of his heart in his chest. That night he couldn't sleep. He imagined the warm skin of her back beneath her shirt. Her blue eyes. Her laugh.

He found the glass of water she had left when collecting the final pages of the translation. He kept it by his bed, sipping it in small doses as if he was drinking part of her. He smelt the velvet cushion on the rocking chair where she had sat. All he smelt was worn fibre and the cheap scent of his step-mother.

"I've fallen in love with the gringa in Raimondi," he told his step-mother helplessly. In five years he had never confessed anything to her.

"What do I do?"

"Fly to Patagonia," she grunted. "I've never seen such a six-foot death wish."

Gabriel missed her so much, that on the fourth day he took the photograph of Elena with her eyes closed to the Salón de Belleza and had Dominica Zumate make thirty copies in different shapes and sizes.

"You must care for her a lot," she said. She knew rather too many women who would appreciate such attention from a good-looking boy like Gabriel.

"I do."

He pinned the photographs to his bedroom wall so that before he went to sleep and after he woke and whenever he looked up from his books he might see Elena in close up, or standing by the jaguar's cage, or with the couple kissing in the background.

But still he missed her.

As the week went on, he went from one pitch of emotion to another. When she comes back, he thought, I must not see her or speak to her. His step-mother was right. What can she see in me? She is white, from a European family. I am a Chinese cholo. We are different animals. I must not expose myself any more. I must put a tourniquet on my feelings.

But he could no more stem his feelings than he could stop the flow of the river he saw every day from the Malecón. In his thoughts Elena became a gazelle – a borrowed image, he realized, never having seen such a creature except in books. A shivering, beautiful animal who might, if he was lucky, edge towards his outstretched hand. But who would leap to the high ground at any sudden move he made, and turn her gaze to another view.

To consult Hipólito was out of the question. Gabriel turned instead to a fellow student at San Agustín. His name was Julio Ángel Medina.

"So what do I do, Julio, what do I do? I'm going out of my head."

"Love is a four-letter word," said Julio. "But it's a good one. Just be cool."

"I am being cool," he screamed.

"Then all I can suggest is manteca de bufeo," said Julio. "Dolphin lard. Rub it on your balls, and you have any woman you want."

"But I don't necessarily want her like that. I want her to feel the same for me."

"It can have that effect too."

"I don't believe you. But if I did, where would I get some?"

"There's a brujo at the end of the Maniti. My brother Bonifacio has directions." Julio smiled. "If it works, let me know."

At first Gabriel resisted the idea of heading upriver to a tributary where the waters turned black from the decomposed forest. Nor had he any desire to take refuge in a witchdoctor's lotion. A week later he stepped ashore at a community of five thatched dwellings called Nuevo Triunfo.

A tin roof balanced over the brujo's hut like a saucepan lid. The mud floor was beaten to a shiny blackness. A table stood in one corner, stacked with perfume bottles containing coloured ointments. There was also a Bible, an astrological almanac and a selection of the *Reader's Digest* from 1957. A calendar pinned to the wall behind showed the motor yacht *Skorpios* among the icebergs of the San Rafael lagoon, Chile.

"Come here," said the brujo. He was an old man with eyes like pockets of cane spirit and the skin of a prune. One of his trouser legs was sewn up at the knee. In Gabriel's honour he had brilliantined his hair and changed into a pair of green trousers.

"Yes, come here," he said. He indicated the floor where he sat, and lit a large home-rolled cigarette.

A fire burned beside him. The empty spit was supported by a black tapir skull and a charred sewing machine.

Gabriel sat.

"Well?"

Gabriel explained.

The brujo smiled.

"What is the reason for living if not the love of a woman. Do you have pictures?"

"Not with me."

"Pity. It's better with pictures." With pictures he could go into the grass outside and when the sun came up he could bury the picture of Gabriel. When the sun set he could bury the picture of Gabriel's woman with some earth, some bones and some leaves wrapped in red thread.

"Then never more will your two souls separate, till death. And you will keep on singing, singing, singing."

"I haven't any pictures."

"I know another spell."

With that he advanced on Gabriel and puffed a gust of smoke down his front. "Nana nee," he began in a high-pitched whine, rubbing the stump of his knee against Gabriel's back.

"Egan nee nee nee nee," he chanted, invoking the spirits of the white ant crawling over Gabriel's leg and requesting that Elena be drawn to him likewise.

"Then I start sucking on your stomach, this side of your neck, your feet. Then you lie down and you promise to diet and you promise to diet well and you promise not to eat chicken or pig. Yes, sir, because the Lord is helping us. The powerful Father whose power is the highest. Sir Jesus Christ who will make her feel love every hour and feel that way all day long. Nee nee nee nee, du!du!du!du!" he continued, puffing deeply on the cigarette, which had gone out, and blowing into his cupped hands. With a final moan it was over.

"What about manteca de bufeo?" said Gabriel.

"As well?"

"Just in case."

"All right," sighed the brujo. "I'll give you manteca." He rose and hobbled to a table. He produced a Nescafé tin from among the bottles.

"Here," he said. "You'd better take the lot."

"What happens when you use it?"

"The person you desire will love you and never leave you. Apply it sparingly."

On the stove the water came to the boil. Gabriel found a tin mug. He stirred himself some coffee, thinking of the Nescafé tin which had caused him such embarrassment.

He had not applied its greasy white contents sparingly enough on the afternoon Elena returned from Lima. He had made a date with her at the Café Nanay. It was her suggestion. He would have preferred another rendezvous. The café was a regular haunt of Don Miguel's which was the reason Gabriel avoided it. He had an abiding vision of Elena's boss sitting at the same table every morning, wiping the crumbs from his mouth with two thick fingers as he heard out X or Y. Invariably, Don Miguel produced a handkerchief from his pocket to complete the job. After dabbing his forehead, he would stretch back, straighten his shirt over a large stomach and, the business done, lean forward to tell a joke, smiling that unfinished smile of his in the knowledge that once again he had concluded the better deal.

That evening, Gabriel's first emotion was of relief that Don

Miguel was nowhere to be seen; his second reaction was surprise on finding Hipólito with Elena.

Gabriel moved to join them. Gingerly, he positioned himself on the other side of Elena.

"Nice jeans," said Hipólito. "New?"

"Why else do you think I'm walking like this?"

"I was just telling her what a stranger you've been. No one's seen you for days. Not even in the library. Where've you got to?"

"Out and about," said Gabriel evasively, and to Elena who narrowed her eyes as she drew on a cigarette, "my step-mother wanted something taken to a cousin upriver. How was Lima?"

She wrinkled her nose. "Horrible – as usual. My aunt spent the whole time dragging me round Miraflores. The shop she wanted was no longer there."

She tapped out a list on her fingers. "She complained about the rubbish, about my job, about the kind of people she imagines I'm consorting with . . ."

Across the table, it was Hipólito's nose that wrinkled.

"What's that smell?"

"What smell?" asked Gabriel.

"I don't know, something funny."

Gabriel moved closer to Elena. On what grounds did her aunt disapprove of these imagined consorts?

"Don Miguel must have said something. Though how he's heard about you two, I don't know."

"He has his fingers," said Gabriel.

"Sacramento, I know what it is," said Hipólito. He leant forward – and dropping his voice, he told them.

"That boy behind us," he hissed, jabbing with his thumb. "That's who's got it on. Don Miguel's son, Mario."

The boy became aware he was the subject of their conversation. He glowered at Hipólito and smiled at Elena.

Elena's face glowed conspiratorially. She encouraged Hipólito to give more details. He needed little encouragement. With large eyes, he told them he had smelled it once before, in a brujo's hut on the Maniti. It was made from the bufeo, the Amazon dolphin, a pink-bellied fish with growths on its stomach like a woman's breasts and a passion for men.

"The fishermen believe that at night they turn into white people. They rise from their city under the water and go to the discos. You, for example," he held Gabriel by the arm. "You can be taken by one into the water. You are young and handsome. You meet this beautiful girl. Toot, toot, boom, boom, she takes you away. You are never seen again."

"Don't be silly, Hipólito."

"The brujos make love to the bufeos. It makes them stronger. They have to do it in pairs, though. The dolphin holds on so strongly, the brujo becomes paralysed with pleasure. Lesser mortals make an ointment from its genitals. Rubbed onto their own," he concluded, "it makes women squirm with an uncontrollable desire."

"No," said Elena.

"Hipólito, you're having us on," said Gabriel.

"Do you know something," Hipólito went on.

"What?"

"I can still smell it."

Unable to contain herself, Elena burst into laughter. She buried her head on Gabriel's shoulder.

"Gabriel?" Hipólito raised an eyebrow.

Elena lifted her lips to his ear. "Sweetheart," she whispered, "it's coming through your jeans."

That was the moment. The moment it finally came home to Hipólito what his friend was feeling. The moment Elena understood what she felt for Gabriel. A moment of supreme embarrassment which only ended when a blushing Gabriel rose from the table and walked to the jukebox.

"What've you put on now?" asked Elena, still laughing.

"My favourite song," said Gabriel.

"What's it called?"

He placed his hand on the back of her neck and sat down.

"'Ojos azules'."

Suddenly she bent forward and kissed him in full view of Hipólito and the rest of the café. So that whenever he played it he would remember her.

Chapter 13

EARLY ONE MORNING in March 1965 Hipólito came to his house. Gabriel was reading a copy of Max Nomad's *Aspects of Revolt*. He heard Hipólito in the front room.

"Morning, Señora Lung. And how is my favourite widow?"

"Tired, Señor Mercedes, tired."

The fly curtain burst apart and Hipólito's energetic face appeared, dividing the bead strands.

"We're going to Lima," he said. A friend at the telegraph office had alerted him to a meeting to be addressed by Federico Fuente, a founder member of the Movement of the Revolutionary Left.

In the end four of them had taken the Faucett flight to Lima. They included Julio, and at Julio's request, his older brother Bonifacio, a man built like a bull who worked part-time at the plywood factory. The address they sought was a house near the gold museum, somewhere in the mist which crawled with the feet of an insect over the face and covered the capital for half the year. A group of men and women sat in three neat semi-circles in front of an empty fireplace. Two men stood like fighting cocks on either side of the grate, arguing.

Gabriel's attention was drawn to the man who had been talking as they entered. Gabriel could make out nothing he was saying, though there was something charismatic about the way he moved his body, his hands, his face. It was the face of an Inca. Dark, deep-set eyes. A high forehead from which the hair rose in black flames. A mouth fluent with defiance.

There was frustration in the room as the four men made their shy advance. No one wished to interrupt the argument, but the new arrivals had to be introduced. The other man by the fireplace inspected them through thick glasses, his Adam's apple pecking at his throat. He thrust out a hand.

"Federico Fuente."

One by one they shook it.

"This is Rolando," he said introducing them to those who stood up. "Néstor, Laura, Emilio . . ." and so on, round the room, until they arrived at the man who stood in silence next to him. He scratched his elbow compulsively. Despite the heat he wore a jacket. Fuente uttered his name, introducing him as a philosophy professor from Ayacucho. The man smiled, showing a mouth of perfect teeth.

The four of them found places to sit. The argument resumed. It was Fuente who began. His grey fanatic's face seemed invigorated by the new element in the audience. His subject was Castro. For an hour he spoke of the Cuban example. Fidel's revolution showed that it was possible to make a genuine revolution. That it was possible to nationalize the big companies created by the monster of the north. That it was possible to make people the owners of their own houses and the land they tilled. That it was possible to recover a sense of national independence and pride. Fidel had showed all this was possible and that it could be made a possibility elsewhere if only arms were given to the people and the people were made aware that the revolution was a historical fact which nothing and nobody could stop and which had to begin now, this moment.

At the end of Fuente's speech, the man from Ayacucho spoke.

"Fidel Castro is a chorus girl," he said.

The room was silent. A stick of dynamite had been rolled into it instead of a quiet sentence of six words. Fuente sat down stunned.

The mandarin from Ayacucho, his hands thrust into the opposite sleeves of his jacket, continued talking. In an even voice he announced he was not against the armed struggle, but that it would be far bloodier, far more violent, far more demanding of sacrifice than anyone had envisaged. That above and beyond all things it had to be an indigenous revolution which accepted nothing, not so much as a single peso, nor a single pistol nor a single bullet from outside. That each of them must be more prepared, much more prepared. That they must first learn the language of the people they hoped to liberate. That the time was not right.

"How many of you speak Quechua?"

Not a hand went up.

"If we act now we throw away everything," he said and sat down.

Gabriel was impressed. As the meeting split into three or four groups, he looked about for Hipólito. He saw his friend holding forth to some older students, next to a lamp which had been caramelized by its bulb. There was a gleam in his eye, a strut in his voice. Gabriel heard him boast about the amount of popular support which existed in Belén, the need to act, the press he owned, his poetry. . .

He moved outside onto the terrace. Fuente was having to be restrained from implementing several angry threats, each prefaced by the words "fucking provincial". Gabriel looked about for the provincial. He returned to the room. Someone told him he had left.

"Wasn't he marvellous?" said Hipólito on the plane. They were playing bingo.

"Yes."

"Fuente, I mean. Not that tiresome man from Ayacucho."

"Bingo!" shouted a woman in front. She fanned her face with a book of horoscopes. Over the intercom it was announced she had won a free flight.

Eight days later, Hipólito received a pamphlet from Lima outlining MIR's policy. It was signed by Fuente with a green swirl and contained best wishes to "our valued brothers in Belén" together with a suggestion that herein might be found the right road.

Hipólito interpreted it as a sign of alert. He became more irritable. He threw his tennis ball harder and harder against his press; against the tiled front of the Booth supermarket in Sargento Lores, against the pavements, against the doors of parked cars, against the wall of Eden Expeditions.

Thud. Thud. Thud.

The noise was always there in the background. Gabriel remembered it loudest during the early days of his romance with Elena.

The news that Gabriel, the mechanic's son, was courting Elena Silves, Señora Guzmán's beautiful niece, had taken that part of the town which cared about such things by a brief storm.

Pía Zumate – La Palometa – didn't believe it until she saw them with her own eyes embracing in the cathedral square like a pair of . . .

exactly – lovebirds. At that moment the scene filled her with unbearable nostalgia for her own youth, or rather, she realized abruptly, with what she might have made of it had not her eyes been blinded by a cinder from a Booth Line funnel called Harry.

Like many others Pía Zumate had always suspected Gabriel's celebrated indifference to girls indicated another taste – a predilection shared by the only other man Pía Zumate had loved. A man she refused to name, not even to herself, but whose advances had terminated after she apprehended him in a scuffle and grabbing of sheets with a tawny rivereño from Nauta.

For a long time she would continue to see Gabriel and Elena as she saw them then, her memory casting its muslin net over the bench to protect their image from the nuisances of the real world.

As she continued her path to Dr Lache's surgery, with a marked spring in her step that made Don García shake his head in a rapture of longing, and say "Qué hermosa!", Pía Zumate felt that if God only exerted himself it was perfectly possible for all to be right with the world.

Why the hell didn't he do it more often?

Gabriel had never been one to hold his wounded finger to the world. But on the day after the episode in the Café Nanay, he told Elena something he had not told any girl. Something he had never been able to feel, despite dreaming of it.

They were sitting on the same ivory-coloured bench where Gabriel had expounded his political theories.

"I love you," he heard himself croak.

Her response was to place a finger on his lips.

"Words come easily to you."

Gabriel remembered a line from one of his friend's sadder efforts. "The gap between the nuzzle and the kiss is the gap between the thunder and the rain." He was thinking of this line and the possible truth it contained when he felt Elena brush his hurt face with her lips, and his lips with hers. Then just as Hipólito's gap had closed, the bell of the yellow cathedral sounded across the square.

Elena pulled away. She looked around. With regret written in her eyes, she said she had to go.

"It's the *Messiah* next week," she explained. "No, you needn't come. I can imagine your position on religion."

"What about tonight?" he asked. He held her hand as she stood up. "What about going to the Dalmacia?"

She looked down at him. Her smile conveyed the expression she had to do something she wasn't particularly keen to do. "I'm sorry, Gabriel. I've planned something else."

He didn't ask what. He was at that stage in love when you do not ask to know more than you are told.

She tapped his nose and walked off without looking back.

"Did you pray for me?" he asked next day.

"Only a little. You don't want to get more conceited."

"Who else?"

"Oh, about thirty or forty others. My aunt, Hipólito, of course, Don Miguel . . ."

"Don Miguel?"

"Yes, I pray for him a lot. Dr Lache says there's little hope."

"Six weeks at most," Dr Lache had apparently told Don Miguel, after finding secondary nodules in his nutmegged liver. At first he hoped it might have been biliary cholic or an impacted gallstone. But the large globulous swelling in Don Miguel's ribs was now the size of a child's head.

Elena finally introduced Gabriel to her aunt.

"She needs cheering up. It's the tenth anniversary of my parents' death. Also, she says it's time she met you."

Gabriel knew the green house well. He walked past it every day on his way to San Agustín. One side, on Calle Raimondi, was shadowed by a palm tree whose leaves grew against the tin roof and curled back upon themselves. The other side, on Arana, had three doors that were never opened. Señora Guzmán was always shooing figures from the steps where they sat eating aguaje fruit. Once a week, she swept the dried peel away with a furious glance which the fruit seller ignored as she had ignored it every Saturday for fifteen years while she scraped the orange flesh with a knife that still lacked a handle, and a smile that said Consuelo could complain till she burst like a melon.

Gabriel knocked on the door at the appointed time. He wore a linen jacket and a sober tie fastened in a tight knot. He was led upstairs to a room filled with books and flowers.

Consuelo was on her second pink gin. Her eyes were bright; her face puffy, causing its white hairs to prick out against the chinchilla shawl on her shoulders.

"I'm draped in black, but perfectly all right," she reassured him. She offered a hand. In her other hand she held a glass rimmed with purple lipstick.

"I thought we'd eat here, in what used to be my husband's study. Elena's still changing, so we can have a word."

She mixed Gabriel a drink, dropping an ice-cube on the floor.

"Don't worry, I'll pick it up later. I hope this tastes all right. I got worried they'd watered the gin. In fact it was the tonic."

They talked, or rather, she did.

"I suppose you're a communist. Young people like you always adore anything left wing. I don't mind. But middle-class people like myself – not millionaires, but middle-class – who have a certain standard of living, we ought to leave. This is no country for our children. I think I will leave now my husband's dead."

She was interrupted by the telephone.

"Hello. Bishop Barrantes? How nice to hear you. Yes. You'll have to shout. Who've I got with me? No. Gabriel Lung. The mechanic's son. Elena's friend. You know, the old garage behind the Cinema Bolognesi." She looked at Gabriel. "I suppose he could be called good-looking."

As she spoke a man in a dirty white jacket entered. She held up her glass. He filled it. Two ice-cubes separated with a loud crack.

"En silencio," she hissed, and gestured at the melting cube on the floor.

"Yes, Bishop. Of course I will give you first refusal." Her brown eyes muddied and strayed to an ivory cross on the wall. It hung above a frame containing the matriculation portrait of Alonso Silves in his rabbit-edged gown. "What? This line's terrible. Yes, yes. If I do decide to sell it – no, I'm not saying I won't – you shall be the first to know."

She replaced the receiver and gave a shudder.

"That man. I could tell you a thing or two about him, though I won't." And then did.

"But you communists," she resumed. "I can see why you want to get rid of the government. It's done nothing for the Indians. Damn all, literally. One thing you'll never change, though, is the Indian's attitude to women. Take Alcibíades. He's a servant and I'm a woman. As far as he's concerned, my proper place is behind him, carrying his baggage. He's been different since my husband died. I'd almost describe him as ungrateful. I suppose he'll go, like the cook – who's a fool." She released a small sigh and glanced at the silver watch on her wrist.

"Look at the time. Where's Elena? Don't worry, I'll ring the bell. But talking of Elena," she said, "I'm worried about her. It's not that she's changed since knowing you – Elena will always be Elena – but she's not happy."

"Why do you say that?"

"I'm an old woman who happens to notice these things. Besides, it's my business." She nodded at another photograph on the wall in a curly mahogany frame. The photograph was of Henriques and Colina. Their faces had been touched up to look like paintings. Their expressions were severe.

"She never knew her parents, poor thing. I have to stand in for them. I have to protect her, but not so she notices. Too much protection can be counter-productive, as I well know."

"Does she need protection?"

Whatever Consuelo was going to say was interrupted by Elena's entrance. She wore her grandmother's blue dress. It had been altered at the waist and shoulders in the modern fashion.

"You look lovely, dear," said Consuelo. "Really lovely. Doesn't she, Gabriel?"

Afterwards Elena asked what he thought of her aunt.

"I liked her," Gabriel replied truthfully.

"She liked you."

"I'm sure you felt it was a chore," Señora Guzmán had said. "But you made me very happy by coming."

Chapter 14

FROM THE OUTSET Elena made it clear she wouldn't make love to Gabriel. Not for the moment, anyway.

"It wouldn't be worth the guilt." Then she smiled in a way that made him want to know what she was thinking.

"I was thinking of my patron saint at confirmation."

"Who was?"

"María Goretti."

"Who was?"

"Stabbed thirty-six times with a stiletto at the age of twelve rather than have sex with the desperate lodger."

"But, Elena, please, I love you."

"And she forgave him."

"But I'm not a stranger. I'm the man who loves you."

She smiled again. "I heard you the first time."

Gabriel accepted her refusal. It marked her out from other girls he'd grown up with, who conceived at fifteen and spent months chewing irritant fruits to abort. So when Hipólito asked coarsely if they'd done anything, Gabriel turned on him.

"OK, OK, I'm sorry," said Hipólito, holding up his hands. "I'm just putting myself in your place. I don't know how you can do without it, that's all."

Hipólito left no one in doubt that his own appetites were being satisfied. In place of Elena, he had found a first-year student at the university, two years older than himself.

"Small, sultry and very extreme. If she has a fault it's that she applies too much make-up."

"What's her name?"

"Edith Pusanga."

On Elena's eighteenth birthday, Gabriel presented her with a copy of Mariátegui's essays. "*My* patron saint," he explained. "I'll give you two days to read him." Two days in which he would refuse to see her. "Then you'll discover what I'm on about."

It was early evening when he next joined her on the bench. He found a girl with a brave face. "I've changed my mind. I don't think you look like Luis Sintra. You look like him," she said. She tapped the author's photo on the dust-jacket. "Admit it's narcissism which attracts you and I'll forgive everything."

"But what do you think?" asked Gabriel.

She had bitten her lip. He was going to hate her. Perhaps she didn't understand. But she thought most of it was wrong.

Like what?

Like Mariátegui's nostalgia for the Inca empire. Even she knew the Inca system of land tenure wasn't a primitive form of communism. Their empire had been founded on conquests similar to Pizarro's. And when Pizarro arrived the whole system was disintegrating.

Then there was Mariátegui's interpretation of religion. His idea that the church and the state should be one. His idea that communism was essentially a spiritual movement. His idea that Marxism sprang from the same impulse as the Christianity of the catacombs, that a revolution was always religious.

Her lips were trembling. Gabriel could see the effort with which she spoke. He couldn't restrain himself.

"But it is!" he exclaimed. In Mariátegui the word religion had a new value. It was a moral not a metaphysical code. Man had only one life. His life on earth. If the Church had fulfilled the teaching of Christ, there would be no need for communism. But it hadn't.

"I don't agree," said Elena. "I just don't agree. That was why the Virgin appeared at Fátima – to warn us against communism. She warned us that communism is the faith of the Anti-Christ."

"But, Elena, just look at your Virgin's Church. You only have to see what it does, to see what it doesn't do. Don't you ever have buried doubts?"

"Of course I do, of course I do. I find God's love hard to understand. I find praying to him tedious. I long for some confirmation. But I don't think I have a right to expect it."

"Mariátegui . . . " began Gabriel.

"Yes, and you know something about your precious Mariátegui? Do you know why anyone heard of him in the first place? Because of an article he wrote on the Lord of Miracles. He even spent time on a retreat in the Descalzos monastery. He wrote a poem about the monks there. Have you read it? No? Well, I have. But that's not really it," she said. "It's the idea that you and Hipólito and Bonifacio are convinced it's upon your shoulders that some sort of burden of deliverance is placed. Only you chosen few know the truth. Only you have the authority to act. You talk about political redemption, about liberating the masses. You don't want to liberate them, you want to dominate them."

"Elena . . . "

She was crying, tears of anger and frustration. "These masses you're acting for, who are they? Those three old men on that bench? Is that who you're talking about? Then go and ask them if that's what they want. Go on."

"Elena, I'm talking about the future."

"The future? I've heard of a rose falling to a monkey, but who on earth is going to be convinced by your Future? The masses? Gabriel, what masses? They're just a convenient symbol. You can't even use their magic lotions without making a complete fool of yourself. You think I haven't been interested in what you and Hipólito get up to? Well, I have. Because to my shame I happen to love you. Oh, but that's not it either," she said, unable to stop herself.

"It's the fact that this can only end in bloodshed. Because I won't let you make love to me, you'll go off and prove yourself in bombs and pistols. Gabriel, be serious. Tell me it's really nothing. Tell me it's just because you're a young stallion. Tell me if I said OK, I give in, let's go to bed, let's spend a week in bed, you'd drop this nonsense. Or is it something more? If it isn't, if that's all it is, then for God's sake go and find yourself a canoeira."

Gabriel didn't respond. He heard nothing. He knew nothing, except that somewhere in her outburst Elena had said she loved him. He sat beside her trying to remember the words, playing them over and over again, but he was trying to trap sunlight in stone. Each passing second eroded them.

"I'm going home."

"No, wait."

He came after her, enveloped in his silence. When he bent to kiss her goodnight she clung to him.

"Is your aunt in?" he asked. He rested his chin on her head. He looked up at the dark windows rising from the single wooden balcony.

"No, she's in Lima."

"And I can't spend the night?" He rocked her back and forth.

"No, Gabriel, not yet. When I'm ready. I promise you, when I'm ready."

"When will that be?"

She was prevented from speaking by a movement in one of the locked doorways. A shape slouched towards them. It stepped into the damask glare of the street light, shaking a black, grease-stained head. With a moan, it stretched a talon towards Elena.

"Get along with you," snapped Gabriel, consigning the figure to the night.

Then, reassuringly to Elena, his face pressed against a cold earring, "Only a beggar."

By accepting back the book of his favourite essays, Gabriel was making a tacit agreement to keep that part of his life separate from hers. Whenever he saw her, once or twice a week, he avoided all mention of politics. He never talked about Hipólito's impatience, nor of his growing impatience with Hipólito.

Nor, when the moment came, did he tell her of the man from Lima.

It was a Thursday night. Gabriel had walked down to Hipólito's shed on the river, built from the planks of an old river boat and now used to store machines awaiting repair – coffee percolators, out-board engines, television sets, sewing machines, goods imported by the very boat which had been metamorphosed to house them.

Here, under a green tarpaulin, Hipólito kept the small press he had acquired when *El Oriente* modernized its offices. Hipólito had originally seen the press (made in Hamburg, according to a metal label on its back, in 1925 – "the same year as Borges' *Luna de enfrente*") as a means of publishing his poetry. In Lima, he had boasted about it to Fuente's followers. He was disappointed, then flattered that the interest they registered had nothing to do with his verse.

The shed was empty. Gabriel was on the point of leaving when he heard a strange tapping. He turned. There was a man leaning in the doorway, drumming a biro against the frame. He had a stringy moustache, short hair swept back from a lined forehead and the tense air of someone more accustomed to the boardroom of a provincial bank than a riverside hut with a dirty concrete floor. "Hipólito Mercedes?"

At that moment Hipólito appeared behind him, drinking a bottle of Inca Kola. "Our friends in Lima sent me," said the man, loosening his tie. His name was Gasco. He had just come from a meeting at Fuente's headquarters on the Urubamba. He had been charged with setting up a foco in Belén – as well as the country around Piura. He hardly knew the jungle, but Fuente had said not to worry, they had a strong body of sympathizers in the city. He sincerely hoped so, he told Hipólito, because things had to start happening like yesterday. Heaving himself onto an empty oil drum, Gasco reached into his jacket pocket.

"I think this is what you've been waiting for."

Hipólito spread out the folded pages. He began reading. Gabriel looked over his shoulder. In small, neat handwriting was declared Fuente's revolutionary proclamation. Armed with both the necessary weapons and the knowledge that they had correctly gauged the people's feelings, MIR called for the immediate dissolution of Congress, a general amnesty for political prisoners, the handing over of large estates to the workers and "the recovery of full national sovereignty".

"At last," said Hipólito. "At last." He glanced at Gasco on his perch.

"Well?"

Gasco nodded at the press. "I want you to print it," he said. "I want you to distribute it as widely as you can. And then, at the given time," he said, slipping onto the floor and rubbing his hands on his trousers, "I want you to go into action."

"But what does he mean by action?" said Gabriel after Gasco left. He was exasperated. "Action against what? Doesn't he know there's only four of us? What are we meant to do? Toss firecrackers at the Mayor?"

"He's promised all the weapons we need in good time," explained Hipólito. "And we'll be told what to do. The point is that the right conditions will be created once everything gets under way. Once we've printed this, once people know what's happening, we'll be joined by many more. You'll see."

Gabriel thought back to the room in Lima and the professor from Ayacucho, who had left Gabriel in no doubt of his desire — expressed quietly and ruthlessly — for what all of them wanted in that room. Yet he had been so sure of himself in advising caution.

What Fuente was proposing seemed absurd.

"No, Hipólito. You don't eat chicken when the meat's still red. Nor do you start a revolution because that's how you happen to feel."

"You're wrong," said Hipólito. He laughed.

"I'm not."

"Does that mean you won't help me print this?"

"Yes."

So it was Hipólito alone who hauled the tarpaulin off the press. He cleaned the italic fount and with surprising speed set the text so that it resembled an introduction to an epic poem rather than a revolutionary proclamation. He ran off four thousand copies and spent a day wandering the town like a seed-sower leaving them in empty class-rooms and in bus stops, on benches and doorsteps and in the hall of the Club de Leones.

As Hipólito predicted, several promised their support immediately; once it was noted how unhurried the authorities had been in removing the posters, a number of others joined them. Lacking any instruction, Hipólito told them to prepare themselves. But the strain was showing. The tread on his tennis ball disappeared altogether. It was now a shiny, bald globe that he bounced off everything in sight, including on one occasion the windscreen of Don Miguel's Chevrolet which braked angrily at the corner of Putumayo and remained there, menacingly still, its doors about to burst open, before gliding off down the Malecón.

"Coward," said Hipólito, retrieving his weapon from the road, then hurling it back towards Edith.

"Here, catch."

She watched the ball roll away without unfolding her arms and only by running hard did Hipólito prevent it from bouncing into the river.

Edith Pusanga was Indian and proud of the fact she had no Spanish blood. She was prouder still of her descent from a Chanca chieftain who wore stolen spurs like sea-urchins and separated from the Incas because he considered them too lenient on Pizarro's brother, Gonzalo. On a captured horse – at first he thought the animal and its original rider one and the same beast – he had led his tribe to a peak near Tarapoto where he founded a city of handsome men whose only blemish was an addiction to human flesh.

Hipólito used to joke that Edith had inherited his tastes.

Gabriel never made such jokes with her, which might have been why she confided in him.

"You're more patient, Gabriel. It runs deeper with you." They were collecting drinks from the counter of a bar which had opened two blocks away from the Café Nanay. At a table by the door, Hipólito was pretending to read Elena's palm. "You're going to be discreetly unfaithful tonight," they heard him saying.

"You're stronger, too," Edith went on. "I feel with him it's only half serious. It's a pose. Something to take his mind off other things."

"Like what?" asked Gabriel.

"Like his poetry. Like the fact he can't write a single line without one feeling embarrassed for him."

"Edith!" He looked into two heavily made-up eyes. "From you of all people."

"You know it's true."

"Because he doesn't write his poems for you?"

"No, he doesn't," she answered. "But that's not the issue. He knows he's a terrible poet, but he drowns the knowledge of this in playing dangerous games. Look at him. What do you really think he feels for the plight of the Indian deep down? Beyond some romantic notion, very little. He's just a sentimental hangover from the poets of the Twenties. A café revolutionary. Could you honestly entrust him with a gun? It would go off in his jacket, if it didn't fall through the hole in his pocket first."

"Are we that different?"

"Yes, we are. What's more we know it. We're in this for real."

"Then why do you stay with him?" Gabriel asked. He gathered up three glasses, leaving the fourth on the counter.

"Because I'm fond of him." She reached for the thin flaring stem. She took a sip. "And sorry for him."

"That's how he gets all his women," said Gabriel. "They fall for him because they think no one else will."

He began moving to the table, but she held him back.

"And you. Why do you think women fall for you?"

"Do they? I don't think they do."

"She does."

"The exception."

"But she doesn't sleep with you."

"Is that a question?"

She turned her kohled eyes on Elena.

"She's not one of us at all."

In the second week of June, news reached Hipólito that Fuente had attacked the Santa Rosa mine in Andamarca and removed a large amount of dynamite.

"It's just a matter of time," Hipólito promised. "Gasco should be in touch any day now."

But he wasn't. Not that it seemed to matter. At last something was happening. A bridge was blown up on the Maraniyoc and another at Comas. Three haciendas were sacked. A police detachment was ambushed and a sergeant killed.

Nor did it really matter that around the city the military began acting as if there was something in the air more urgent than the threat from Ecuador. It proved they weren't dealing with a handful of horse thieves, as the government was branding Fuente's men.

Then, towards the end of June, Hipólito received a roneoed letter from Fuente. He was taking advantage of a halt in his march, he said. He was writing things "as they came into mind". There was a lot to say. Events had not only justified initial expectations, but progressed further than could have been hoped.

The support given by the peasants had been enormous. Even after a disastrous ambush when a comrade, since reduced to the ranks, had let off his rifle prematurely. It had been an extremely valuable experience. For three days they had fallen back, and learned from their mistakes. Measures were under way to restore contact with the masses.

"It doesn't inspire confidence," said Gabriel. He passed it over to Edith.

Hipólito ran a hand through his hair. "We've got to do something soon. We've got to. Where is that fucking Gasco. It's all slipping like water through our fingers."

"Wait, Hipólito," said Edith. "Give him a chance."

"Gabriel?" Hipólito challenged him.

Gabriel retrieved the pages from Edith's lap.

"I think he's had it," he said.

Hipólito snatched the letter from him. He was furious. "Observe, observe, observe. That's all you ever do. You never act, ever. Well, I'm an actor," he snapped, unconscious of any irony.

And the vigil went on.

One afternoon Gabriel called at Señora Guzmán's house in Raimondi. It was a hot day, hotter than usual, and the few people about kept to the cooling tar of the shadows.

Consuelo's side door lay in full sunlight. The heat made it painful to the touch. Gabriel knocked hard once, then less hard a second time and waited.

He was taking Elena to a film at the Bolognesi. He hadn't seen her for ten days and for all of that time, as for all of the times when they hadn't seen each other or spoken, she had been a shade in his mind.

For ten days he had imagined the evening ahead; the short walk to the decrepit cinema near his father's old garage; the two hours spent watching Luis Sintra's famous love story, daring to press the hand he held in his lap when one of the scratched scenes seemed an apt commentary on their own situation; and afterwards, the frustrating walk back through the warm night to her aunt's house, into which he would have to condense the thousand things he had stored up to say.

"She hasn't come home," said Consuelo, walking onto the balcony. Gabriel took two steps back and looked up. She had her father's crucifix in her hand. She was rubbing it with a cloth. "Try the office."

He walked to Eden Expeditions where he found Elena behind her desk, typing.

"We're late," he said.

She apologized. But Don Miguel had detained her with a last-minute booking. She'd come in early tomorrow to complete the forms.

"It's the least I can do. You may not like him, but he's dying, Gabriel."

"How long has he got?"

"Dr Lache says a matter of days."

They made their way to the cinema. As they walked, a helicopter flew overhead and deafened the square with its chatter.

"Wait." She reached for him. "It's saying something."

Gabriel stood, shielding his eyes. Above the engine noise, he heard the rasp of a loudspeaker. The machine descended and a flock of leaflets tumbled from its belly. A group of schoolchildren scattered to retrieve them. Gabriel snatched one from the air. His lips enacted a silent curse.

"Gabriel, what are they saying?"

But as the helicopter lowered itself closer to the square, dipping the trees and sending an old man's straw hat into the road, no interpreter was needed.

Armed agents were abroad. They were in the pay of foreign governments. Their aim was to subvert the nation. Anything suspicious must be reported. Anyone concealing weapons or spies would be punished. For those attacking the established order, the penalty was death.

"Come on, or we'll miss the film."

"No." She pulled away. "Don't patronize me. I don't mind if we miss it. What's going on, Gabriel?"

"What do you mean?"

"You know perfectly well what I mean. Look at me. Tell me you don't know."

"I don't."

"Then why is everyone forbidding me to see you?"

"Who is . . . ?"

"My aunt . . . "

"I thought she liked me!"

"Don Miguel."

"Screw Don Miguel," cried Gabriel. "Why is he so bloody important all of a sudden?"

"He isn't, but he's the reason I was late. He told me seven soldiers have just been tortured to death at Yahuarina. He said he never wanted to see you in the office again. Or Hipólito."

Gabriel's face tightened.

"So do you want to end it?" he asked. Somewhere in his mind the soft cold nose of a gazelle was drawing back. He felt its tense body preparing to leap.

"I don't know," said Elena. "What do you want? All I know is that I can't go on like this. I've never felt so lonely. It's as if you're afraid of talking to me."

Gabriel put a hand on hers.

"No, Gabriel, you can't deny it."

"You're always busy in the evenings. You're always doing something."

"So, you suspect someone else," she flashed, putting her hands on her hips and throwing up her chin and looking suddenly like the photograph in Consuelo's house of her mother, Colina.

"I don't know what to suspect."

"Well, you're right. There is another man."

"Elena . . . "

"And not only one. Twenty, thirty maybe." She laughed bitterly.

"Boys with no legs, children who can't speak, men who can't eat or walk or smile."

A man walking by quickened his step.

"Where do you imagine Sebastián goes at night? Have you ever thought, you who are so busy changing the lot of the poor? Have you ever stopped to ask yourself what kind of roof he has over his head, or hundreds like him? Have you ever stopped to think what his head actually looks like? No," she said calming herself. "Of course, you haven't. He's just another abstraction. Well." She drew breath. "I know what his face looks like. I know what sounds he makes when you feed him. And I know where he sleeps. It's where I go to at night. I go with the Belgian sisters. There are four of them. They look after the handicapped children who have been thrown into the street like chicken bones. No clothes. No food. No love.

"Last week we ran out of rice to feed them. I told one boy with cerebral palsy there was nothing to eat. He smiled and said 'Don't worry, Elena, we'll pray.' That's all he said. And I thought . . . pray to whom, I thought. You can't live on prayer. It's not something you can eat, not something you can drink. I felt more confused and useless in that moment than I've ever felt. And I'm not much help. I don't suppose I'm any help at all. But I'm learning. And I feel at least it's better to do something – anything, however small, even if it's only washing someone's hands or heating a bowl of soup – than to talk about it."

She looked up.

"But it's not Sebastián I'm worried about right now. It's us," she said. "I try not to think of your politics, of what you might be getting up when you can't see me. I try to suppress these thoughts, but I can't. I've never loved anyone before, but never for a moment did I imagine love could mean this."

They arrived too late for the film. The foyer was deserted. Elena leant against the locked ticket booth, creasing the posters tacked to its red chintz surface which showed the black and white hero of *The Rubber Man's Daughter*.

Gabriel looked at the girl he loved, who would not let him love her as he wanted. He looked at the posters behind, of Luis Sintra, the native of Coimbra who left Portugal to make his fortune in the jevea forests of the New World; the legendary cauchero, the man of mathematical genius who could paralyse ladies with his smile, but who had only ever smiled at one of them, the Rubber Man's daughter.

He looked again at Elena. An eyelash had lodged on her cheek. He wanted to wipe it away. Involuntarily, like a sneeze, he reached out his hand. She flinched. "No, I'll do it. Just tell me where." Taking one of her fingers he brushed it back and forth across her face.

"There."

"All clear?"

"Let's go to the Dalmacia," he said suddenly. "Let's go dancing."

She looked into his eyes, through the thickets where his mind was stumbling.

"All right," she said. "Let's do that."

They went that night. Elena wore her grandmother's blue dress and they danced and danced until the afternoon was forgotten and Gabriel could finally put his arms around her without feeling they embraced a tense girl who might turn her back on him at any second.

"You're appallingly beautiful," he said, affected by the music and the lights. She kissed his ear. "That's like a corny line from the movie we missed."

He felt the texture of her dress.

"Can we make love tonight?"

The words tumbled out before he knew it. They were dry and pleading. His fingers went on kneading the blue small of her back.

"Not now," she said, detaching herself. "But soon."

Soon. The promise sustained him when, at the beginning of August, the air force bombed Pucuta and captured three guerrilla bases in the mountains nearby.

All this absurdity would soon be over, he thought. He wouldn't have to make a choice between Elena and Hipólito. Soon Hipólito's revolution would be buried for good in some remote southern valley and he could devote himself to winning round both Hipólito and

Elena to the revolution he believed in.

His hopes grew when a US Marine Corps adviser in a combat jacket was spotted on the cold slopes leading up to the Mesa Pelada plateau. There in the ichu grass, it was thought that Fuente's men might have regrouped.

Then came unconfirmed reports that napalm had been used against them, that one of Fuente's own men had betrayed him when he made a break for Amaybamba, that the guerrilla leader had been sat on a crate of dynamite and blown sky high.

"I'm not waiting for Gasco," said Hipólito on hearing the news. He slammed his ball against the shed door and walked out.

Next morning, positioned between advertisements for car-hire and bedding, a notice in *El Oriente* called for all those who supported the heroic actions of Comrade Fuente to assemble at the Café Nanay at four o'clock.

"You're mad," raged Gabriel. "You're out of your fucking skull. You might as well pack up now. It was lunatic of you to announce the revolution before it happened. But to invite everyone to turn out in broad daylight as if you were throwing a tea-party . . . "

But Hipólito was radiant. He seized Gabriel by both arms. Didn't Gabriel remember what Fuente had said about the Peruvian peasant? How he was slow to make up his mind, but how when he finally reached a decision he was unmoveable? That was one of the reasons this revolution had taken so long. But that's why when it happened, it was going to be the most effective revolution in the whole history of the world.

"And we've got to make it happen right this minute, before it's too late."

"All right," said Gabriel grimly. "Since you've forced the issue. But we'll skip thé-dansant." He would round up those he could. They might be able to count on eight, ten at most. Then there was the problem of weapons.

"Come," said Hipólito. He left the shed. Gabriel followed him. They walked round the back to an allotment where a neighbour kept manioc and chickens and the rusting carcass of a Toyota pick-up. Hipólito lifted the seat. In the cavity below, badly wrapped in pages of *Caretas*, were ten rifles.

"Arrived last week," explained Hipólito, "from a contact of Edith's in Leticia."

Gabriel stood with his back to the pick-up. He looked at the pale afternoon sky. "Look," he pointed. "A full moon."

Hipólito followed his gaze. "The man in the moon," he said. "He's smiling on us."

"You can't seriously think that looks like a face?"

"Yes," said Hipólito. "I do." His eyes dropped to the ball in his palm. He drew back his arm and threw it with all the strength he had in him.

They watched the ball rise above the roof tops and the buzzards, above the finger-shaped clouds, above the nail-coloured moon, until it disappeared in a flash of sun.

They only heard the nearby thud as it fell on Vásquez's roof where the barrowman's wife had spread two paiche skins to dry, and the subsequent plop as it bounced among the tiny, faded boilersuits which Vásquez had never suffered to be washed until that morning, and the brown meadow butterflies which Francisco, his son, attracted with a paste of mashed banana and urine, and the north end of the market where he sold them in camphored matchboxes, and the frail stands on the steps down to the Plaza Clavero which supported buckets of writhing black carapama, like prehistoric toys, and kerosene for termites, and bootleg cassettes, and perfume with names like Royal Wynsor and Happened Love and Wild Leather, and bottle after bottle of thick creamy lotions for chicken pox and eternal love which Don Emilio recommended only after you had exhausted the powers of the ayahuasca which he sold, whistling like a Tunchi, with a promise that if you crushed its roots and boiled it for seven hours and drank it warm, you would live for a thousand years without ever feeling sickness, somewhere in this teeming, noisy world in the middle of the jungle, Hipólito's ball bounced out of sight forever.

Inspecting his bare hands, Hipólito spoke.

"I'm prepared to go it alone, Gabriel."

Gabriel had pledged his support believing there was still time to persuade Hipólito that his scheme was ludicrous. As Gabriel understood it, this involved boarding the evening packet to Requena and striking overland to join Fuente's last known redoubt in a valley near Manzamari.

In the hut he searched for a piece of paper. The only piece to hand was one of Hipólito's proclamations. Turning it over, he scribbled a note to Elena. He wrote that he would be gone a week, or perhaps two, he didn't know how long exactly. She might hear things but she must not believe them: he would be back. He loved her very, very much, he wrote. She had no idea how much. After entrusting Pía Zumate to deliver his letter – a matter of the heart, he explained, knowing her history of delicate lusts – he went down to the river.

They had assembled on the bank above the Requena wharf. There had been five of them, Bonifacio materializing at the last moment in a floppy denim hat.

"The boat's late," said Edith. She raised her sunglasses and squinted at Gabriel with the sun setting behind him. "Could be later this evening, could be tomorrow."

Gabriel glanced at the pile of canvas bags. "We can't stand here. Let's find a hotel."

Julio agreed. It was risky to be seen in town. He had just come from the cathedral square. The police had blocked off the entrance to the Café Nanay. Its owner would love him for that, said Hipólito, smiling. No one said anything. All of them had misgivings about his advertisement in *El Oriente*.

They carried their bags to a pension two streets behind the waterfront. Hipólito disappeared upstairs to the caballeros. They agreed to meet him at a bar on the Plaza Clavero. Edith left to buy some cigarettes. Julio's request for something to smoke had revealed the five of them had neither cigarettes nor matches.

"How would we have set off the bombs?" one of them joked later in the bar. The others tried to laugh, but their laughs were dry and without humour. The truth was, they were scared stiff. Gabriel saw his moment to stop them. He cleared his throat to speak.

That was when Hipólito began telling him about the dreams he'd been having in which no one talked to him.

That was when Don Miguel walked by with his tart and realized that the guns he'd let through customs with such a magisterial nod could not possibly be destined as hunting rifles for the Club de Leones. Those rifles, he realized, catching sight of Gabriel and Hipólito and the black bundle at their feet which contained them, might tumble something out of the trees but it wouldn't be a turkey cock.

Chapter 15

FROM EDITH'S WINDOW Gabriel could see the floating church where he resurfaced.

He had taken two deep gulps and dived again, following the contours of the hull until he was certain it shielded him from the opposite shore. Then he came up for air.

He coughed as he took in a mouthful of water. His feet found the bottom, but to stand there would have meant sinking in mud. He used his hands to propel him to the bank. One of his espadrilles was missing and his arm was bleeding from where he had torn himself against the hull. But he heard no more shots. When his breathing was steadier, he rose.

A police launch throttled into sight. It sent up large waves that rocked the floating church. Across the river, the crowd were pointing at something in the water. They were pointing at Hipólito, thought Gabriel with a lurch as blood and water dripped from him onto the oily mud.

He made for Hipólito's shed, where Elena found him two hours later. He lay in a heap against the wall, squeezing his arm to stop the blood.

"Oh, my darling," she said. She rocked him in her arms. "My poor, poor darling."

When Pía Zumate delivered the letter, she had rushed immediately to the cathedral and begun a fervent prayer. In the middle of it she heard gunfire. She opened her eyes and found herself looking at her grandfather's Annunciation. As she stared at the Virgin and the Archangel, she realized with horror that she knew the reason for the shots. She had run to the river. All along the waterfront people were talking about how a dangerous terrorist had been killed while escaping. Another terrorist was thought to have drowned, swallowed by Yacuruna, the angry river god.

"I thought it was you they had shot. They hauled this body onto the deck of the police boat. They tried to hide it from us but I saw Hipólito's shirt. I was so relieved. Isn't that terrible?"

She spoke through her tears, as if to herself. "But I knew you would be with Hipólito and I prayed and I prayed that you were still alive, that you hadn't drowned or been shot as well. And I waited while they searched the river and found nothing. Then I decided if you were alive there was only one place you would go and I climbed up here, and sure enough I found you," she said, looking at Gabriel's head in her lap and bending to kiss his muddy forehead. "In this horrible place."

"Come, it's not that bad," said Gabriel. He sat up, grimacing. "Who knows about it?"

"Only a few."

"Is it safe for tonight?"

"Think of somewhere safer."

"I'm going to get you some dry clothes and medicine."

She left and it began raining. No one would look for him in this weather, thought Gabriel, listening to the sting of water on the roof.

Elena returned after dark. She poked her aunt's umbrella through the door. "It's me," she said. She carried a plastic bag. It contained sandwiches, a bottle of iodine, a clean shirt and a pair of jeans. The jeans were too tight around the waist.

"You must leave first thing in the morning," she said. "You were on holiday in Leticia. When you come back you can say you had nothing to do with this afternoon."

Gabriel laughed. "No one's going to believe that."

"But what have you done?" she asked. She dabbed iodine on his wounded arm. "Nothing," she went on. "Precisely nothing. Which I dare say is a major problem for a firebrand revolutionary, but which also means they can't accuse you of anything."

"They'll find something. I was a friend of Hipólito's. That's enough."

At his name, Elena knelt back on her heels. She bit her lip. "I'm so sorry about Hipólito," she said. She stared at the bare floor. "I know what he meant . . . " she added helplessly, and then unable to find the words, her chin dimpled like choppy water and she was about to cry again.

"I know what you and he . . . " but in a sudden movement Gabriel reached out and stopped her mouth with his own. He clung to her, losing himself in the kiss, until, relaxing, she responded and the two of them slowly leant back on the floor.

"Now," said Gabriel.

She made no reply. Then she said, "Let me get rid of this."

She sat up. He saw she was still holding the bottle and the ball of cotton wool. Caressing her arm, he waited for her to screw the top back on.

She looked at him. Her blue eyes had never been brighter. He smiled. He bent to take the cotton wool and the bottle from her hand.

When he raised his eyes, she was still looking up.

But no longer at him.

Chapter 16

A NOISE interrupted Gabriel's reverie. Edith was in the room. She was saying something.

"What?"

"I said the police are everywhere."

"Is that unusual?"

"Very." She placed her basket on the table.

"No one saw you yesterday?"

"No."

"Not even Bonifacio?"

"Bonifacio?"

"He found me in the market just now. He said he'd tried the door."

"No," said Gabriel. "He didn't see me."

"It's better he doesn't know you're here."

"Why?"

"I don't know. It could be dangerous." She began emptying her basket. "He blames you for his brother's death," she went on. "He told me they'd found Julio's body. In an unmarked grave near the beach at San Bartolo."

Gabriel remained silent. Edith continued tonelessly. "He's just come back from Lima. He flew down to confirm Julio's identity and give him a Christian burial. He had to steal the body. He told me he was lucky to find it at all. Some of the bodies had been given false names. The military are still denying everything."

She unpacked a jar of coffee on the table, from one of the contraband stalls in Sargento Lores which had mushroomed under Don Miguel. Then a bottle of nail varnish remover from Dominica Zumate's pharmacy.

"Bonifacio now looks after the explosives."

"Edith . . . "

"He's a bastard," she said filling the kettle, raising her voice above the water. Her hands were shaking.

"Edith . . ."

"All right," she let out, through closed teeth, before spinning round to face him. "We'll talk about Elena. What is it you want to know?"

"Only if she's been here."

Edith sat down. She avoided Gabriel's eyes.

"Yes, she came. About three years ago."

"What did she want?"

"You," said Edith. "She wanted you."

"What did you tell her?"

"I told her where you were. I told her I didn't know when you would be released, if ever. She appeared to understand. She's not stupid."

"Did she know about Don Miguel?"

"Yes. She didn't say much about it, only that she'd heard."

"What else did you talk about?"

Edith pulled her face around and looked at him. "It's all right. I didn't tell her everything."

"I didn't mean that. Did you find out where she was going?"

"She didn't say. I'm not sure she knew herself. She wanted to see me before deciding. I think I was her main chance of finding you. I had the feeling she didn't expect much to come from it."

"And that was three years ago?"

"Yes."

"When three years ago?"

"I can't remember. Sometime during the Niño."

"And you haven't seen her since?"

"No, Gabriel, I haven't seen her since, not since she walked out that door."

Gabriel stood. He picked up her purse from the table. He extracted some notes.

"Gabriel. . ."

"I'm only going to the church."

Edith swallowed. "This meeting with Ezequiel. If you go looking for her, I don't think I can recommend you attend."

Gabriel reached the door. "I know," he said, opening it.

*

Gabriel walked purposefully through the market for three blocks and turned left down a wide tarmac street towards the river. This was Santa María. It led directly to where Hipólito's shed had been.

Nothing remained of the building. In its place and dominating the area, rose a large basilica with a jelly-mould dome and two grey towers the colour of thunder. To the left, was a modern convent. To the right, stood the abandoned foundation of what was to have been the Bishop's new palace.

Gabriel approached the gate. A woman sat on a rug selling prickly pears and lottery tickets. On the bars behind hung the religious effigies celebrating the appearance of the Mother of God at Belén. Key rings, medallions, statuettes, and ashtrays with the figure of the Virgin Mary and a girl kneeling rapturously at her feet, unrecognizable as Elena.

In the months after the visions, 26,000 cases of holy medals and rosaries had been shipped upriver to Belén – not to mention the candles, the postcards, the bars of commemorative chocolate.

Gabriel entered the basilica. The church was empty. The only sound was the tape-recorded chant of a choir. It came from a loudspeaker on a pillar near the altar. On a ledge beneath was an angel with a lace mantilla and a bent tin wing. Its enamelled gaze was fixed on the silver altarpiece.

A girl with red hair appeared behind Gabriel. She dipped her finger in a shell-shaped bowl. The bowl was empty. The girl crossed herself and advanced along the left aisle to a cabinet containing the Virgin. She touched the glass. She lit a candle. She began praying.

Gabriel looked about him. He found it hard to imagine that somewhere under this golden dome was the patch of land where the press had stood. The arches, the cedarwood pews, the mosaic letters which rimmed the dome spelling La Inmaculada had extinguished all traces of the dirty wooden shed.

He came across Elena's favourite painting in a small apse by the altar. A framed notice explained that the Silves Annunciation had been bequeathed to Santa María at Elena's request. An earlier inscription gave the provenance of the painting, believed to be the work of Fra Angelico's favourite pupil and donated to the municipality of Belén by Alonso Mario Silves, 30 September 1911.

It was the first time Gabriel had seen the painting.

Alonso's Annunciation had been heavily restored. The Archangel delivered his message beneath a thick layer of varnish. His long wings quivered, two yellow axes embedded in his back below a waterfall of golden curls. He stretched forward. A mysterious wind wrapped his scarlet robe. One hand, holding a lily staff, pointed at the Virgin. The other at the sky. His eyes were focused on the importance of what he was saying. "Hail, thou that art highly favoured, the Lord is with thee. Blessed art thou among women." The words curved over a number of small holes where the polilla worm had fed. They reached the Virgin at the level of her halo.

She looked up from her book. She saw the Archangel. She crossed her arms against her crimson chest. Her instinct was to recoil, but what he was saying drew her to him.

Under the varnish, her listening face was phosphorescent.

Gabriel retreated to the altar. He forced his eyes to the crucifix. He thought of the time when Bonifacio had defecated on the lace cloth and inserted a number of consecrated hosts into the pat – "like one of mother's cakes." And the time before that when, a week after the basilica's official opening, he had doused the altarpiece with petrol.

"O Gabriel, it burned beautifully," he heard him saying, this man now arranging a Christian burial for his brother, Gabriel's palanca. "I was transfixed. Can you believe it? I stood watching, feeling totally at peace with myself."

Only in thinking of the flames could Gabriel easily look at the altar. And as he looked his mind cleared and the basilica dissolved and he was back in Hipólito's shed on that rainy night twenty-one years before.

"A voice was speaking to me, calmly and distinctly. I thought it was your voice. I said to myself, what's going on, what's Gabriel up to? Then I saw this light. It was more brilliant than the sun – yet the extraordinary thing was I could look into it. I also wanted to look into it because I began to see the silhouette of someone opening their arms. I saw this person as I see you, but all of a sudden I felt so insignificant I didn't notice the details. Even now I find it impossible to describe. All I know is that my heart was on fire."

And what had he seen, kneeling in a pair of jeans too small for him, a ball of cotton wool in his hand?

He had seen Elena's face as she stood and walked to the door, then out into the rain. He had watched her advance step by step through the manioc patch until she fell to her knees a few yards from the Toyota pick-up. He had looked as she tilted her face to the full moon, all the while nodding and moving her lips. And following her eyes, he had seen the candle-end of moon begin to tremble until it appeared to spin on its axis.

It was the rain, he thought – though later he was certain no water had fallen on either of them.

It could be explained by his state of shock.

But seeing Elena kneeling on the ground, he remembered thinking she had never been so beautiful.

It was a different person who stumbled to her feet. "Oh, Gabriel," she whispered.

He led her back inside. "What have you seen?"

She looked at him as if he were out of his mind.

"But didn't you see?"

"Who was it?"

"Didn't you hear?"

"Was it the Virgin?"

"A priest," she said. "I must see a priest."

Gabriel covered their heads with the green tarpaulin. He took her over the river. She refused to believe he had seen nothing except a trembling moon. Had he not seen the face, composed of a light as white as the river at Rapoto where the kingfishers plunge into the fall? Had he not seen the curls of hair which fell like gold lace onto clothes made of no colour she had ever known? Had he not heard the words, words which she was asked to repeat and remember and which reiterated that God existed, that there was but one God, one truth, and that the people must no longer try to advance without God, as if man were his own creator?

"They were not empty words like we use."

"Of course not, Elena," said Gabriel soothingly. "Of course not."

"I must return the same time tomorrow."

"You will, you will."

The rain had stopped by the time they reached the cathedral square. Gabriel removed the tarpaulin from their shoulders. He folded it while she waited. Then they continued across the square to the Bishop's palace.

He paid no attention to the three men on the bench.

"She told me to return at the same time tomorrow."

Gabriel was only half listening. He was ringing the Bishop's bell. At the same time he was trying to zip up his trousers. Before he could do so, the door opened and it was not the Bishop, but a strange man, a gringo, who told them in heavily accented Spanish that the Bishop was away in Lima and that he was just staying a few nights before. . . He was about to say before joining his mission in Delicias, but at that moment he saw the girl and decided they had better come inside.

Chapter 17

FATHER PAUL MABY was a Franciscan who had been in the jungle five years. He came from a village fifty miles south of Tulsa built of clean, fresh-painted houses and surrounded by fields of furry wheat that seemed to go on forever. A mile outside the village was a well. The most popular form of suicide in the area was to throw oneself down it.

Paul was the youngest of three brothers who had loved the same girl. For the rest of his adolescent life his dreams would draw on the memory of the twelve-year-old who stared down into the darkness where David and Martin had vanished without a sound, having expected him to keep his word and follow.

Paul Maby's hands were gripping the bricks to propel him from the rim when a mortar bee flew under his nose and he toppled backwards into a lavender bush.

Its scent reminded him of the girl he loved – the daughter of a psychotherapist from Maine. Paul had begged for some miracle which would make her love him. But smelling the lavender, he was possessed by his first certain knowledge of the difference between good and evil; also by the idea – which would never leave him – that life itself was the miracle.

Paul Maby had not broken his word since. At the age of twenty-six, he had left home to escape his father and because he heard a bishop at the seminary give a talk on Peru and ask for volunteers. His had been the first hand to go up.

"A vision, you say?" He looked at Gabriel. After five years in the jungle he knew when a man ceased to be responsible for his actions. "You'd best leave her with me."

Dazed by Hipólito's death, by his own escape and now by this, Gabriel was in no state to look after Elena. He placed an arm on her shoulder, his tired lips on her cheeks and left with a promise to see her next morning.

An hour before midnight the Bishop's door opened. The two figures of Elena and the American priest hurried down the steps and into the Bishop's car. The white Volkswagen beetle coughed three times before making a circuit of the square. When it reached Raimondi it turned left. A hundred yards on, it halted outside Señora Guzmán's house.

At five minutes to nine the next morning, Corporal Velarde could be seen knocking at the door with a loud, steady rap. In his pocket, inside a polythene bag in case of rain, he carried a warrant for the arrest of Edith Pusanga, Julio Angel Medina, Julio's brother Bonifacio, and Gabriel Rondón Lung.

Velarde was a little irritated by the impatience with which Don Miguel, the person responsible for the warrants, had treated him. He knew Don Miguel was gravely ill, but that meant he should be taking things easy instead of looking over the corporal's shoulder as if he didn't trust him to wear his trousers on his legs instead of over his head.

Twice in the night Don Miguel had called at the station.

"Nothing at all, señor. As I said, we're looking."

Velarde had removed his new Ray-Bans for Don Miguel. He wouldn't do that for many people. After all, what happens when men with sunglasses remove them? Their eyes look raw and tender at having to confront what they see.

But Don Miguel was different. Velarde's eyes had nothing to hide from Don Miguel.

Perhaps the corporal should not have worn his glasses on that day when his captain was sick and it became his job to check the boats come in from Ecuador. Perhaps then he would have seen what he wasn't meant to.

"How much do you earn a month, Corporal?"

Velarde had told him, adding a few pesos because he suspected what was coming. Don Miguel wouldn't be asking that question if the next thing he was going to say was How's the wife and baby? Not with Velarde standing awkwardly beside him on his deck, having routinely opened one of Don Miguel's cupboards and finding there such a big bag of powder.

It would take some purchase to whiten the money Don Miguel would make from that.

"Three hundred soles, Señor Minero."

Velarde saw him reach inside his jacket. Mother of God, was he reaching in there for a gun?

"Here's thirty years' salary."

You had to have a reason to turn down such an offer. At the time Velarde couldn't think of one, though now he could think of lots of them, despite his Ray-Bans and his neat little house by the airport, and the gold ring on his finger and the gold in his mouth, and his car, which had been dented by some round object on the very day it was delivered from Brazil, and his daughter, who was going to be a handful he could see just by the way she walked across a room, and his wife whom she took after, who only loved him because he bought her alpaca jerseys from Arequipa and who insisted on wearing them when she showed her love, which was three nights a month before her flower-time, and which she liked to wear because they made her sweat in the torrents she had seen in films but which made him come out in a rash as if he had been bitten by several brigades of red ants. Yes, now he could think of reasons, but on that boat his mind had been a blank, and from that moment Don Miguel had his screws in him. Though why he should be showing interest in a teenage revolutionary who couldn't revolve a door defeated reason.

Señora Guzmán stood before him. Velarde removed his peaked cap and explained to Elena's aunt the nature of his visit.

"If you insist, Corporal. But be gentle, she's rather confused."

I bet she is, he thought, stumbling against a step he hadn't seen and then against the lion claw of a chair which finally persuaded him to remove his sunglasses and fold them with a snap into his shirt pocket.

He bet her sweet ass she was.

What was her story? Velarde asked Elena, who sat holding her hands on a sofa, with her legs crossed. His tapir eyes flicked over her black hair. Where was she last night? Where was Gabriel Rondón Lung?

But it wasn't going to be that kind of interview, he realized. Oh, no. As Elena told him what she had seen the night before, it became obvious even to Corporal Velarde that whatever she was describing lay outside the authority of Belén's police force.

Gabriel stood before the altar and shivered. He sought the cloister.

The arcades contained the original allotment; the land where the car had been and the row of manioc bushes where Elena had knelt. Two of these bushes remained, grown from shoots of the original plant. They were protected by a waist-high circular wall. Around the wall, a number of flowers sprouted top-heavily from shoe-polish tins. An open drain gurgled in the corner.

But here on the following afternoon some ten thousand people had assembled to witness the Virgin's return.

They took to the oozy paths leading up to the shed, trampling over the chicken field. People used to seeing their auguries in cloud formations and the entrails of birds; people with incurable scabs, ulcers, and varicose veins; men, women and children seeking some sign that in these dangerous times of shootings and angry helicopters, the forces of the supernatural were on their side. By bicycle and boat they came. On the tops of lorries from the Nanay, on motorbikes from Quistacocha, on the ferry which Don Miguel, forgetful of his interest in Gabriel, had chartered to bring them from as far upriver as Jiron. There they stood in the manioc, warming their soup over candles, blowing their whistles and waiting.

Ten thousand of them, said *El Oriente*.

At seven o'clock there was a stir. "Make way for the girl who's seen Our Lady," came the shout. Then Elena appeared, followed by Father Maby, Consuelo and Corporal Velarde.

Gabriel stood with four others on the roof of the Toyota. From where he stood he could see her face. She was wearing a thin necklace – a present from him – made of paiche scales. Her hair was arranged in a tidy plait.

She seemed relaxed. When the American priest said something, she laughed with her whole body.

A rug was produced for her to kneel on and there was a hush. Her hands joined in prayer. Her face looked up, alert.

"It was a clear night," said the report in *El Oriente* next morning. "The stars were salt across the sky. The moon had swum free of the trees."

From the shed's roof came a bright flash. "Our Lady, Our Lady," a woman shouted, but it was only the newspaper's photographer.

All eyes were on Elena, kneeling there. She stiffened. Suddenly her head jerked back to catch sight of something above her. At the same time a light spread through her face.

The crowd murmured.

"Look, look, the moon," someone cried. Everywhere people fell to their knees in the mud. To *El Oriente*'s correspondent, the light glowing on their backs seemed "as if it were shining down through a church window, altering everything and everyone."

A yard behind Elena, Corporal Velarde made a sign of the cross. He brought a man forward to the rug. The man produced a stethoscope from a leather bag. He pressed it clumsily against Elena's chest. He gestured for a candle to be brought which he raised and lowered before Elena's eyes. Holding it beneath her chin, he lifted the flame to the skin. Finally, after fumbling with his spectacles, he applied a needle to her arm.

All this while, Elena looked at the sky.

According to *El Oriente*, she smiled 36 times, gave 23 nods and moved her lips on no fewer than 17 occasions. The electro-encephalogram performed by Dr Lache confirmed that she was neither dreaming nor in a state of epilepsy. Her pulse was faster at 79 than the average 60. Her eyes blinked less than was normal and the pupils were dilated. Otherwise she was suffering from no sort of tension. Having examined her afterwards in his surgery, Dr Lache was obliged to declare Elena Silves to be of sound mental and physical health. He could offer little explanation as to why she failed to react when a needle was pricked in her arm – though he agreed to meet the costs of laundering the bloodstain he had caused on her shirt.

As for why her chin showed no signs of burning though he had placed a candle against it for 15 seconds, he preferred not to speculate.

"It was as if for that particular period," Dr Lache later told the elder of his two wives as he removed his spectacles for bed, "she didn't exist in our world. Either in space or in time."

"What did the Virgin say?" asked his wife, an agoraphobe who could only walk between Dr Lache's house and the supermarket on the corner of Nauta – and so remained ignorant of the separate ménage he kept in the next street.

"She said she would return again one final time tomorrow."

Then, rubbing his eyes, he went to sleep with a corner of his sheet in his mouth and his mind fixed firmly on the things of this world, such as who would pay for his evening's work.

The municipality – for surely it was something that involved the whole town. Or perhaps, that man who had telephoned him in the first place, the American priest. Or perhaps, when he returned, the Bishop.

Chapter 18

IT IS MIDDAY by the Swiss clock on the cathedral tower. The bell has rung and the square is full of schoolgirls gossiping on benches with their socks about their ankles. A baby balances on a flower bed that burns with the pink waxy flames of torch ginger. A blind woman walks by, guided by her daughter and son-in-law. The heat makes rippling shadows on the pavement. The air is inflammable with exhaust fumes. Don Wenceslau's false teeth shine in the sun, washed by the first of the masato he has drunk from Vásquez's barrow. Already his pupils are dilating.

"Why is it," he asks, "everything tastes better out of someone else's glass?"

Don García chews on a chicken leg. His hungry eyes appraise the tourists walking by. Two girls have already prompted a spurt of concupiscence. This he tries to satisfy by eating.

With his mouth full, so his words are not quite clear, he says, "One of those things, Don Wenceslau. Ask Don Leopoldo. He'll know."

Don Leopoldo shifts. He has been dreaming of the Amazons who attacked Orellana's expedition — women who lived alone, with hair that touched the ground. He has been thinking of the arrow quivering in the magnificent buttock of Fray Gaspar Carvajal. Disturbed by the conversation on the bench, he clears his head. He opens his eyes. He sees his fustian friend, Wenceslau. Ah, well, he thinks, he who sleeps in a pond wakes up a frog.

"I want to tell you what happened on that day," Don Wenceslau is saying.

Don Leopoldo sighs. There are few experiences more tedious than to be told of something he has himself actually witnessed. Most especially by Don Wenceslau. But listening to him has become a ritual, like putting out your hand to say hello, goodbye. It confirms Don Leopoldo's conviction there are only so many stories to be told, only so many characters, and these repeat themselves.

"We must have gone about this time of day. I was with you, Don Leopoldo, remember? We had crossed the river together. We wanted to be there early. You were telling me how sceptical you were. You had read an article about the Virgin's last appearance in Lithuania. You remembered her promise that she would next be seen in Egypt. You didn't believe any of it. Your friends at the Club de Leones had said Boy, are you going to have fun."

Don Wenceslau chortles. "It was you who saw it first.

"You said Look! Wenceslau, look at the sun.

"I said you shouldn't look at the sun, Don Leopoldo, it's bad for your eyes. After all, your eyes are your profession. And we aren't in Egypt. Nevertheless, I looked . . . and there it was, not hurting me in the least, but coming towards me, in, out, in, out. Then you arrived, García."

Don García nods sombrely. He assaults another piece of the chicken beside him, wrapped in the pages of *El Oriente* like a greasy flower.

"Never look at the sun, you repeated. But I wasn't listening. I said Look, for God's sake. And slowly, very slowly you looked. Heavens, you gasped, wait a minute, what's it doing? What's happening up there? And very soon all three of us were saying Look, it's coming towards us and going back and stopping. All three of us were seeing the same thing.

"But you know something, it was as if the sun was looking at us and not the other way round. As if it was talking to us in a funny sort of way, in a ridiculous sort of way. Don't you remember, Leopoldo?"

"Yes, yes, Wenceslau. I remember."

"You even hoped it might cure your haemorrhoids."

Don Leopoldo splutters. "Nonsense, Wenceslau. Never."

"Anyway, the whole point of the story . . . "

And all of a sudden, Don Wenceslau runs out of steam. He has forgotten what he was going to say. It is the fault of the man next to him. He is a patriarch, Don Leopoldo. A dampener of conversation. A misery boots. Never happier than when staring into that bag at his feet. In Don Wenceslau's marinated eyes, Don Leopoldo's bag has the messy shape of their country. He squints at the long neck contracted at the mouth. He tries to think of something pertinent with which to conclude his story. Nothing comes to mind. He looks at Don García eating.

"I used to like that part of the bird," he says cheerfully. "Until I realized it was its arse."

Chapter 19

THE BISHOP hadn't liked it. Not one little bit. He had heard the news in Lima while conducting negotiations with the departing Italian ambassador over a Sienese cross.

"Seen this?" said the wiry plenipotentiary. He came from Sapri and took scant care in concealing his desire to return there.

"The eyes of the world are on Belén," read the Bishop in amazement. It had always been his belief that few and far between were those who had heard of his city in the jungle. Now apparently the whole world would know.

To the powers that be, he thought, drumming his chubby fingers on the aeroplane's armrest, and trying to distract himself with a game of in-flight bingo, it would look very bad indeed.

Eucario Barrantes was, as one of his numerous critics put it in special reference to his glibness, the kind of man who had no trouble writing amusing entries in visitors' books. It was often said of him, and not always behind his stooping back, that he was a man on the make. His grandmother had said it. His mother had said it. His fellow seminarians at Ocopa had said it. They had said it at various times in Lima, in Arequipa but most often of all in Piura where to make his mark he had held a mass for the glorious hero of the Pacific War, brandishing, so he imagined, Admiral Grau's black and gold sword. (Actually, the sword had been donated by a group of Peruvian women in Europe long after news reached them of the tragic fate of the glorious iron-clad *Huáscar*.)

None of this worried Barrantes, a small, slight man with a lacklustre face and brightly polished shoes. What worried him was the possibility that the Cardinal Archbishop of Lima might be saying it.

Since his appointment as Bishop to Belén eighteen months previously, Barrantes had made a conscious effort to swim with the tide. Increasingly he was finding the exercise a strain. Though he bore the coveted title of Bishop, Barrantes found himself the primate of a diocese answerable not to Lima but to Rome. Due to the paucity of missions in the region, Belén was ranked as an Apostolic Vicariate rather than a fully-fledged Bishopric. It was a distinction Barrantes could not help feeling keenly.

After a prelature, an Apostolic Vicariate struck him as the lowest form of life. It suggested the local Church was not mature enough, at least not in the pastoral sense. It also meant the Church was serviced by foreign personnel.

People like Father Paul Maby, he thought, poking a finger through a number on his bingo card which corresponded at last with that announced on the intercom.

For eighteen months Bishop Barrantes had felt caught between the demands imposed on him by the Curia and his ambitions to rise in the hierarchy nearer home. Keeping both masters sweet would have been a difficult task at the best of times. This was not such a time.

The Vatican's second Ecumenical Council was drawing to a close and Barrantes had a nasty feeling that in general the tide was turning. Vagabond lily he may be, but some of the modifications proposed by the Vatican struck him – and, he suspected, his Cardinal Archbishop – as unappetizingly modern. Nevertheless, in accordance with Rome's instructions he had steeled himself to show a face of the Church that was of and with this world. A face, he reminded himself, that believed in a community of equals.

Stepping down onto the tarmac, it was a face of unconcealed irritation that he showed the American priest who had come to meet him. Only momentarily, when a reporter approached his diminutive presence at the baggage check, did the expression arrange itself more beatifically.

The Church had not pronounced itself, he smiled. Nor must it be too quick to label whatever was happening in Belén as superstition.

Not until he had sat in the front of the car did he address a word to the American. Then looking pointedly at him, he opened his minted mouth.

"Now," he said. "Tell me about this apparition on the manioc bush."

*

In his last year at the seminary, Eucario Barrantes had submitted a dissertation on Jean Gerson, the fifteenth-century rector of Paris University. It was a modest piece of scholarship, remembered by the invigilator for its curious mixture of pedantry and prurience.

Barrantes had obviously relished his investigation into the rector's pronouncements on lesbianism. Also into the surprising absence from Gerson's canon of what seemed to Barrantes a pertinent commentary on the mores of his contemporaries – and a key interrogatory for the medieval confessional: namely, the priest's demand to young women as to whether they had marinaded a small fish by placing it between the labia minora and then delivered it in a dish as a means of bewitching their sweethearts.

In a footnote, Barrantes speculated that the fish was probably a sardine. The invigilator was inclined to suggest red herring.

Barrantes' dissertation was only marginally preoccupied with deviancy. Its main thrust concerned Gerson's manual relating to cases of fraudulent sanctity, especially among women.

On the aeroplane, Barrantes repeated to himself a fragment of the rector's Latin. According to Gerson, the visions and sayings of women were "to be held suspect unless carefully examined, and much more fully than men's." The reason? "Because they are easily seduced." Before he even knew of Gabriel Rondón Lung, Bishop Barrantes had decided that the visions of Elena Silves were suspect and suspect for this very reason.

The problem remained, what to do?

The truth was that, listening to Father Maby's patient testimony in the front of his Volkswagen beetle, Eucario Barrantes felt undecided and, contrary to the impression he might give the outer world, he had never thrived on indecision.

He was anxious to be seen implementing whatever the Holy Synod desired, but what it desired for devotees of the Virgin Mary was, in his opinion, opaque. Next to Papal Infallibility, Mariolatry was the greatest barrier to Christian reunion. Barrantes had followed closely the events in Rome, but remained in several minds as to whether the barrier had been removed, fortified or simply left untouched.

The Virgin had been subjected to possibly the Vatican's closest debate ever. Should her doctrine be contained in the schema on the Church or be granted a separate chapter? The propaganda was intense. Bishops from the Ukraine and India stood on the steps of St Peter's and forced leaflets on those who entered. There were stories of an unseemly collaboration between advocates for the separate chapter and the Vatican Press Office. It was rumoured that a pontiff from Madagascar had thrown a clumsy punch at the Bishop of Toledo after the latter had argued that Mary was a most exalted co-operatrix with Christ.

Barrantes did not know exactly what he should admit to thinking on this issue. But as one who combined a legalistic frame of mind with a reverence for the scriptures, he did know that there was nothing in the Bible to justify Mary's extra dignity and status. She was mentioned a few times in the New Testament with something approaching casualness. Even Christ had shown signs of impatience.

"Woman what have I to do with thee?" Wasn't that what he had asked at Canaan? And was there any indication that he was aware of the few miracles with which she had been credited? For the Immaculate Conception and the Assumption, Barrantes argued to himself, there was no biblical basis whatever. They were inventions of the clerisy. Inventions as doubtful as the special shrines and prayers and effigies which proliferated everywhere and exalted the Mother above the Son. They couldn't even decide whether she was buried in Ephesus or Jerusalem.

According to the report in *L'Osservatore Romano* there was an audible gasp when the votes were cast and it was decided by a majority of 1114 to 1074 against the granting of a special treatise.

In his jungle, Barrantes rejoiced. Since the days of his seminary he had always been suspicious of Tradition as a source of revelation. He had also been secretly disgusted when in the 1950s the Assumption became the one doctrine to be decreed as an article of faith since the definition of Papal Infallibility. The new biblical enthusiasm of Vatican II suggested that the cult of Mary would now be contained. At the end of the Third Session, however, the Pope announced his decision to confer on her the title of Mother of the Church. Not only that, but he encouraged a rosary and a daily prayer. Then, by way of achieving a total volte-face, he sent a Golden Rose to her shrine at Fátima.

Where that left Eucario Barrantes, Eucario Barrantes was unclear. Where it left him now that the Virgin had apparently blessed his own parish was a matter of graver doubt.

"You say you saw the moon move, then next day the sun," he said, gritting his teeth as the car bounced with a clang in its bowels over a large pothole Father Maby had seen too late. "And that there's another vision planned for this evening?"

"Right."

The Bishop looked at him. Father Maby's presence in Belén was beginning to be as welcome as a dog at Mass.

"You were correct to insist on the presence of a doctor," he said. "We have had so many impostors. All the same, it's not exactly stunning, is it, what Our Lady said to her? Less charitably, one would call it trite."

The man beside him tooted at a bicyclist and shrugged.

"Playing Devil's advocate, doesn't she come to each of us on our own terms?"

The Bishop snorted. He was not a man who cared for such advocates. "One could argue that. One could also argue that Our Lady should make her identity and intentions a little bit clearer. Why is it that she always appears to young girls in the back of beyond who hardly have a clue what's happening to them?"

"Nazareth was the back of beyond," replied the American. "And I won't pretend I'm not confused. I spend my life meeting drunken messiahs in the jungle who may well be the Second Coming but who wouldn't know the Lord's Prayer from a hamburger stall. I'm also familiar with all that Fátima and Lourdes guff. But when you meet Elena Silves you'll realize this isn't a case of some little shepherdess on the hill with her lambs. For a start she comes from a good family."

"I know about her family. I know her aunt. I know the girl. I see her every week in the choirstall. What I want to know is what's going on in her mind?"

The American said, "I would say two things. One, she's as honest as a blush. Two, she's just extraordinarily happy."

"Wasn't there some specific message," the Bishop went on. "A secret only the Pope can see. A heavenly sniff of roses. A magic spring. Didn't she ask for a medal to be struck or a chapel to be built. Were there no angels with pretty fluttering wings?"

"No," replied Father Maby. "No angels."

"Why does the Virgin always look like some Murillo archetype instead of a girl in first-century Galilee? Why, if she appears today, doesn't she wear a . . ." He looked at passing houses to see how young women in his parish dressed. Failing to find them, his eyes veered to the car roof.

"Why doesn't she wear . . . a bikini?"

"Bishop . . . "

"Sorry, but I'm angry. I would almost have preferred a weeping icon." He remembered with a twitch the occasion when his maid returned from Cuzco bearing a piece of wool wrapped in red tissue and wet with the tears of a saint.

"Could it be narcotics?" he asked optimistically. "Or lack of food?"

Too late, Father Maby braked before another hole in the ground. He apologized. "I'm not used to these gears."

"Could it be an optical illusion?" the Bishop pressed on through the grinding of machinery. "I've often stared at a bright object in a dark background and thought I'd seen things."

The man at the wheel said something.

"What was that?" asked the Bishop.

"Devil's advocate again. I was thinking of the moment our whole faith rested on the appearance of the risen Christ. Before that I was thinking of the light the shepherds saw in the sky."

"Oh," said Barrantes. The Volkswagen was turning into the square when he spoke again. "Satan himself is transformed into an angel of light," he quoted. His driver raised an eyebrow.

"Saint Paul," the Bishop explained, opening the door. "Your namesake."

The Bishop went to see Elena Silves that afternoon. Two policemen leant against a car outside Señora Guzmán's house. They had been posted there following the cable he sent from Lima urging the Mayor to provide protection for the girl. They raised their hands in a salute.

"Why, it's the Bishop," Consuelo chuckled on opening the door. He didn't know if she was enjoying herself – or intoxicated. She led him to a room upstairs.

"One minute a revolution. Next minute a revelation. I can't keep up. She's in there." And she tottered off leaving Barrantes to find Elena with a smile on her face that reminded him with a heavy heart of that woman who ran the Hotel Liberty.

"So," he said, crossing himself and kissing her for good measure on the crown of her head. "Tell me all. She who does not speak is not heard by God."

A grim expression came to his face as she spoke, although, as she talked, he couldn't help noticing Alonso's ivory cross poking tantalizingly between her hands. He replaced his tongue inside his mouth. "What did this figure say?"

"Return to prayer," said Elena. Nothing was more important. The face then disappeared like a blown candle.

"Nothing can replace the sacrament and holy prayer," he agreed. "Not even an apparition." But he felt uncomfortable as he walked back across the square to his house. What was the Church to do with someone whose line to Christ appeared more direct than its own? How was one to bridge the gulf between a trainee tourist guide who had spoken to the Mother of God, and an official representative who had not. Mindful of the bishop who had been deprived of his authority after the apparition at Beauraing in 1933, he voiced his doubts to Father Maby.

As he did so, he began to wish there was someone else he could confide in. The American obviously believed the finger of God was here. It made him suspect. In fact Barrantes was beginning to believe the whole thing was a hoax put up by the Franciscans. If he hadn't been in Lima none of this might have happened. He could have talked the girl out of it, he could have suppressed the news.

"There are thousands of Peruvians who want to believe in

something like this. Our country has never been in more need of mothering, but that doesn't mean she saw what she claims to have seen."

"I don't want to believe it," said the American. "My whole training is against believing it. As I said before, in the jungle I've witnessed lots of so-called visionaries. Like you, I take the Church's position that all visions are false unless they can be proved true."

"Well, then."

"On this occasion I'm convinced, absolutely dead convinced that she is seeing something – whether this something is inside her or whether it exists. She could not lie. If I was to say to her, Say this, she would say But that's wrong, Father."

"Why didn't anyone else see it then? Why didn't you?"

"I didn't see the face of the Virgin Mary," said Father Maby. "But in Elena Silves' face I saw the reflection of something like it."

"I return to what this apparition is meant to have said. It seems so banal. It seems entirely without logic."

"This is a mystery which has leap-frogged over logic. After all," said the American, "we know what happens when men have recourse to argument. They argue."

From the expression on the Bishop's face he saw he had struck a chord. "At least," said the Bishop, "what was uttered is free of theological error. We can be thankful for that. And the crowds are gathering in a spirit of prayer, some who can't have experienced the sacrament for twenty years. But why has Our Lady chosen to come to Belén? Why here, of all places?"

"Because she found faith?"

The Bishop looked at him in genuine astonishment. "My dear fellow, if that is the case she must have got lost. Belén, as you must have noticed by now, is no halt on the path of simple virtue." No. Something was not right. He felt it in his bone marrow. What he needed was time, he thought, unlocking the door to his study.

Normally he would have paused, taking pleasure in the crosses displayed on the wall – a modest collection of fifteen crucifixes purchased with rather too much of his stipend. On this occasion he made directly for the bookcase by the window. He couldn't remember whether he still possessed the Latin document. He hadn't seen it since he wrote his dissertation. But there it was, between a rare copy of Miguel Alberto's *Stimuli Divini Amoris* and a first edition of Sarah Grand's *Babs the Impossible*.

He sat at his desk. In a long and carefully worded telegram to the appropriate authorities in Rome and Lima he outlined the circumstances and gave assurances that he was proceeding with extreme caution in full accordance with the *Norms of the Sacred Congregation for the Doctrine of the Faith About How to Proceed in Judging Alleged Apparitions and Revelations.*

Later that afternoon, the Bishop visited Belén. He insisted to Father Maby on going alone and in disguise. He wore a shapeless macintosh with its collar turned up around his plump cheeks. He looked like one of Velarde's plain-clothes men, thought Don Miguel recognizing him instantly and careful not to charge the full fare across the water.

Even at half the cost, the Bishop judged the price of Don Miguel's ticket exorbitant. Don Miguel may have resembled a death mask, but he had no business to be making money out of this. He must be raking it in, the Bishop reckoned crossly as the crowd pressed him further along the ferry's deck. He had never quite approved of the man. Nor had he felt the appropriate sympathy on hearing the news of his illness. The fact that Elena Silves worked for him made the whole thing worse, he thought, rubbing off the damp rust which the rail had left on his palm and taking a sharp breath as a woman trod on his foot.

He joined the procession up the bank. A white ribbon was strung out along a number of posts. Behind it, some workmen were constructing a concrete path. Further up, a man was selling white loaves on a table. At the summit, a notice warned pilgrims against looking at the sun. The day before, if one believed *El Oriente*, fifty people had to receive medical attention for eye-injuries.

The field was strewn with fish heads and piles of rice and the boiled-out skulls of goats. It smelled of urine. Near the shed, an area of land had been fenced in. It was guarded by a policeman, who prevented anyone leaving more of the tokens which festooned the manioc leaves.

Standing on tip-toe, the Bishop could merely catch glimpses of this shrine. Dozens of people ringed the fence, men and women in bare feet or in fine leather shoes, who stared at the manioc plant with the same look on their faces, hoping it might cure them of incurable ulcers and Pott's disease and lumps in their chests the size of coconuts.

They listened to a loud-hailered voice read from Saint Matthew's Gospel. "But immediately, after the tribulation of those days, the sun shall be darkened, and the moon shall not give her light and the stars shall fall from heaven and the powers of the heavens will be shaken; and then shall appear the sign of the Son of Man in Heaven: and then shall all the tribes of the earth mourn . . . "

At five o'clock Elena appeared once more on the arm of Father Maby. They were protected by three policemen. As they walked through the crowd, the voice on the loud-hailer began leading them in the rosary. Immediately, the crowd knelt to reveal an embarrassed policeman, the parcel of land on which Elena had seen her vision and, at the back, the figure of Bishop Barrantes.

Barrantes arranged his macintosh and reluctantly joined them in the mud, feeling nothing except acute irritability and a dull ache in the region of his bladder.

When after an hour the Virgin failed to appear, Barrantes experienced a wave of relief. After two hours this approached something very near ecstasy. He returned home on winged feet to find the telephone ringing in his hall. It was Corporal Velarde. He was calling to inform the Bishop of the guard he had posted at his request outside Señora Guzmán's house, and to tell him that he was increasing it by a further two officers. Not only for Elena's own peace and quiet. But also to prevent Gabriel Rondón Lung from attempting to reach her.

"Gabriel Rondón Lung?" said the Bishop.

Velarde explained. He had in his hand a letter. He rustled Hipólito's leaflet into the mouthpiece. It had come into his possession by the prompt action of Señora Guzmán. (Having promised to keep secret the incident of Gabriel's letter, Pía Zumate had finally unburdened herself. It was one thing to protect a terrorist in love. It was another to continue doing so when the Holy Mother was implicated. Velarde had used her testimony to wrest the letter from Elena's aunt.)

It was written from the terrorist to Elena Silves.

"It is," said Velarde, rereading it and experiencing a momentary pang of regret that the days had passed when he and Señora Velarde felt such passions, "a love letter."

That did it, thought the Bishop. He was exultant. Gerson was right. These visions were nothing more than a dammed-up libido. What had des Brosses said on seeing Bernini's Saint Teresa? "If this is divine love, I know what it is." Hadn't Barrantes known this all along? He was pouring himself a libation of whisky when the telephone rang again. It was the American. He was speaking above the noise of a bar in Plaza Clavero.

He didn't quite know how to put it. Something extraordinary had happened. It concerned Don Miguel who had begged Elena for help in curing his cancer. Elena had touched him as she left the site. Her employer had visited Dr Lache's surgery directly.

"And what is Dr Lache's diagnosis?"

"The cancer has been arrested."

"How does he know?"

"Apparently this Don Miguel had a lump in his side the size of a new-born baby."

"And?"

"Well, it's disappeared."

"This is something," the baffled doctor was at that moment telling an excited press corps, "which upsets all our acquired notions of pancreatic pathology."

"Bishop, you still there?"

"Yes . . . yes, I'm here."

"It's being talked of as a miracle."

The town was in turmoil. In the bars and cafés, in the brothels, the churches and the post office, in the market stalls and on the benches of every square there was talk of nothing else. Don Miguel's rescue from certain death was truly a miracle which only the intercession of the Mother of God could have effected.

Hipólito's death and the escape of his fellow terrorists, which two days before had occupied *El Oriente*'s front page, might never have been.

Instead there were phone calls from Buenos Aires and Madagascar and Quito and from a peculiar denomination of Italian mendicants near Cortona. There were planes scheduled to arrive at the town's small airstrip from Miami and Bogotá. There were even rumours that the Pope's favourite theologian, Urs Von Balthasar, had caught a flight from Zurich.

At eleven o'clock next morning, in a state of abject depression, the Bishop took his telephone off the hook and went to replenish his supply of Amplex from Dominica Zumate's pharmacy. Hidden behind the stacks he overheard two girls wondering if the Virgin looked like Martha, reckoned the most beautiful blonde in Iquitos, or Vásquez's daughter, a sultry brunette called Alejandra.

Plainly, he thought, reaching through a mound of Peter Pan bras for his Amplex, it didn't matter a damn that the visions had ceased. The important thing was to remove their cause from public scrutiny. Too big a candle could burn down his whole church.

An hour and a half later, at twenty past twelve, Elena Silves left her aunt's house for an unknown destination, clasping a small overnight case.

At two-thirty *El Oriente*'s correspondent revealed her whereabouts in the care of some Canadian friars near the Nanay.

At five o'clock the situation repeated itself when a journalist from *Oiga!* managed to enter the Bethlemite shrine in Moronacocha through a lavatory window.

With the arrival of Faucett's afternoon flight from Lima containing 119 more journalists and two television crews, Bishop Barrantes realized his task was hopeless. He was left with but one option. This he exercised that evening. Wearing his macintosh – though it was not raining – and leaving Father Maby in charge of the house, he walked through the streets until he reached the

Benedictine hostel by the waters of Sachachorro.

The smell from the rubbish dump was such that he had to hold his nose while rooting for his mints — in which slightly ridiculous position the Benedictine father found him. He told Barrantes, as he led him to Elena's room, that the indefatigable reporter Alejandro Berlaguer of *Caretas* had called once and, not at all satisfied with his answer, had promised to return.

Barrantes remained standing as he informed Elena of his cogitations about her future. She was to enter a convent. It was to be far away from Belén while remaining in the department of Soreto. It was to be a closed order.

"You understand I can only suggest you stay there as a postulant. The decision to enter the religious life has to be made freely and it can only be made by you alone."

The Bishop continued. "Once you have decided, you must on no account tell anyone where you come from. You must not tell anyone who you are. You must not say a single word about what has happened here. You will have a completely new name. Only one person in Silar will know your true identity. The Mother Superior."

His voice softened as he concluded. "This is the price, my dear, for being blessed with a vision from God."

"When do I leave," asked Elena.

"Tomorrow morning. Tonight you stay with me in the Bishop's palace."

Chapter 20

FOR THREE DAYS Gabriel had heard nothing but whispers. How Elena had transformed Don Miguel into a man thirty years younger with the complexion of a grapefruit pith. How Don Miguel was set to make $700 a day from his company's tour of the site. How the Sacred Congregation for the Doctrine of the Faith was already deliberating on whether to nominate Elena for the sainthood.

The wilder the whisper the more frantic Gabriel became. He was a wanted man. He had nowhere to hide except the warehouse on the Nanay where he had spent three sleepless nights under a boiler. He had no idea how to reach Edith or Julio or Bonifacio. Far worse – and the occasion for his sleeplessness – was the fact he couldn't see Elena. The police outside her house made it an idiotic risk to shout up at her window and Consuelo Guzmán had followed Barrantes' example and cut off the telephone.

He bumped into Consuelo by chance. It was the morning after the Bishop had removed Elena from the Benedictine hostel, when the stories were so extravagant that *El Oriente* was consigning one in every three to the spike.

Consuelo was walking through the contraband market with a basket clinking of gin. At first she appeared not to recognize him. She withdrew her arm as if he was a bag-snatcher.

When he mentioned Elena, begging to know where she was, she relaxed. But she was distressed. They had taken her away. She didn't know where. Some religious institution. They hadn't told her the name of the latest one. They said it was to protect her. But Elena didn't need protection. She was happier than she'd ever been. If anyone needed assistance it was Consuelo. Her husband would have known what to do. She was too old to suffer these traumas on her own.

And why was Gabriel asking after her? Wasn't it true he had a price on his head? So that ugly corporal said, forcing her to go looking like a spy in Elena's bag.

"I ought to leave," she said, suddenly forgetting Gabriel, his letter and her niece, and thinking for no reason at all of her very first memory, a picnic given by her father at which the Portuguese Vice-Consul had lifted her high into a cloudless sky with the words "So you're Consuelo."

"I will," she said, her eyes descending to find Gabriel instead of a man in a white uniform. "I will go to Portugal."

Gabriel watched her disappear into the crowd. Nearby someone turned up a radio which had been playing American music on a stand selling Patum Peperium. There was a news flash.

" . . . We have just received this statement from the Bishop's office. 'The public is understandably anxious for the Church to say something about the events in Belén where Elena Silves claims to have seen the Virgin. Advised by the Holy See against reaching any hasty conclusions, we cannot for the time being attribute a super-natural character to these events. Only time will tell if the Church can deliver a judgement of heavenly origin. Meanwhile all might make private pilgrimages to the site for the purpose of devotion, worship and conversion. Official pilgrimages led by the Bishop are not permissible. Signed; Eucario Barrantes, Bisho of Belén, 13 August 1965'."

A fanfare followed. The announcer spoke again. "As for Elena Silves, who today leaves the care of Bishop Barrantes for a safe sanctuary, it doesn't need me to say that she departs her native city with its fullest blessings, with its sincerest hope that she will return . . . "

Those who wished to see Belén's most beautiful daughter one last time were advised to make their way with all haste to the cathedral square where news had been circulating of Elena Silves' imminent departure for the airport.

It took Gabriel seven minutes to reach the square. He ran through the narrow stalls of Sargento Lores overturning a table of cream crackers from Dublin. He ran headlong down Juan Próspero into the traffic of cars and motorcycles and motorcycle taxis which swerved and hooted at the sight of him advancing towards them in the middle of the road with arms and legs pumping, his shirt-tail behind him and his face a picture of agony.

He ran into the back of the large crowd which had gathered around the entrance to the Bishop's house and he only stopped running when having elbowed Sebastián out of his path, then Pía Zumate, then Don Tonsurans and finally Dr Lache, he no longer had the breath nor the strength to push his way through to the front.

He stood on tip-toe, panting, looking over the backs of men and women jammed tighter than pilchards.

He saw three rows ahead of him the Bishop's white Volkswagen, protected from the crowd by twelve policemen with machine-guns. He saw Father Maby run down the steps and slide awk-wardly across the passenger seat to a position behind the wheel. He looked at the door from where the priest had just run. He saw it open and three people descend to the car — Corporal Velarde, Bishop Barrantes and Elena. He saw Elena. He saw the shape of his gazelle on the high ground. And he screamed.

"Elena! Elena!"

Hearing his heart-rending cry, the crowd fell silent.

"Elena!" he screamed again. With a superhuman effort he thrust himself forward to the car. He pressed his head against the window at the back where Elena was sitting. He screamed again, pounding the glass with his hand. She turned her face away. When she turned her face away, he tried to open the handle. He was about to punch the window when Father Maby engaged the gears, released his foot from the clutch and accelerated forward in a jerk that threw Gabriel back into the arms of the police.

The crowd followed the car. Forgetting Gabriel, they surged after it, singing and waving and touching the white bonnet. Not until he had driven unsteadily for two blocks did Father Maby lose them.

Only the three men on the bench saw what happened to Gabriel.

"Is he dead?" asked the youngest policeman.

"Who cares," said another. He kicked the face at his feet with such force that the whole body rolled off the pavement and into the gutter. He could promise one thing, though. Not even that bigamist Dr Lache would be able to tell if this face belonged to a Juan or a Juanita.

Chapter 21

GABRIEL EMERGED FROM Santa María and stood in the sun. The bell sounded above him. It was one o'clock. He needed a drink. He entered a cebichería on the corner. He ordered a beer and sat at a table overlooking the sandflats.

The sandflats had grown since his last visit, built from the soil of the crumbling river banks. Everything had grown. The number of houses on the rice fields. The price of kerosene chalked on the board.

"OK," said the customs officer at the next table. "You pay a hundred only. But next time it'll be more. Tell Mario that."

The cost of bribes.

Gabriel's beer arrived. He poured it, feeling the chill against his fingers. As he drank he heard laughter. A man at the bar was telling a story. The man turned, responding raucously to his own joke. He turned in Gabriel's direction. When he saw him his smile froze.

"Che, Gabriel," he said, pointing a finger. He walked over to Gabriel's table.

"It *is* you."

A grin returned to the lager-flecked lips. "Aren't you meant to be dead?"

"Not yet, Bonifacio. Not yet," said Gabriel, making rings on the table with the damp bottom of his beer bottle.

"But weren't you in the dormitory?" The man drew up a chair and sat down on it the wrong way round with his dirty fingers on the rim.

At the bar, the other men turned their backs.

"I'm sorry about your brother, Bonifacio. He was a good compañero."

"Weren't you?" hissed the man.

"I had a palanca with him."

Bonifacio hiccuped. "Yes. With my brother. With my fucking

brother. I supposed you knew what was going to happen." There was menace in his voice. His mouth was a fresh scar. He was drunk.

Gabriel poured the rest of his bottle. When the beer foamed up he placed a finger on its head and took a swallow.

"Why don't you pretend we're coming into Requena," he said, "and piss off."

"Why are you here?"

"None of your business," answered Gabriel. He rose to his feet. He put on his jacket and left an inti note on the table.

"I'll make it my business," shouted Bonifacio. The words hung in the beery air. At the bar, the men's backs were a row of trees braced in the wind. Gabriel stopped. Standing there, looking at his feet, he seemed about to swing around.

Bonifacio stabbed a finger at Gabriel's face. "It's that gringa whore, isn't it?"

But before he could put the question mark in place, Bonifacio lay on the floor like an upturned bicho, the rim of the chair back at his throat and Gabriel's body pressing down on him between the metal legs.

"You just listen," said Gabriel, holding Bonifacio's hair and slapping his head against the ground once, twice, three times.

"Did you hear what I said? I said I was sorry. You think I don't know what I owe Julio? You think I would forget?"

He leant harder on the chair.

"No, Bonifacio, I haven't forgotten. But if you want that tongue to taste beer again, don't let it mention Elena Silves."

That night Gabriel lay smoking on Edith's couch. She had not seen him with a cigarette before. He had said nothing all afternoon.

Looking down at his etiolated body puckered with scars, she was reminded of a tormented Christ in the cathedral. She scratched her leg. It was the only sound in the room, like a rat in the skirting.

The cigarette glowed and dulled. He coughed and rubbed the stub out on a plate. She couldn't tell whether he coughed out of illness, or because he wasn't used to tobacco.

She took a deep breath and looked down at the floor where their clothes lay. She knew what she was about to say contained an end to everything between them.

"They say she went to see Father Maby."

There was no reaction in the figure beside her. She turned her head. She saw his stomach lit by a spear of moonlight from the shutters. It trembled with his heartbeat.

"Who says?" he asked at length.

"I heard it from Pía Zumate."

"Where is Father Maby?"

"He's still at Delicias."

Chapter 22

I'M GOING TO TELL YOU something you'll find fascinating. . ."

Don Wenceslau is proposing to tell his story of the Amazon dolphin, the bufeo. The others have heard it before, but they let him talk. After lunch there is never any stopping him.

They can smell his breath, a raw-liver breath of food that has rotted between the few dark dominoes in his mouth and the masato which has swallowed his pupils. When the masato is the stronger smell it is better to listen.

Beneath his trilby Don García closes his eyes. At intervals he gives an appreciative nod. But his mind is not on Don Wenceslau. His mind is on women. The problem isn't getting them, he convinces himself. It's getting rid of them. That's why he likes the Teletroca . . .

Don Leopoldo gazes glumly at the shells by his feet and flicks them with a finger into a rough circle. He raises his eyes to the Admiral. He reads the words on his plinth. The words are compressed together. Some of their letters are missing, like Don Wenceslau's slurred speech.

8OCTOBERI87
FOLLOWHISEXAMPL
SOL HOP

Don Leopoldo looks at the green epaulettes, parroting the bunches of iron grapes which hang from the windows of the Palace Hotel. He looks at the Admiral's face. He looks into his bronze eyes. Through them he sees the mist lifting from the sea off Antofagasta on that historic day of 8 October 1879.

On one side lies the ocean. On the other, the bare, scarped cliffs of a grey cordillera. Admiral Grau peers at the morning coast through the turret of his iron-clad *Huáscar*, the 1130-ton "Lion of the Pacific". On this boat and on its companion, the *Unión*, rest the hopes not only of the fair women of Trujillo (who have embroidered the ensign now visible through the mist), but of his whole country.

He rotates the hand-worked turret. Off the point of Angamos, at the extreme tip of Mejillones bay, he sees three pipe-cleaners of smoke. He swivels the turret. On the north-west horizon, three more!

Six ships to two, but for champions of Peruvian liberty, for Grau, and for his predecessor Lord Cochrane after whom, irony of ironies, one of the Chilean funnels is named, these are everyday odds.

He signals the *Unión*'s captain. He instructs him to make his escape. If both ships are destroyed, the country will have no navy. With infinite regret, Captain García y García – the author of a volume of sailing instructions for this stretch of coast – turns about.

"Full steam," orders Grau, the sole hope of Peru.

"Fire!"

The fourth salvo from the 40-pound Whitworth guns passes through the *Cochrane*'s galley. There are hidden cheers. They are smothered by the sound of a shell starting the bolts and breaking an iron beam in the *Huáscar*'s turret.

Escape is impossible. Grau decides to ram. The *Huáscar* advances on the *Cochrane*, shooting wildly.

300 yards.

100 yards.

50 yards.

The *Cochrane* replies.

The only fragment to remain of Admiral Grau who has given his lasting inheritance to Peru and earned his deathless fame is an inch and a half of knee-bone.

Don Leopoldo has not seen it, but he can picture the relic on its red velvet cushion in Callao's Merchant Marine College.

"It was Good Friday," Don Wenceslau is saying. "We were coming from the Puruha river. There was this young woman washing clothes on the bank. We had gone thirty metres past her when we heard shouts and screams. We looked round. She wasn't there any more, only the clothes she'd been washing. We looked everywhere. Nothing. They had taken her. The bufeos had taken her. We told the witchdoctor. He said she was under the water, alive there somewhere and living with the dolphin who had stolen her.

'Always carry a cross,' he said, 'and nothing like that will happen to you.'"

Don Wenceslau's fingers mount to the crucifix at his throat. He looks at his two companions. "That's what I did and nothing has happened."

Don Leopoldo waits to see if the story is over. Satisfied, he rubs the earth from his fingers and leans back.

Don Wenceslau drags a sleeve across his bluish lips and burps.

"Don Leopoldo," he asks softly, "do you believe in the Amazon dolphin?"

"No," says Don Leopoldo.

"No?"

"You know I don't."

Don Wenceslau sighs heavily. "What about you, Don García? What do you think?"

Don García's expression implies he is not quite sure what to think. His concentration has been drawn to a girl on the bench opposite. She reminds him of a woman who used to cross her legs behind his back. His mind returns to his own bench. The bufeo. Don García knows the gallons of water which Don Leopoldo pours on this creature of myth, but he remains an agnostic. He too has heard strange stories; how the bufeo lives at the bottom of the river near big cities; how it enters town at night in the shape of a white man or woman with different coloured eyes; how you can tell a bufeo by its deformed feet and four-fingered hands and the blow-hole under its sombrero.

Perhaps Don Wenceslau is such a creature. He has the requisite bulging eyes and the smell of swamp moss and when he stands up he is slightly bow-legged.

Don García crosses himself so Don Wenceslau doesn't see.

What else has he heard? He has heard of fishermen who fuck dolphins. As a young man he met one. They were very clean animals, the man said. Not greasy, and much tighter than women. When you fucked them, they moved their tails.

"Imagine every ecstasy you ever had, Señor García. Multiply it by whatever age you are. That's the ecstasy you feel when they move their tails."

Don García attempts a crude algebra and decides to think of something else. Such as the woman his father knew who had given birth to a child that was half Christian, half bufeo. The wind of the river, she told her husband. It was a sorry sight, apparently. When they burnt it a voice cried out with the mother's name.

But why a Christian? That is what puzzles Don García. "Why do bufeos always appear as white strangers?"

Don Leopoldo replies in that lecturing manner he adopts when he believes he knows about a subject. "Because our continent has always been dominated by white strangers. Think of Pizarro, think of the missionaries, think of the Spanish, the Portuguese, the British, the Dutch who have inflicted themselves on us. That's what the bufeo represents. It's a symbol."

"A symbol," Don Wenceslau repeats. "Like this cross."

"Like your cross, like that church, like that car, like everything that has been transplanted on us."

"Like communism," says Don García who is keen to demonstrate his grasp of Don Leopoldo's polemic.

"Like communism."

It is all too much for Don Wenceslau and not in the least what he expected when he began his story. The masato has fortified his hazy belief that whatever has been said he is right.

"Fucking communists," he mutters. "Fucking terrucos." He thinks back to what Vásquez told him barely an hour before, shaking his newspaper with a rage that rattled the barrow. What type of man is it that can send a child scampering into Lima's Crillón Hotel to explode into a hundred thousand pieces. Not a day goes by without some incident like this. He thinks of the recent mutilations at Cabaña. He thinks of the town now buzzing like a jostled termite's nest with strange soldiers from Lima and helicopters that whisk his hat away. His poor country. Overrun by the communists, by the military, by the police.

"I doubt if they'll blow up the Liberty," says Don Leopoldo, unable to resist following Don Wenceslau's line of thought.

Don Wenceslau suppresses another belch. "Pity," he says. "They might take a few tourists with them."

"What about my beautiful Argentine?" says Don García in tones of mock anguish. "Pía tells me her music is quite out of hand. The guests have been complaining. There are cracks in the ceiling where she dances . . . "

"But Pía never speaks to you," observes Don Wenceslau.

"All right, all right," he replies. "She told Capitán Velarde who told me. Satisfied? What's more Velarde told me her name." Don García looks as if he is about to cry.

"Yes?" say Don Wenceslau and Don Leopoldo together.

"She's a man."

"Called?"

"A gringo called Riddle. A writer."

"As I thought," says Don Wenceslau. "An Irishman."

Don Leopoldo is unruffled. "I wonder if he's anything to do with the Major Riddle credited with discovering the electric eel."

"Whoever he is, Pía tells Velarde he's got appalling taste in music."

"Why tell Velarde anything?" asks Don Wenceslau. "I thought she hated him. Even more than she hates you."

"They're checking out the hotels. Not just the benches," says Don García, glad to get his own back. He doesn't know the reason, but whatever it is they have left him alone. His trilby he supposes. They could tell he was an artist. Even brutes like that.

"Louts," says Don Wenceslau with emotion, reminded of the incident which had sent him in a fury to Don Vásquez's barrow.

"Asking for my documents. Who does Velarde think we are. Agents from Ecuador. You'd make a fine agent, Leopoldo," he says. He prods the man beside him. "I suppose he thought you had a bomb in your bag."

"How's the great work?" Velarde had said, inspecting Don Leopoldo's identity card, faded like a patch of old cotton, and the photograph of the young historian before he blundered into the cobwebs.

"Coming along, coming along," Don Leopoldo had muttered, peevish and embarrassed.

Bad enough to humiliate his companion like that, but to Don Wenceslau far worse was the way they had upset his own ritual. Just as he was stretching the toes in his Duckers in anticipation of his afternoon shine, just as he had summoned the boy and just as he was counting the change in his pocket with two coins extra for the tip, one of the policemen thrust out his boot and ordered him to clean it then and there.

He recognized the man. He was one of the bastards who had messed up Gabriel Lung all those years ago.

That was it! Don Wenceslau realizes. What an utter fool he's been. They must've found out about the Chino.

"They must've found out about the Chino," he says. "That he's not dead after all."

Part Three

1986

Chapter 23

THEY HAD WALKED all morning from the tributary where the boat dropped them, Gabriel and a boy from Dos de Mayo called Alan. For 200 intis, Alan had agreed to guide Gabriel through the jungle to Delicias. He knew a short cut that would halve the journey there by boat. "Coming back," Alan promised, slanting his hand through the air, "you glide."

He had a black dog, who criss-crossed the path in pursuit of butterflies, and a glass eye where his brother's machete had struck him while cutting cane.

After an hour Gabriel heard a wild turkey flap its way up a tree. Then some red paraqueets flew over, screaming. The rest was jungle static and the slash of Alan's machete.

Cobwebs marked Gabriel's face, thorns tore at his clothes, creepers tripped him. It was a long time since he had been in the jungle. Sliding on rotten logs and damp paths, he was breathless in its mosaic light.

After five hours they emerged from the jungle into a river bed with flat stones and a rut of brownish water. Even the dog was tired.

"Let's sit," gasped Gabriel. He fanned his face with a leaf. He had not expected this exhaustion. But his strength had been sapped from him. His torture, his illness, his years in San Francisco prison had scored him like a rubber tapper's knife.

"One more hour," said Alan. He patted the dog and pointed through the thin trees fringing the river bed.

Gabriel sat on a rock catching his breath. He followed Alan's hand to where the clouds dropped jaguar spots on the mountains. He relived the last time he had been in the jungle, fleeing through it with a price on his head, Edith at his side and his face a feast for every insect in miles.

*

He heard himself moaning. Someone was trying to open his eyes. He saw a dark shape blocking the sky. The moans were Sebastián's.

His step-mother stopped her rocking when she saw them in the doorway. She rose from her chair. She thanked Sebastián in an unbroken voice and led Gabriel through the coloured plastic strands to his room. She sat him on his bed while she fetched a bowl of water. She said nothing until she had washed his bleeding face and groin.

Then she said: "You can't stay here, son. Not unless you want to find yourself in the Moronacocha."

With that she left Gabriel on his bed, to buy some antiseptic cream. Gabriel knew she was leaving him to decide. He wondered why he felt no pain. He looked up.

Everywhere he saw his photographs of Elena and her face before it broke into a smile.

When his step-mother returned from Dominica Zumate, she found Gabriel standing calmly in the middle of a million fragments. He was staring at the wall above his bed. In the blank space from which Elena's images had been obliterated, he was picturing the face of the man from Ayacucho.

He found Edith in a house owned by her cousin. She sat in an empty room. Her hands were looped around her knees. She was staring at nothing. Above her a grey parrot fidgeted in a cramped cage. It pecked unblinking at an empty water tray.

"We're going to Ayacucho."

She looked vacantly at him. Tears had blotted her make-up into an oily smear below her cheeks. He held out his hand.

They reached Ayacucho in three weeks. They caught the boat to Requena after hiding for five days in a scatter of huts on the Maniti. (He wouldn't be able to find it now. Probably it was no longer there. The Indians had a habit of moving on once the thin jungle earth had given up on them.)

From Requena they took another boat to Pucallpa and then a lorry through the mountains. Gabriel sat with Edith on the truck's floor. Through the back they saw donkeys loaded with roof tiles and cattle dragging ropes along the road. As the lorry passed them, girls held out their hands for money.

At one village they were joined by an Indian band heading for the ice festival at San Juan. There were six of them, presided over by a squeaky-voiced Lord of Misrule. They wore silk scarves on their backs, patterned with a woman on horseback in a black hat.

The band played the same tune again and again. Their falsetto leader kept them awake by hurling orange peel at those who threatened sleep.

On the second day the tarmac ended. Gabriel looked out at the bleakest landscape he had ever seen. Mountains without vegetation. An implacable sky. A sun that could blister the stones.

As they climbed between a high pass of shaled sand, dust rose between the boards, covering their clothes and faces. They tasted its chalkiness, they felt its weight on their eyelashes, they sneezed it into their sleeves. By the time the lorry reached Trapala, they were statues of grey flesh.

"The man downstairs says it's one more day," said Edith. She was washing her mask away in their hotel room. Gabriel caught her eyes in the mirror. He had never seen Edith without make-up. Her face was revealed for the first time, the face of a Chanca Indian.

"Two at the most." She bared her teeth.

Gabriel spoke. "Come here," he said.

She turned. She walked to where he lay on the bed. He pulled her to him. She did not resist.

Afterwards he felt a tugging. He raised his face from the ticklish darkness of her hair, spread out on the pillow. The movement released her head. Her face came into focus. She was looking at the ceiling.

"What are you thinking about?"

She told him.

"I loved him more than I thought," she said.

"That's why we're going to Ayacucho. To see he didn't die for nothing."

"What about Elena?"

"I must never think of her."

Already Gabriel was burying her memory with the dry, colourless earth of his revolution. Instead of the seraphic glow in the sky, he was thinking of the crowd glimpsed from the Toyota roof, the sudden convergence of men and women that nothing on earth could have stopped.

The first thing Gabriel noticed about Ayacucho was its light. It struck everything with the same force – the lizard tiles, the thirty-three churches, the equestrian statue of General Sucre raising his tasselled sword to the hills.

Gabriel also noticed how thin the air was. Just to walk up the slope of the colonial square made him dizzy and exhausted.

"Your professor" – as Edith called him – had returned only recently from a trip to China. They arrived in Ayacucho in time to hear him lecture on it. His talk was given in a large room on the first floor of the faculty of education. The room was full of undergraduates and professors. Even the sharp-nosed Dean of the University in a lace bow-tie was there. Because of the low voltage, it was easy for Gabriel and Edith to pass themselves off as students. It was a time, the students used to say, when you almost needed a match to find a light.

The professor arrived punctually at six. He was accompanied by his wife, a dark-browed woman who sat next to the Dean smoothing her black and white check skirt.

There was a hush as he made his way to the platform. He produced a bundle of papers from his case. He began arranging them on the table.

He was simply dressed, in a long-sleeved shirt. An orange cravat was tucked into its open collar, hiding his neck. He had the same gleaming hair, dark eyes and white teeth of the man who had stood by an empty fireplace in Lima. But there was something severe about his face. His defiant mouth was now a hawk about to plunge.

He raised his head. "Close the door, please."

The lecture lasted an hour. It was devoted to his seven-month sojourn in the People's Republic of China and the state of that country since the Sino–Soviet split.

He began by describing several field trips made in the company of a colleague from the university – a bearded man who sat nodding in the front row. There were no slides, but every so often he produced a chalk and grated some words on the blackboard. Gabriel remembered two phrases: a quote from Mao—"without intellectuals there is no revolution" — and the derivation of the word religion — "from religare = to bind up".

For the first time since childhood Gabriel became aware of the country Achin Man Lung had left a century before.

"That's why I let you in," said Ezequiel, with a gaze that made him feel like a beetle caught between a beak. "Your Chinese blood."

The lecture concluded with the observation that China had a great deal in common with Peru.

There was a tremendous silence in the room. Then he began speaking again, this time without notes. Unlike China, Peru was a land which had not come to terms with its last 400 years. It was a place, not a country. A no-man's-land which was aware of its boundaries only through the boundaries of others. It had no pride in its sovereignty, no fairness in its government, no future in its present condition. It was a land which refused to see its own reality – that it was a land of Indians.

But he believed the secrets of the Inca empire were not lost. He believed it was possible to restore a sense of national identity. He believed it was possible to do this by overturning the entire system.

Only a violent revolution on the Chinese model would enable this to be achieved.

"Only a violent revolution," said the professor scratching his elbow, "will give us back our identity and pride."

Later, Gabriel and Edith found a bare-bulb room in the Hostelería Santa Rosa. They registered in false names, then returned to the Plaza de Armas where they sat with dangling legs in an arcade overlooking the square. Gabriel followed General Sucre's swordthrust to the mountains. Their folded slopes were faces without features, but they reminded him of his father who had died without seeing a mountain, who believed that mountains were where the earth had shrugged when the wind changed.

On the other side of the sierra was fought the famous battle of Ayacucho. Gabriel watched the tiger-eye sun roll over the peaks. He found himself able to look at it without blinking, and as he looked it became Hipólito's ball, coming to rest at the site of the battle which had finally liberated the continent from Spain, when, outnumbered two to one, the patriot forces comprising William Miller's hussars, and men who had fought at Borodino, and a division of sightless soldiers, snow-blinded in the Andes, followed General Antonio José de Sucre on his horse, a massive charger with bollocks larger than avocado pears from whose nostrils snorted trumpets of mist as it paced the heights called Condorcunca – worthy of the condor – and, spurred on by the flash of the General's sword, put the silver-headed royalists to flight in such a way that when the Spanish Viceroy Canterac rode down to surrender, he could only say to the English general who offered him tea, it all appeared a dream.

General Miller, he said, again and again and again, as the wick lowered on the sky, and also three centuries of Spanish rule, ésto parece sueño.

Chapter 24

ON THE RIVER BED, Gabriel threw away the leaf. He rose to his feet. "One hour more," Alan repeated.

At three they reached Delicias. They came out of the trees into a grass bank that rolled up towards the village. In the river a group of naked children stopped their splashing and watched them. Over the ridge came the thump of drums.

"They're preparing the pot for you," joked Alan.

The drums grew louder as they climbed the bank, followed by the children. Gabriel traced the noise to its source in a clearing bordered by stilted huts. Three Indians sat outside one hut on the rungs of a ladder. They wore grass skirts and green feathered head-dresses. One man beat an upturned plastic bucket. Another piped a flute carved from a section of hose-piping. Another shook a pair of rattles.

"They caught so much yesterday," Father Maby explained, "they don't have to work for two days. They've been drinking masato all morning. That's how it is in the jungle. You live for today."

When the Indians saw Gabriel, they stumbled groggily down the steps. The one with the bucket made a V-sign against his lips for a cigarette. Gabriel gave him his packet.

"Stay here," said Alan. "I'll find the Father."

Gabriel took his place on the bottom rung. The three Indians converged on him, puffing their cigarettes. The man with the hose-pipe flute crowned him with his parrot head-dress. The others touched his cheeks and forehead with their fingers. It was a while before Gabriel realized they were painting him in yellow patterns like their own.

When Alan returned, he covered his mouth with his hand and whooped. The Indians yelled along with him, not quite understanding. The dog barked.

"The Father?" Gabriel asked.

"He's ill," said Alan, his glass eye on Gabriel's yellow cheeks, his other on the musicians who had resumed their playing. "But he wants to see you."

"Do I remember her?" The words were non-committal. From his hammock Father Maby took in Gabriel with eyes rusty from malaria. The priest's face was gaunt, tapering into several chins which the disease had left untouched.

"Yes," he said decisively, slipping from the hammock. His feet searched for sandals on the floor. He shuffled to the quivering fridge. He took out a can of Pilsen. As an afterthought, he produced a second.

"What the hell. If my liver's going to be ruined, I'd prefer to do it with booze, not pills."

He opened the door with a foot. With the beer cans he gestured at a table overlooking the spongy forest along the Yagua.

"Of course, I remember her. More to the point, I remember you."

It was twenty-six years since Paul Maby first walked up from the hard, ribbed sandbanks of the river below. He liked to think the mission he founded inside Henriques Silves' old rubber station was one of the Church's more worthwhile achievements in a region known – if known at all – as The Devil's Paradise.

Since making the journey from Tulsa he had not cared to leave Delicias. Disaster had usually struck the moment he had done so. Or controversy.

Even today, reminded of the incident by his pale, unspeaking visitor – a man he long had wanted to meet – Father Maby did not know whether the Church had forgiven him for the stand he took over Elena Silves' vision. He did not care either.

"A vision. You say she's seen a vision?"

Confronted that night by the two figures on Bishop Barrantes' doorstep, his first thought was to send for Dr Lache. So often in the jungle he came upon trances induced by an overdose of ayahuasca, the root of the dead. But in the dark, Gabriel's excited explanation of an apparition that had evidently passed over his head seemed more consistent with Messianism than hallucinogens.

"Let's get this straight. You're telling me the Virgin has just appeared to this girl. In a shed across the river?"

Father Maby had allowed himself an inward groan. He still hadn't forgotten the end of the world, as prophesied by Melquíades Góngora, a lathe-operator from Chorrera.

How long before had that episode taken place? No more than a year, but the details were fresh in his mind. It had been a Wednesday – he remembered this: after all, what if the man had been right? – when Góngora appeared on the river with news of his return from Heaven.

God, said Góngora – who seemed to be suffering from a catalepsy of the jaw – had entrusted him with the following message. Only those living on the Yagua river and who followed his teaching – which so far as Father Maby understood it required disciples to dance in figures of eight to the words "Elbu, elbu" in emulation of Góngora's affliction – would be spared the apocalypse intended for that night.

To be certain of deliverance, they should give Góngora their pigs and chickens. The more generously they gave, the surer they were to escape burning, the quicker they would ascend to Heaven. In Heaven, said Góngora reasonably, there was no need for pigs or chickens.

Góngora's message reassured a frightened crowd, amongst whom Father Maby recognized several of his own flock.

Three figures stood out. A wizened woman, and two elderly men who hummed in loud voices – voices fuelled by cachaza from an Allsopp's Pale Ale bottle – a familiar but maddeningly elusive tune.

This group were distinguished by their sounds. They were also distinguished by their dress. Each of the men had on a lady's crimson blouse. The woman wore a pair of trousers on her head, fastened by a band of egret feathers.

Almost at the same time that he realized this drunken trinity were none other than the Holy Ghost, Saint Joseph and Saint Mary, Father Maby deciphered in their wailing an aria from *Lucia di*

Lammermoor.

He had gone to bed early and been pleased to wake with the world and his credibility intact. But when, all those months later, Father Maby switched on the light in the Bishop's porch and saw the girl standing beside Gabriel, he knew he was witnessing a different phenomenon.

For one thing, Elena Silves wasn't suffering from catalepsy.

For another, she had obviously seen something.

He swallowed a mouthful of beer, half waiting for a belch that never came. He would let Gabriel do the talking – at least to start with.

He looked at the man sitting beside him on the bench, who gazed unseeing into the blue distance where the forest ended and the cerrado scrublands began their climb into mountains not even Father Maby had visited.

His unexpected guest did not look well. The only colour in his cheeks belonged to a patch of yellow paint. His hair was thin, his lips dry and the corners of his mouth pulled down as if hooked by some unseen fisherman. Father Maby was no psychiatrist, but he would say it was a very delicate filament which lit the heart of this man.

Gabriel scratched at a scar on his arm. In the chlorotic eyes of the priest, it had the shape of a chicken claw.

"Where is she, Father?"

"No idea. She left a week ago. Without a word. The children are still waiting for her. I haven't the courage to tell them –" There was hurt in his voice.

"Where was she going?"

"I told you, no idea."

"How long was she here?"

"Three years. More or less from the time she left Santa Clara. She had become more vital to the community than I am. They loved her . . . " His voice disappeared.

Gabriel clawed his hands together, until the knuckles whitened.

"Tell me, Father, what she was like? What did she say? Anything.

Anything at all. Please. You may not understand . . . "

"Oh, I understand," said the American priest. "I understand a great deal."

"You may think I have no right –"

"Bullshit. Everyone has the right to stew in their own juice. But we could do with another beer."

Father Maby was fond of illustrating the difficulty of his calling with a free translation of a local Indian saying. The idiom "putting up with Christ", he explained to the few clergymen who made it to Delicias, could be roughly translated as "dealing with an idiot". It was not until Elena Silves appeared from the carob trees and walked across his lawn, that he fully understood the phrase.

After eighteen years in the convent, her eyes held to the ground, avoiding contact with anything around her.

"Look at me!" he would shout. "Not there. At me."

But when he learnt what she had done, he knew there was no going back. If she was to survive in the world she had stumbled into, the sooner she looked it smack in the face, the better.

She spent much of the first fortnight asleep. Once or twice he caught her awake at six in the morning, staring from the verandah into the vast, uninhabited dawn. The first time, she tried to break the silence. It was the hour of prime, her first canonical prayers.

"I . . . I can't seem to say them."

Father Maby took her back inside. He told her if that was the case then she needn't say them. She needn't say anything.

"But when you do, when you're ready, I want you to promise me two things. The first is you won't ever lie to me."

"And?"

"So is the second."

It was a month before she was ready to speak. In that time she attended mass regularly. She seemed to need the ritual, rather than the message it contained. She had suspended her faith, put it on ice, along with the beer in Father Maby's fridge. But she couldn't forget its ceremony. It had spoken to her at a deep level for a long time. It still comforted her in moments of terror. And in those first months there were many such moments. Terror, after years of conditioning, that her life was not legislated for in all its details. Terror at the huge expanse of space that confronted her. Terror at a jungle which was so unlike the Silar desert in its seething fertility that a monotheistic belief seemed impossible.

On the day she was ready to speak, she had been treating a sore on a child's leg. She said: "Silly, isn't it? I've had to leave the convent to do one of the things I entered it for."

"Which is?"

"Live for others, I suppose. Which is what I had begun to do in Belén."

Soon she was spending most of her day visiting the sick and deformed, those whom the community traditionally placed at arm's length. She never interfered with their customs – Father Maby insisted on that – but she would sit with the witchdoctor sipping his masato so that she came to appreciate them.

She only intervened once, when the witchdoctor ordered the burial alive of a young girl suffering from leukaemia. She rose to her feet. Standing there, she acknowledged her promise never to poke her nose into the tribe's affairs.

"But the killing of an innocent is against every custom I know."

If the family would allow it, she would care for the child. In the end she got her way and the girl moved into the house. She died a year after, but she was given a Christian burial – Elena had made him baptize her – and practically the whole tribe, including the witchdoctor, attended the service.

Little by little, Father Maby learnt of her life at Santa Clara. When she caught him boiling a toothbrush – one of the few things to survive intact the journey from Tulsa was his love of cleanliness – she joked how he reminded her of the Mother Superior. Only in this respect, she added quickly.

"What was she like otherwise?"

"Oh, I think she hated me for having had a vision. She hoped I'd show signs of pride. She was ready for those. She was like a cow who couldn't jump over the smallest fence. After a while that's what I must have been to her – a small, insurmountable fence."

"Why?" He removed his saucepan from the boil.

"I suppose in the early days I knew what I thought. None of the others knew until the Vatican told them. They existed in a pleasant, irresponsible limbo, drifting down a half-lit corridor to a door that ended in God. But I felt proudly I had already seen inside. I felt that what I had seen was an answer to all the prayers I used to offer for those maimed, broken bodies. I believed what I had seen was a truth I could not forget once the door shut again. And it was not a truth that made it easy for me to pass my days making rice pictures of Saint Teresa.

"Of course, this took years to come out. To begin with, I was more preoccupied getting rid of my feelings in order to accept God's love. And I so nearly made it. So nearly. In fact when I finally changed my name and put on my bridal dress I really did think I could admit no lover but Himself. Deep down I honestly was the bride of Him whom the angels serve and at whose beauty the sun and moon stand amazed."

In front of her, Father Maby walked to the mesh door. He threw the steaming contents of his saucepan onto the grass.

"I couldn't have been more wrong," said Elena.

Another day, after he had said Mass in the small church, she stayed behind. She ran her hands over the communion table – the varnished trunk of a lupuna tree he had rescued from the river. Suddenly she said: "God's love should be enough for anybody. But I was lonely, unutterably, shudderingly lonely. Stupid things, like no one remembering my birthday. No cinema, no radio, no books, no poetry."

She laughed. "Not even a travel brochure to pit my wits against. Just myself, this lifeless, mediocre vessel – and God. Of course, I'd been well prepared for temptation. From the very first day it was drummed into me what a vile time Saint Bernadette had suffered in her convent. Not a week went by without me taking solace in our holy mother Teresa. And she spoke so eloquently. It was all there, the extreme desolation that comes after ecstasy, the absence I sometimes felt of God, of even a sense of him.

"And I took the greatest solace of all in her idea that once you reached this desolation, once you had your heart and soul consumed by it, you were really beginning to know God. It wasn't till I'd been in Santa Clara ten years that I began to think of the love that no amount of apostolic love can replace.

"A man's love.

"And I remembered the love of the man I had loved, and before I knew it I was remembering his face, his particular way of laughing and scowling and dressing, and when I caught myself doing this I forced myself, seriously forced myself so that sometimes I had to bite the inside of my cheeks, to think of him as just muscle and bone.

"How can you contemplate betraying God, I would say, for something that's three quarters water? Something that wouldn't even fill a shallow bath. At the end I was even praying to God for help, but by then He must have seen it was too late. He had looked down on the lowliness of His handmaiden and found her wanting."

She turned to Father Maby. Her blue eyes were glistening.

"Do you know what finally did it? A song. A simple pop song. I can't even remember the words. They sang it the day the rain came, ending the drought. I think they were drunk. Hearing it, I suddenly thought: Here am I who have been blessed with a vision from God, who has been chosen by Him, who knows she has stood in the presence of something infinitely greater than herself, here am I – and yet can I say to myself or to anyone else that it has actually been a blessing."

She was crying now.

"And I couldn't. I just couldn't . . . At that moment it was as if I had been inflicted with the knowledge of God, not blessed with it. At that moment I felt the knowledge of God was nothing more and nothing less than a plague."

She wiped her cheek. "And to crown it all, I find I've given up God for a man who has taken away the only life I've breathed into anyone."

Father Maby handed her the paper tissue with which he had wiped the chalice.

"If anyone deserved that, it was Don Miguel," he said.

"Don't be stupid," she laughed – one of those laughs that can only be made when crying.

"Then do you regret it?" Father Maby was aware as he said it, of how stupid the question sounded, but at that moment, by the altar, beside this woman, he could not think of anything else. He wanted also to know the answer.

"No," she replied, letting out a breath that seemed to come from the earth. "I don't. Not at all. You see, by that time I'd also discovered something else."

"There is a time for penance," Father Maby told Gabriel, "and a time for partridge. Let's eat. If you want to kill a friar give him lunch late and no siesta."

A large Indian woman with no teeth brought a dish to the table. They ate it in silence. After the meal – the minced remains of a tapir – the priest swallowed two Maloprim tablets and retired to his room.

Gabriel walked to the village a hundred yards away. Some children were kicking a ball. When they saw Gabriel they hopped across the grass, struggling to push their arms and heads into their brown cushmas.

They re-emerged in a long orderly line led by their father. He smiled. He had an arrow in his hands which he pointed to a hut in the trees. Three women sat in the shade of this hut. They were joined by the children who stood shyly by a boiling kettle. Behind, some ceramics dried in the sun. A calendar for 1968 – eighteen years old – flapped from a beam overhead. March showed Christ on the cross and an advertisement for tractors.

A girl washed out a gourd bowl. She gave it to her mother who poured masato into it. The girl offered the bowl to Gabriel.

Another girl offered sticks of yucca on a white tin plate. The man spat and sat on his haunches. He laughed as he watched Gabriel eat and drink.

When he had finished eating, Gabriel thanked him in Quechua. The man continued to laugh. He didn't understand a word, thought Gabriel. He asked something else, in Spanish. The man looked bashfully down at his arrow. He poked its tip between his toes.

Gabriel thought of the years he had spent in the villages around Ayacucho. Cleaning irrigation ditches, clearing the terraces of paddle-shaped cactus, claiming the people's serrano confidence inch by inch until the time he could plant in their minds the idea that life was a much longer thing than the span of their generation.

Gabriel thought of these Chinese years in the field, working, working, working, interring in that same ungenerous soil his own identity, his own past, his own passions in order to understand the customs and the ways and the language of those Ezequiel wanted to liberate. Yet here in the jungle, in the department of his birth, he couldn't exchange a sentence.

The man raised his arrow. He pointed it at Gabriel's chest.

"Elena," he said. The word unlocked the children behind him. They came forward on their hands and knees.

"Elena," they repeated. Elena, Elena, Elena.

"What would you say to a drink?" Father Maby stood in the kitchen wearing a clean pink shirt.

"Perhaps you'd like a Bourbon. I think we'd both of us could do with a Bourbon."

He handed Gabriel a large tumbler and took a gulp from his own. This he kept in his mouth before swallowing.

"That's better. That's what I call high-class holy water."

Dinner was a repetition of the same dish they had eaten at lunch, with rice. For a time the only sound on the verandah was that of cutlery on china. Somewhere in the night a bird called. After a while Gabriel cleared his throat.

"More?"

Gabriel held up his hand.

"Father, why did she come here?"

Father Maby did not answer immediately. Then he said: "Perhaps because I was the first person who believed her. And I doubt she had anywhere else to go." He broke a ryebread cracker. "She also wanted a safe place, where she could wait until you came out of prison. I don't know whether or not she had forgiven you for Don Miguel, but she didn't want that to be a barrier. She hoped you might make the same sacrifice that she had made for you."

He swallowed more of his muddy holy water. There was a burr in his words when he spoke again.

"She was living for you, dammit. For the life you would have together, for the children that would come of it."

He heard her voice as she knelt on the grass with his photograph album. "Everywhere I looked, Father, there were frescoes of the Virgin with a child in her lap." She had looked up from the photographs they had sent him from Tulsa of a niece he was unlikely to see. "I was surrounded by reminders of the children I couldn't have."

His speech sweltered with fever and Bourbon. A drop of sweat trembled on the tip of his beard. He forked up some food. It fell to the table.

"Goddam," he cursed, brushing it to the floor with his napkin. "I never could eat rice." He dabbed his forehead and retucked the cloth under his chin.

"Tell me, Gabriel Lung, why *have* you been released?"

So Gabriel told how he had discovered the newspaper cutting; how he had arranged a palanca on the remote chance it might be Elena who had escaped the convent in Silar, how he had followed the trail from Bishop Barrantes to this mission on the Yagua.

At the mention of Barrantes, Father Maby changed colour.

"Barrantes wouldn't say shit if his mouth was full." He waved his fork in the air. "That man was so mean he wouldn't have given a rice grain to Saint Peter's cock. But tell you something, that was one weird situation. I think a small part of him wanted to believe in Elena's vision, but another part, the larger part, the part that collected those crosses, felt he shouldn't. Anything that fouled up his relations with Rome or the big-wigs in Lima was out, out, out. And there was I who didn't want to believe it, whose whole training and instinct was hostile to believing it, but who came to believe it. He saw me off, though. Chased me back to the back of beyond." He spoke the last words in English.

"It can't have cost him a minute's sleep to make her disappear into a closed order while he sat back and reaped the unofficial benefits. It takes no fool to work out how he bought his crosses. What he had going with Don Miguel would have filled the Prado."

His hand jutted out to the bottle.

"You know, when your people burnt down the mission here, he

refused to visit me. He felt it would be 'badly interpreted' – as if what you had done was God's way of punishing me. He didn't give me anything, not a jumping bean, even though my vestments had gone up in flame."

"What burning?" said Gabriel.

"Don't, don't, don't." Father Maby's voice rose. "At least be decent enough to take responsibility for your actions."

"I know nothing of this," Gabriel insisted. "What burning?"

In the poor light, Father Maby could see the palpitating scar. What the hell, perhaps he didn't know. If so, it only confirmed his experience that after twenty-six years in this country, he had met no one outside the jungle who knew their butt from their elbow.

"OK, buddy." He pushed away his unfinished plate, and lit a cigarette. He had sat on the packet of Hamilton Lights and it poked from his lips like a broken pencil.

"Since you continue to plead ignorance, I'll tell you what happened here while you were fiddling with the masses."

It had happened two years ago. They had come at six in the evening, forty or fifty of them. He had been in Lima, seeking advice on a hydraulic pump to bring water from the Yagua to a reservoir nearer the village.

"Elena was delivering anti-biotics to a hamlet an hour away. When she heard the explosions, she hurried back. She was found on the path by a group of children. Fortunato, the village elder, had sent them to hide her. She was concealed in one of the pits used for trapping wild boar.

"They were looking for both of us. Instead they found an empty village. The people had fled like chickens. All except an old father, quivering behind the altar. He told them the two gringos were in Lima.

"They started burning the mission. They set fire to the house. They set fire to Elena's room. They set fire to the hut with the medical supplies. Last of all they threw dynamite at the tabernacle.

"It was a woman who led them. The children saw her through the grass. They said she had war paint on her face. She stood back from the others as her henchman kerosened the church. She was watching a nest on the roof. She was watching the birds as they tried to rescue their young.

"When the church collapsed the sky was filled with birds on fire."

He poured more Bourbon.

He closed his eyes.

He drank.

"I arrived two days later. The Indians were gathering. They came down from the hills all painted black and stamping their bows on the ground while a drink was mixed which wound them into a state in which they either had to kill those responsible or kill each other.

"They gathered in the square. There were so many that they spread into the compound here. Fortunato said to me 'Do you agree Father, we should kill them.' 'Fortunato,' I said, 'remember when you asked me to baptize you, what you promised? No vengeance. You too, Román. Egalimento, Leonidas, José, Pablo,' I said, looking at those I had baptized. 'Remember what you promised.' Suddenly Fortunato let his spear fall. He burst into tears. One by one the others followed. You can cut an Indian's arm off and he won't show emotion, but there they all were, weeping like a lot of willows."

Father Maby rubbed an eye stung by his smoke. "One way and another, you can say I saved a few lives that day. Theirs, as well as your friends'."

He shook a finger at Gabriel. "But lighten my darkness, will you? What did you have against us? What possible threat was posed by a middle-aged nun and a Yankee priest who for no reason he could explain, except his whole heart told him so, believed that a long time ago this woman saw the Mother of God?"

Gabriel was not listening.

"Edith . . . " he mouthed. Anger squalled his face.

Father Maby sniffed and carried the plates to the kitchen. His voice came through the kitchen window. "Tomorrow I'll show you what's left of the damage." A moth floundered against the wire mesh. Inside a plate clattered.

"Dammit, dammit, dammit."

Father Maby appeared in the doorway.

"I've spilled that tapir all down my front."

*

Gabriel spent the night in a wooden outhouse twenty yards from the main quarters. It had been built for Elena after the burning down of the mission. The room was empty except for a bed. Gabriel ran his hands several times over the blanket. Then he lay down and slept.

In his dreams he dreamt of Elena and Ezequiel. Their faces alternated. But the face of Ezequiel was the clearer. It was the morning after Ezequiel's lecture twenty-one years before. Gabriel was knocking on a door in Calle Libertad. The door opened and there stood the professor. The sky was cloudless, but he still wore his jacket. He was chewing a pen. (He had been marking a thesis.) Behind him a hose was watering the grass, its damp crackle the only sound in the garden.

Gabriel was shown to a white wickerwork chair. He told Ezequiel that listening to his lecture was like listening to himself. He confessed he had been one of those in the room with Fuente. He described his involvement with the northern foco in '65.

"I want to join you."

Ezequiel heard everything Gabriel had to say. He removed the pen from his mouth. Come back in a week, he said.

A week later they were walking by an empty river bed.

"Do you really know what's required of you?" Ezequiel scooped up a handful of pebbles. He threw them into the ditch where the water should have been.

"I'm prepared."

"You have to be a lost man. A man without interests. A man without belongings. A man without a name."

"I know."

"You'll have to live without your family, your friends, your girl." He threw the last stone. "You have a girl?"

"No."

"But you did have."

"There was one . . . "

"I know."

"How do you know?"

"Edith told me." Edith.

Then Gabriel saw them together. They were walking out of a café in the slanting square where the students drank pisco with tea. Ezequiel stumbled. Edith helped him. "Thank you," he said. That was all, just those two words, which caused no suspicion until the day when Gabriel discovered Ezequiel had vanished.

But that was more than ten years later, years which he had spaded into the soil, with his head down, his eyes on the terraces, never thinking of his own life, only of the harvest the revolution would bring.

A week after Ezequiel's absence all those years later she turned up in the "thank you" café. Gabriel was sitting with Julio and Bonifacio. The two men had come to join him in the fields near Chuschi. Julio brought him news of his step-mother's death. Bonifacio scratched a crop of spots on his shoulder as he told how he had burned down the church the Bishop had started building, then desecrated the altar. There wasn't much other news. Pía Zumate was thought to be having an affair with Dr Lache. The Bishop had decided after all not to move into his new palace. Don Miguel was going to stand for the council.

"And that aunt of Elena's, remember," said Bonifacio.

"What about her?"

Bonifacio gloved his answer with a smile. "She died." That was when Edith entered. She had driven Ezequiel and his wife to Arequipa. They had gone underground, she explained. For the final stage.

Gabriel woke.

He saw a smear like lipstick on the pillow where his gums had bled. Since his torture, they bled all the time.

He dressed and walked outside. Father Maby crouched in the stiff grass with a butterfly net.

"Catching the Holy Ghost, Father?"

The priest made a fisherman's gesture with his hands. "The biggest swallow-tail I ever saw – and I missed it." He put down the net. His fever was passing.

Later, they walked to the Yagua, to where the river was fed by a tributary from an overhead cliff. They stripped, leaving their clothes on a rock and entered the sparkling barley-stick of water.

"Sorry I lost my cool last night," shouted Father Maby. He raised his face to the spray. The water pummelled his head. A bird swooped into the fall. It disappeared behind the dazzling curtain.

Gabriel didn't reply. He shouted again. Gabriel muttered something.

"What?" yelled Father Maby.

"It's I who am sorry."

Father Maby looked at him, standing in the roaring white mist, his ribs a shipwreck covered by sand, his scars shiny in the sun. This was the man who had been chosen over God, he thought.

"I believe you."

They dressed, except for their shoes, which they held, and walked back. Half way up the hill, Father Maby left the path and made into the trees.

"There," he said. "Our old church. Where the rubber station used to be." He indicated a statue of the Virgin on a stretch of concrete cracked by roots and creepers. Her crown was melted, her head a black char brushed by grasses.

"I couldn't bear to throw it away. Don't you think her expression is . . . beautiful's not the right word, but can you see what I mean?"

They stood looking at the twisted shape which had been her face. As they stood, a large blue butterfly danced like broken paper over the concrete.

"Sonofabitch," said Father Maby. He watched it disappear into the trees.

They continued uphill. "I've been thinking more about that stingless bee, Barrantes. He's like all those for whom the means are the ends. They miss the bolt. OK, we've got the Pope's infallibility. OK, we've got the Immaculate Conception, but where does that take us? I'll tell you where." Father Maby dropped his shoes to the ground. He wiped the sand from between his toes.

"It takes us to a world where everyone's a Catholic and no one's a Christian, where everyone celebrates the cross but forgets the Christ. When Elena saw what she saw, the Church was still in diapers. A father had more confidence in his sixteen-year-old son than the Roman Catholic Church in a man of sixty. It was a triangle of Pope and Bishop and People – which meant that everything was translated into inaction.

"Much of it hasn't changed. Barrantes' Church still likes to force-feed its people with dogma as if they are Strasbourg geese. It makes them swallow the idea of an invisible God when they already have the sun and the moon.

"And what happens? They come to think Holy Water is a medicine they can buy. They come to think that prayer is something to mouth, like an American pop song they don't know the words of."

He wriggled his feet into his shoes.

"That's not my Church. In my Church the people matter more. Put character at the centre of your faith and all the obstacles fall away."

"Even sin?"

"I don't believe many people sin. What we want is a conscious-ness of sin, not a list of sins. It used to be like a Sears Roebuck catalogue. I would have men say to me, Father, I've committed a sin. I'd look at them and say Do you really believe that? They'd shake their head and say No, Father. And I'd say, Come back when you believe you have."

Father Maby turned to Gabriel. "No good explaining this to you, of course." He held out his hand to a girl who had run onto the path. When she saw Gabriel she chewed her fingers.

"Do you honestly think these people give a monkey's about Mao or Mariátegui? Any more than they care about Catholic dogma. I tell you, I came here to teach the Indians Christianity, but I found they had more to teach me. They don't steal. They don't lie. They don't covet their neighbour's wife. The only thing I've been able to teach them is money — so they're not robbed by the rivereños. Hardly something to be proud of.

"But I also learnt something else. You can't impose anything on them, politics or religion. It's like putting a plaster on a dog's nose. The dog just scratches it off."

He sent the girl gently away. "I don't know, perhaps we're both clawing at the moon."

"I hate God," Gabriel said. "I hate him so much I used to dress as a priest."

"You only hate what you fear."

"Don't tell me you've never had doubts."

"I have had doubts," replied the priest. "But I'm almost certain – no, no almost – that God exists and that I will have to tell Him what I have done and that in staying here I will have made the right choice."

"Why here?" asked Gabriel. "Why not the shanty-towns in Lima? Why not the pueblos jóvenes in Piura or Puno or Trujillo?"

"If I'm not here, soon no one will be. Unless someone protects these people, they will be chased out, corrupted, murdered by the mestizos from the mountains, the narcos from upriver, you lot. They haven't much time. But they've all the time I've got."

They faced each other on the path, their hands spidering their hips. Gabriel thought of Fuente and Ezequiel in the drawing room, by the empty fireplace.

He smiled. "And women?"

Father Maby laughed. "You know what they call a Franciscan? A man who fucks well. When women ask me why I'm not married, I tell them I am. I have been tempted, naturally."

"What do you do?"

"My job is not to do anything."

"What do you feel?"

"I feel I must pray harder."

They reached the top of the hill where children were playing football. When they spotted Father Maby, they kicked the ball towards him. He returned it awkwardly so it bounced off the pitch. A boy running to retrieve it said something. It included the word Elena. Father Maby shook his wet head.

"They'll have to know the truth," he told Gabriel.

"Which is?"

"That she's not coming back."

"How do you know?"

"After a lifetime in the Styx, one knows these things. Like one knows one will never catch that homerus swallow-tail. Like one knows there is no man in the moon."

"Like one knows that she saw what she saw?"

Father Maby didn't answer.

"I'm going to have to tell you something," he said at last, "for which I will rot in hell." He rubbed his malarial eyes. "But it involves us both."

It was something that happened the day before Elena left Delicias. A rivereño had beached his boat on the sand and walked to the house. He wanted to sell the priest a case of sorghum whisky. Fortunato had interrupted their negotiations. He had a query about the ditch they were digging for the reservoir. Father Maby had left the rivereño with Elena.

"She was milking him for news of the big wide world."

After dealing with Fortunato, Father Maby came back to pay for the whisky. When the rivereño had gone, Elena came into the kitchen. She wished him to take her confession. Not in the morning. There and then. Father Maby was surprised, but said nothing. They went into the church. Elena knelt. She nodded to the altar. Then turned her blue eyes on him.

She had something to tell him. Something she had kept secret for twenty years, since the night of her first vision. She spoke her words deliberately, with the care of one who had thrust their arm into a deep hole and one by one drawn a nest of eggs to the surface.

The vision Elena had seen was not of the Virgin Mary.

It was the vision of a man.

She had been too ashamed to admit this at the time. She had accepted the version put upon her first by Gabriel, then, imperceptibly, by everyone else. By the third day, it was too late to say anything.

She hadn't felt fraudulent about it. Nor had there been any reason to. The voice she had heard and the visions she had seen were obviously those of the Archangel, whose effigy was the first image to meet her eyes when she heard the sound of guns as she prayed in the cathedral.

She remembered the initial apparition at Fátima had not been the Virgin. It had also been an Angel. And that anyway, Saint Teresa had always impressed on everyone the unreliable nature of visions.

It was years later at Santa Clara, listening to the music from the river that Elena came to realize that what she had heard and seen was not a vision of the Archangel Gabriel, but instead a revelation and an affirmation of the beauty of human love . . .

The priest looked at the children playing. He looked at the church he had rebuilt with his own hands. He looked at Gabriel's hand gripping his shoulder. His eyes were heavy with tiredness.

"Yes?" stammered Gabriel.

Father Maby heard the words flutter from her caged mouth.

"It was a vision of you," he told Gabriel, "dressed as the Archangel."

Chapter 25

GABRIEL LEFT DELICIAS on a raft of logs nailed together in an open semi-circle. He stood at one end, his ankles washed over by the water rising through the beams. The river soon carried him out of sight of Father Maby on the sandbank.

At the point where the tributary joined the Amazon he caught a launch to Dos de Mayo. From there he boarded an empty packet to Belén.

The boat was one of the old steamers used to carry barbasco and curare in the days after the rubber boom. The blades of its paddles were rotten and splintered. The paint had flaked from its hull, removing its name.

For most of the passage Gabriel stood alone at the stern rail. Occasionally he spat into the Amazon.

To the captain he seemed a figure from a book, a figure of romance. To the captain's mate, a man with one green eye, one brown eye and a face pitted by verruga fever, he looked like a howler monkey.

"Engineer, missionary or gun-runner?"

The captain, a man of semitic appearance, scratched his chin. "None," he said. "I'd say he was a man down on his luck. A musician who has lost his instrument."

Pleased with the image, he spread some tinned fish onto a slab of bread. He opened the cabin door and offered it to the *Libertad*'s only passenger, who refused.

"Gun-runner," said the mate. "Definitely."

Gabriel was not hungry. He gazed at the stern rail into the wake, smelling the sharp scent of foliage on the afternoon breeze. He was remembering his call to arms and the death of Don Miguel six years before.

*

One March morning he walked into a small hotel in the town of Satipo. He climbed the uncarpeted stairs. He thought how long it had been since he had seen Ezequiel's handsome face. He knocked. The door was opened by Augusta, Ezequiel's wife.

He entered.

Someone was standing by the window with their back to him. Gabriel recognized the outlines of Ezequiel. He was wearing slippers. He appeared to be reading. His body has thickened, he thought, looking at Augusta looking at him and becoming aware of her implacable stare.

"It's Chino," she said.

Ezequiel turned.

In the light from the window, Gabriel saw a face covered with pustules. Its mouth, nose and eyes were hardly recognizable as features. Somewhere in the white and scarlet sores, Gabriel detected the professor from Ayacucho.

Ezequiel walked towards him.

"What's the matter," he said. His voice was the same soft voice. "Don't you like my face?" He made another step towards him. Suddenly Gabriel understood. Ezequiel was going to kiss him.

"I'll leave you together," said Augusta. She edged past and descended the staircase with her black and white dress swelling in the air.

"Psoriasis universalis." Gabriel felt the rough vegetable skin on his cheeks. Ezequiel drew back. That's why he had gone underground when he did. "It had reached my face." He took Gabriel's hand.

"Something to show you." He brought Gabriel to the window. He held up a piece of paper. Even the skin under his fingernails was affected.

"The final decision of the Central Committee," he said. "To begin the revolution."

Gabriel breathed out. "At last," he said.

Ezequiel explained. He wanted Gabriel to return to Belén to prepare a cell. He needed someone who understood the Soretanas and their jungle. He didn't want a recurrence of the mistakes that were made in '65. Edith would help him.

"I've told the others," Ezequiel said, scratching his elbow.

"I wanted to do so personally because, for security reasons, they are unlikely to see me again. And that goes for you too."

"I understand, Comrade Ezequiel."

"Not Comrade, Chino." It was a mild chide. "Nor Professor." There was a trace of humour on the mother-of-pearl scales where his lips should have been. "Presidente."

"When do we begin?"

Ezequiel gave a date. "The day Túpac Amaru was pulled apart in Cuzco." He referred to the last great Indian revolutionary and the belief, common in the Andes, that Túpac Amaru's severed body had been regrowing underground until the day he would rise to liberate his oppressed people.

"The choice of date is Augusta's," said Ezequiel. It was merely a coincidence that it was the date of the presidential election.

"And remember, Chino, if ever you have a creeping doubt, as you will do, as I have done, as we all have done, it's not numbers that are important. It's faith." Pizarro, he reminded him, had taken a continent with 180 men. Columbus, with 90, a hemisphere.

"What we are about to make isn't just a revolution for Peru." His smile was a compass indicating he was no longer concentrating on Gabriel.

"This is an example to the whole world. This is the start of a people's war to liberate all humanity."

Gabriel left the hotel in a trance. He paused at the bottom of the staircase to steady himself. He took several breaths, then walked out.

As he crossed to the square, Gabriel heard the words of a song. He stopped in the middle of the street. The words were in English, the singer American. The voice was familiar. Turning, Gabriel followed the music back to its source on the third floor of the hotel.

A light was on. It haloed the dark shape of Ezequiel, motionless but for a blur where his fingers scratched. The words drifted down from his window.

"I'll find you in the morning sun," Frank Sinatra was singing.

"And when the night is new,

I'll be looking at the moon,
But I'll be seeing you . . . "

When Ezequiel sent Gabriel back to Bélen, it was his first visit since Hipólito's death. Much had changed. His step-mother's house had become part of a school. San Agustín College had moved premises to a modern building in the Plaza Clavero. Señora Guzmán's house was shuttered and ambulantes sat on the steps among the dry fruit peel, no longer admonished.

Posters papier-mâchéd the front door and the tiled wall. They showed the thick lips and beseeching smile of Don Miguel who was standing for Mayor.

Gabriel noticed the changes but they didn't trouble him. He had returned for a purpose. He had come back as an active participant in the people's war. The theoretical part of his life, the years of preparation were over. The time had now come to bloody his hands.

For two weeks he stayed in a hut on the red road to the zoo. He rarely left it. He spent his time planning several operations and organizing leaflets. The leaflets exhorted the people to avoid deception by a presidential election which would prolong a brutalizing oligarchy. But he was angry. At Edith, for never having confided in him about Ezequiel's illness. At Ezequiel, for, among other things, having confided in Edith. He was also angry with Julio and Bonifacio who turned up from Ayacucho a week later than expected.

At the end of April, Gabriel sent a message to Satipo. He was ready.

In May 1980, the Belén cell of the Shining Path attacked the Banco de Crédito in Calle Morona. The cashier, a niece of Pía Zumate, saw a mother enter the main hall, pushing a pram. The baby was crying so much that the mother gathered the bundle in her arms and walked up and down, whispering soothing words in its ear and humming a ballad. The cries grew louder so she went outside leaving her pram unattended.

Four minutes later it blew up.

When the police arrived, the bank had been robbed of 50 million soles by two men who materialized through the smoke. One was dressed as a priest. The other wore a military uniform. Both carried guns. On the wall above the upturned filing cabinets and their smoking contents was daubed: EZEQUIEL OR DEATH.

It was November before Gabriel's unit captured Don Miguel. By then the man cured of terminal cancer by Elena Silves had been sworn in as Mayor of Belén.

Edith drove the car – a blue Peugeot – to Don Miguel's house behind the university canteen. It was past eleven at night. Two men sat on the steps of the billiard hall on the corner of Ucayali. The streets were quiet. The evening air smelled of oil from the refinery.

Bonifacio stood at the entrance to a lane on the left of Don Miguel's door. Down that lane, men would walk to the soggy meadow known as the Colchón Verde. On the Green Mattress, on nights when it had not rained, candles lit the feet of prostitutes waiting for clients in the long grass.

Bonifacio was dressed as a colchona. He wore a wig of loose blonde hair, a brown cape and a bag over his shoulder. When he saw the car, he waved.

"Park by that Ford," said Gabriel, adjusting his dog-collar. He drew back a sleeve to look at his watch. "Fifteen minutes." He looked out of the window. A girl with red hair was crying in the front seat of the parked car. He watched her for a while. Then he said, "Let's go."

Don Miguel opened his door. He had been at dinner and his mouth was full of chicken. He was surprised to see the two figures of a priest and a woman in a brown cape. The woman was moaning uncontrollably. She had thick calves, he noticed approvingly. He was less sure about the purple lipstick.

He swallowed his food.

"Yes?"

"Don Miguel?" said the priest.

"What you want?"

"The señora, she's had a terrible experience."

Through his confusion, Don Miguel absorbed the priest's appeal.

"You'd better come in," he said. As he shut the door behind them, the woman reached into her bag. Instead of a handkerchief, she drew out a hand-gun. Don Miguel said nothing, perhaps because he felt nothing. The priest held him by the wrist. It was already slack, as if he had given up the moment he realized his mistake.

The car headed out of the city. On the windows a mist formed, smeared there by the tension of the occupants. Every time Gabriel wiped the windscreen with his sleeve, the mist returned.

"Wind down your window," said Edith.

A kilometre beyond the electricity works, Edith turned off the road. She braked in front of a two-storey building. She kept the headlights on until Gabriel and Bonifacio had disappeared inside.

The house was used as a metal forge for the plywood factory. Near the window an anvil was bolted to the floor. Saws and soldering irons hung on the wall.

Don Miguel was placed in a chair. From his seat he watched the girl with thick calves transform herself into Bonifacio. In front of him the priest defrocked into the person of Gabriel.

A damp patch grew under his arms.

His captors sat behind a table, a plywood sheet on trestles.

"Don Miguel Minero," Gabriel began, his dog-collar loose around his neck. "You have been arrested by the members of the Peruvian Communist Party. This is a revolutionary trial." Edith raised a camera and took a photograph. Bonifacio toyed with a metal-worker's mask. Don Miguel said nothing. Under his arms the patches spread.

Gabriel looked into the Mayor's face. Until this moment the man had been not much more than a shape behind the frosted glass of Eden Expeditions. Yet this was Elena's miracle, he suddenly realized. This was the living proof of her vision.

Gabriel was reminded of a badly stuffed animal in the museum at Quistacocha. A long nose dented with wide pores, hair tumbling from his ears like moss on a dead tree and still, grey, artificial eyes. He imagined the faded label. Common name – Don Miguel Minero. Scientific name – Mayor of Belén. Family name – Bourgeois Reactionary.

"By executing you," he thought to himself, "I'm beginning to topple the whole structure. With your death, nothing can be the same again."

Gabriel listed the charges against Don Miguel. The shooting of the early martyr Comrade Hipólito. Corruption of Customs, corruption of Police, corruption of the Church . . . Occasionally Don Miguel answered "I don't remember that." It was when Gabriel mentioned the circumstances surrounding his father's death that Don Miguel appeared to recognize him. His face went the colour of a man who has swallowed cordite.

"Don Miguel Minero," said Gabriel. "The tribunal has found you guilty of treason against your nation and your people. You will be executed shortly."

The vest showed through Don Miguel's shirt like a girl's swimming costume.

"Could I shave?" he faltered.

"We have no razor," replied Gabriel.

"You must let me have a priest. A real priest."

"There's no time."

Don Miguel wiped his forehead. Even the Rotary Club badge on his lapel had lost its glint. He took a comb from his shirt pocket and ran it through his damp hair. The gesture seemed to tranquillize him.

"What about my family?"

"No charges exist against them."

"She will never forgive you for this, you know," he said.

For an instant, Gabriel did not understand. When he registered what was being said he stood up.

"Gabriel!" Edith held him back. "No. Not now."

"Let's get this over with," he said.

He pulled Don Miguel to his feet and led him to the staircase.

"Down," he said.

"You're not going to kill me in the basement?"

"Bonifacio, the anvil."

In the basement, Gabriel stood Don Miguel against a wall. More tools hung on a rack behind him. Snapped saws, bent drills, blunt screwdrivers. Bonifacio's hammering began. The noise came through the ceiling, reverberating about the small underground room – not in a natural beat but in a steady metallic rhythm of its own.

"Faster," shouted Gabriel. "For God's sake tell him to go faster."

Edith handed Gabriel her pistol. She disappeared up the stairs.

The secret was not to look at the eyes.

"At least tie my laces?" Don Miguel's words had a reasonableness about them. With his shoes undone, the Mayor of Belén seemed ludicrously unready for death.

Gabriel pointed the pistol at Don Miguel's stomach. He lowered himself onto his haunches. When he saw the shoes and their trailing laces he realized he would have to use both hands. It was during that hesitation, to Bonifacio's quickening tempo, that the stuffed animal came alive. Don Miguel jerked a knee into Gabriel's face, grabbed a saw blade from the wall and lunged out, slashing Gabriel in the cheek. His arm was raised to strike again when there was a shot.

Don Miguel turned casually to the floor.

Gabriel looked at him through fingers squeezed against the pain in his face. He knew Don Miguel was hurt as well. It was the first time he had seen him with a finished smile.

Edith placed the pistol to his forehead. She timed herself against two of Bonifacio's strokes on the anvil. In tune with the third she fired. The body went limp. The blade fell to the floor. It was followed by Don Miguel's comb.

Edith spoke. "When the snake is dead, its poison is dead."

They dropped his body by a rubbish heap near the airport. Bonifacio placed a week-old edition of *El Oriente* over his head. Edith pinned a notice to his shirt.

"There is no town, no home, no bed where you can hide if you are an enemy of the people. The armed struggle will always find you because no one can hide from the people. They are the eyes of Presidente Ezequiel."

They drove to the Malecón. Edith parked the car above the Requena wharf. She saw the night ferry at the bottom of the bank. Sparks from the funnel fireworked into the night. The decks milled with people. The boat was on time. By tomorrow morning they would be another world away.

They got out of the Peugeot. Edith and Bonifacio supported Gabriel between them. His arms lay over their shoulders like broken wings. The blood fell from his ripped cheek. It fell over his dog-collar, his shirt, his shoes.

"Wait," said Edith. She slipped away. She walked back to the car. From the boot she took out the brown cape Bonifacio had worn as a colchona. She draped it over Gabriel's head and shoulders.

"We'll say he has la uta."

The boat paddled on through the dusk. On either bank, the orange fires of the river-dwellers flickered through the trees. Once or twice a fish dented the silver river.

Looking into the wake, Gabriel thought of Ezequiel who wanted to change the face of the world. Was it vanity which fuelled his secrecy, a vanity only someone like Edith would understand? He thought of Elena's vision. Had it, in fact, been as flawed as his own?

Above all, he thought of Elena.

A light went on in the wheelhouse. From a cupboard, the captain's mate produced a bottle of cachaza and two tumblers filigreed with dirty fingerprints. He placed them on the varnished sill. He splashed out the dark rum. Behind the glass, in silence, the two shapes began drinking.

And the boat moved on towards Belén, a ghost boat gliding beneath the full moon.

The police picked up the trail next day.

It was Abel Fonseca, the cine-projectionist, who alerted them. He was carrying three reels of *The Rubber Man's Daughter* from the Cinema Bolognesi, where the film had enjoyed a long run, to the Cinema Grau, where it was about to open.

He was walking along the Malecón in the early hours of the morning, the romance of Luis Sintra balanced on his head, when he noticed, at irregular intervals, marks on the mosaic pavement.

Abel Fonseca was not the most intelligent of projectionists, and it was a bother to have to put down the heavy cans. But he had spent a life watching popular films and he had no doubt that what he saw when he crouched on the pavement and dipped his finger into it was blood.

He told a police sergeant who told Lieutenant Velarde who followed the drops along the Malecón and down the path to where they disappeared by the empty berth of the *Victoria Regia*.

Lifting his eyes to the Amazon, Velarde cursed He would bet a week's whoring in the Teletroca that whoever had murdered Don Miguel was no longer in Belén.

He returned to his office. He removed his sunglasses. He rubbed his eyes, then his chest. Sacramento. Just when he hoped for promotion. Just when he'd expunged from his record the disaster of that episode with the poet.

Velarde's failure then had set back his prospects of promotion for a good ten years. Whatever benefits had come by way of Don Miguel's handout – the mountain of jerseys, the daughter's school fees in America, his four thousand shares in Electro-Peru – that thirty-year salary cheque had not helped his career. He hadn't tracked down a single one of those terrucos with Hipólito Mercedes, not one. Of course, given time, he would have found them all, but then the military suddenly burst in on the scene, removing the president from his palace, still wearing pyjamas, and handing out pardons to every mother-fucking cholo criminal in sight as if they were tickets for the lottery.

Since when Velarde had eaten shit with the patience of a novice. And after all the shit he'd eaten, it was looking as if finally, finally things might be paying off. Only last month his superior got brandy-drunk in the Club de Leones and told him he was being considered for Deputy Police Chief.

Then this had to happen.

He knew his duty as a policeman. He rang the station in Requena. "If you know the difference between a jerk-off and a fuck," he told his opposite number, "you'll be on that wharf when the Belén ferry comes in. And, Pablo, careful. Whoever this Presidente Ezequiel is, he's just made chicken crap of our Mayor." Velarde put down the receiver. Later he would hear how a man had been apprehended, hiding under a blanket, without so much as a fistfight, and how pleased Lima was, even though they hadn't found anyone else and how Pablo must make it back to him sometime . . .

Don Miguel, he thought. His dead Mayor. Did he feel sorry? No, he didn't. The man had been a braying, stubborn, corrupt, unpleasant ass. For more than twenty years he'd made Velarde follow him. The Lieutenant picked his nose. He inspected the result. He turned it into a very small ball and rubbed it on the wall behind him.

Twenty years. And all that fucking time he'd had to smell his wind.

The sun had finally set. The sky was the pink of a dolphin's belly, leaping to swallow the moon. In the wheelhouse the two men raised their glasses again.

Gabriel moved towards the bow. They were rounding the Padre Isla. Soon they would see the lights of the city. He lowered his head until it rested on an arm. Seeing Gabriel lean like that on the bowsprit, the captain opened the wheelhouse door. He slopped down the steps to join him.

"Señor." He swallowed before speaking again. When he opened his mouth his breath was sweet. "Señor, a drink."

He held the bottle out to him. There was something placatory in the gesture, as if he might be afraid of rejection a second time by the musician who had lost his instrument.

Gabriel was on the point of waving a flat hand to say no when he changed his mind. He looked at the bottle, the surface of its brown liquid bobbing with greasy slicks. He reached out and held it.

"It's good," slurred the captain. He watched Gabriel's Adam's apple rise and fall as he swallowed the rum. "The best."

He rested his arm on the rail and looked at the night. "Tell me, señor, what do you play?"

"What do I play?" asked Gabriel. He wiped his mouth.

"Yes, what do you play. Guitar. Pipes. Drums. Clarinet?"

"Ah, what do I play. I play . . . " He thought a second. "I play the flute."

"The flute?" The captain was pleased.

"Not any old flute," said Gabriel, raising the bottle again. "Not one of those cane flutes that go peep peep peeep. No. My flutes are made of bone."

"Bone?"

"Yes, human bone." He stared joylessly at the captain. "Have you ever heard the sound of such a flute, Captain?"

"No, señor." The captain drew back.

"But it is a beautiful noise, Captain. Once you have heard it, I promise you never forget."

"Indeed," said the captain stiffly. "And how does it sound, this flute of yours?"

Gabriel took a deep breath. He screwed his face in preparation. But the captain was not listening. He was staring into the dark.

"Strange," he said.

Gabriel's face went slack. He let the air out through his teeth without a whistle.

"What's strange?"

"Belén."

"What about it?"

"Look."

"But there are no lights."

"That's what I mean."

And sure enough, gazing into the night, the phosphorescent waves beneath him, Gabriel saw that where the town should have been was a blackness as dark as Sebastián's hood.

Chapter 26

THE MAN KNOWN TO his followers as the Fourth Sword of the World Revolution woke earlier than usual.

He lay in a cold, bare room. A loose wire ran down the wall beside his bed. There was a framed photograph of Paris on the wall and a lithograph by Cossio del Pomar of six Apristas who had been executed at Chan Chan in April 1932. The only furniture was a side table and a red chair, grey with dust.

He rose from his bed and unbolted his door. He felt his way to the lavatory over the landing, careful not to stub his toes. The building was silent, like the jungle outside. Thinking of those asleep below, he did not flush the bowl.

He returned to his narrow bed and swallowed a pill containing a solution of potassium arsenite. He shook the bottle. Only half a dozen remained, and his psoriasis was worse, definitely. He felt himself possessed by a powerful alien. The disease had a life of its own, overtaking his own. He raised a hand to his elbow and began scratching.

He slept.

A dog barked.

He woke.

He raised himself from the bed. His face corrugated with the effort. He limped to the shutters. He looked down through the slats onto the roof of the next-door building, the café. A ladder connected the flat roof, one storey below, with his own building. The ladder was out of sight from the square and led to a door at the rear of the landing.

He concluded it was someone he knew. Already the dog was scraping a tongue along its back searching for fleas. He stood in the centre of the room facing the closed door. In the fragment of mirror hanging from a nail he saw the cravat around his neck and an expanse of red shirt. He lowered his head to complete the reflection.

Behind his lips he still had perfect teeth.

There was a knock on the door. "Ezequiel? Presidente Ezequiel?"

Recognizing the voice, he unbolted the lock.

"I don't know why I bother," he said half to himself. He rattled the bolt back and forth. "There is no gun."

Edith came into the room. She walked to the table. "Here," she said. She produced two batteries, then a small bottle from a bag.

"Sorry they've taken so long. Dr Lache wanted a fortune."

He sat down on the bed and inspected the pills.

"Everything fixed for this evening?"

She nodded. "I'll go straight there from the meeting. I have the keys. The explosives are ready."

"You approve?"

"Yes. It'll mean another move for you. But we're not throwing anything away. Not after Cabaña," she said.

"What about the meeting? Can everyone be there?"

Edith's eyes fixed on the collar of his red shirt.

"Everyone except Chino." The words were devoid of emotion.

"Chino?" he frowned. "But he was in the dormitory?"

"He'd arranged a palanca with Julio Medina."

"And why can't Comrade Chino be with us?" asked Ezequiel. He shook his bottle.

"A woman."

"A woman. That's unlike Chino."

"Bonifacio will take his place. He'll come with me to the plant." She raised her eyes above the collar. "Ezequiel, is there anything else?"

"What?"

"Can I get you anything?"

"No, no." The man shook his head.

"If that's all, I'll see you this afternoon."

"Yes."

"Chau, Ezequiel."

"Chau, Edith," he said as the door closed. Then, remembering something, he shouted, "Edith?"

The door opened.

"The tapes. Did you bring any?"

She looked miserable. "I found one in Sargento Lores, but you already have it."

"Which one?"

"*Point* of something."

"*No Return*," he acknowledged. "You're right."

"But Augusta promised she'd bring some from Lima."

The door closed. He waited until she had disappeared from the roof. Then, careful not to be seen from the street nor dislodge a row of batteries recharging on a sheet of tin foil, he pushed open the shutters.

The sun burst in, thickly, as if it had been accumulating against the wood. He took off his shirt. He threw it on the bed. In the light he examined his body; the psoriatic patch returning below his arms, the scaly lesions coalescing about his elbow like a pile of silver coins thrown carelessly onto a gaming table. His fingers moved gingerly down the soft felt of his skin.

"I must not scratch, I must not scratch," he told himself. If he didn't scratch, his skin built up a dry white crust. If he did, it became red and shiny. If he pulled off a flake too near the new skin, it wept.

He moved to the side table, slapping his chest with alternate hands. He picked up the two new batteries. He fitted them into the bottom of a small cassette recorder and inserted a cassette. He pressed Rewind, then Play.

"I'll be seeing you

In all the old familiar places

That this heart of mine embraces

All day through . . . "

It was twenty years since Ezequiel's discovery of Frank Sinatra. He possessed most of his recordings, and a dim understanding of the words. It was an insidious passion, he knew, one that irritated and amused him. But in the songs, which he played when no one could hear and which he accompanied unmelodically, he found things that had continued to stir him.

For a man not allowed to eat cebiche – his favourite food – nor smoke, nor drink, nor take tea or coffee, it was a harmless pleasure.

"I'll be looking at the moon," he told himself as he limped up and down, a half-naked man pottering through the shadows. "But I'll be seeing you."

But his mind today was not on Frank Sinatra. It was on the man with Chinese eyes who had risen from the dead. The man who couldn't attend his meeting this afternoon because of a woman.

A funny thing, but last night he'd dreamt of Chino. He was turning down Lima's Washington Street on his way to visit José Mariátegui when out of the night loomed Gabriel Rondón Lung.

"Where are you going?" asked Gabriel. Ezequiel told him. "Can I come too?" It was vaguely appropriate. He had detected a similarity between the young man and the socialist. The same green eyes, the same pale, wasted face, the same falsetto voice. Or perhaps he didn't have a falsetto voice. He couldn't recall.

They found Mariátegui lying on a chaise-longue, a tartan blanket over his leg, a curl of hair making a black cedilla on his forehead, a bow-tie drooping over a starched collar.

There were others in the room. Mariátegui was telling them of the night he saw Naska Rouskaya dance in the cemetery to the strains of Chopin's funeral march. How the girl from Buenos Aires had whirled her indigo dress against the tombstones and lifted her Porteña chin to the stars.

"That was the night I gave up believing in God," he whispered. He glanced at Ezequiel. And then all of a sudden it wasn't Mariátegui who lay along the chaise-longue looking into his eyes, but Gabriel Rondón Lung, the man who had pleaded his way into Ezequiel's house in Ayacucho twenty years before and through that door, two steps up off Calle Libertad, into the revolution.

A woman, he told himself.

He stopped his pacing and looked out over the glittering calamina roofs to the jungle.

A woman. The psoriasis had put paid to that.

"To be a lost man. A man without a name . . . " How aware had he been of the sacrifices he demanded? Here he stood, a man debilitated by illness, a man trying to restore the past, yet for ten years without a past of his own – just the memory of hotel rooms in Piura, Chimbote, Puno, Arequipa, Satipo, Belén.

Wasn't that why he'd come to Belén, because it was the safest of the lot? No one in the square below, nor the houses beyond nor the country beyond that knew if he was alive.

Only the dog on the ledge below, catching sight of him at the window gave a whimper of recognition.

"In the small café,
The park across the way,
The children's carousel,
The chestnut trees, the wishing well . . . "

Ezequiel closed his eyes and raised his face to the sun, recharging his batteries.

They sat, the seven of them, cheek by jowl in Ezequiel's room around the table which rocked whenever anyone moved.

A poster hung on the door, covering the mirror – which made a bump beneath. It showed a line of soldiers firing at a mass of prisoners. The prisoners carried the communist flag and they rose from out of the sun. The sun was Ezequiel's unblemished face.

"Glory to the fallen heroes. Long live the revolution!" went the inscription. Ezequiel thought he detected the influence of Goya and Delacroix in the design.

Augusta was talking. She sat on a stool opposite, her face between her hands. She was speaking for him.

The prison massacre was a tragedy. But they must avoid panic. Comrade Edith's operation at Cabaña was a fine example. What they needed now was a single concerted action. That night the whole country would witness it.

She outlined Ezequiel's plan: a simultaneous blackout in all the major cities. The only light would come from bonfires. They would burn on the mountain-sides of Piura, Puno, Lima, Arequipa and Trujillo. They would blaze out the name of the man opposite.

She crossed her legs and made the table rock. Ezequiel leant back on his chair. He picked an empty cassette box from the side table where he kept his Dead Sea salts and violet bergamot that smelt of tea. He slid the cassette box under the guilty leg.

"Are we together on this?" he asked, speaking for the first time.

"Abimael?"

"Yes."

"Emilio?"

"Yes."

"Edith?"

"Yes."

"Bonifacio?"

"Yes."

"One final item," said Augusta. "The case of Comrade Chino."

There was silence. Then Bonifacio spoke. "His behaviour puts us all in jeopardy. I recommend he be tried by the Central Committee."

Several elbows descended in the murmur of consensus. Ezequiel was pleased to notice the table did not move. He fastened his gaze on the poster, stroking the folds beneath his chin.

"Comrade Edith," he said, displaying his perfect teeth. "You find him."

One by one the members of the Central Committee embraced Ezequiel and left. Only Augusta remained. She touched his cheek. She didn't bother to hide her concern. He wrapped her in his arms, embarrassed.

"I'll get us something to eat," she said.

Ezequiel walked to the balcony. The sun was setting. He looked at his watch. They had been talking for four hours. A plastic box flickered into life on the right of his balcony. The blue neon letters illuminated the corroded ironwork and the empty plant holders. LIBERTY they flashed. From where he stood, the letters read back to front.

He watched his wife bob across the square and into a shop. Reminded of something, he went inside and opened her bag. What was the name she said? Jones? Not a name he knew. He switched on the cassette recorder. For the first time in three years he dragged a chair to the balcony. He would catch the last of the sun which his ancestors had worshipped. It was meant to be good for his skin.

"The green, green grass of home . . ."

From inside the room came the voice on Augusta's cassette.

Whoever this Jones was, he didn't bear comparison, thought Ezequiel, looking down through the ironwork, onto the roof where the dog was dream-shivering in its sleep and the corner of the iron house where Sebastián was rattling his bowl and the square beyond where three old men sat watching him.

Chapter 27

NOW NIGHT APPROACHES the square. The sun is setting. The sky is full of masato. One by one the lights come on in the Hotel Liberty, in the Bishop's palace and in the fountain where the water shines bright green like Inca Kola.

The square is an ovation of flowers. The smell of copa de oro which has pervaded it since early morning now mingles with acetylene as Don Vásquez ignites his lamp. Suspended from a coat hanger, the lamp illuminates his bottles of red alcohol, his steaming tray of chicken pieces and his newspaper, folded to a syndicated article on Bolívar's journey into exile and an interview, in her Fort Lauderdale home, with a former lavandera from Iquitos.

With the exception of Don Wenceslau and Don García, no one has bought anything all day, but now they queue for chicken; girls rubbing insect-repellent on their shins, a mother wiping her daughter's face, a pair of shoe-shine boys arguing over a sheet of lottery tickets.

In the middle of the square, the benches fill with smartly dressed couples. They watch the flies cluster the lights, they whisper comments about those passing by and, tapping their polished shoes, they listen to the naval band facing the town hall. As the white uniforms break into "Sin ritorno", the younger men snake an arm around necks dabbed with Caliope, Caribe, Madame D'Orly.

"Ah, look!" says Don Wenceslau. "La Palometa!"

Her mouth leafed in red, her hair piled in a hennaed bun, her moustaches swirling, Pía Zumate crosses the square towards the islamic pillars of the Sociedad Española de Beneficiencia. Dreaming of the evening ahead, she smiles manically.

"Tut, tut," says Don García. "Stockings."

"Look!" says Don Wenceslau. "The British lord!"

They follow his quivering hand to the balcony where Ezequiel sits, partially obscured by the ironwork. Don Leopoldo reaches down into his green bag. He produces a leather spectacle case. From it he extracts a pair of half-moon glasses.

In the dark the three men peer, Don Leopoldo most of all.

"There's something not quite right with his face," he says.

But suddenly Don Wenceslau is not interested.

"Look!" he says. "A shoe-shine boy!" He inserts a finger to his mouth. He whistles. At long last he feels ready for his second polish of the day.

Don Leopoldo removes his glasses. The lenses have also brought Eiffel's iron house into focus. He adds another line to his cheeks as he thinks of himself in fine Scotch tweed, drinking rum-coloured beer in the Club of the Dead Parrots. He folds his spectacles and slides them back into their case.

At the other end of the bench, Don García nurses his disappointment as a man joins the girl opposite. It is a disappointment only a visit to the Teletroca will cure.

Next to him Don Wenceslau stretches out his Doocares. "Now that's red, boy, and you know it is . . . "

The three of them are too far from the electricity station to hear the bomb. When the power cuts out, cowling the city and causing the monkeys to howl in their cages behind the Meloka Restaurant, the clock in the cathedral tower is striking half past eight.

They come into the square from Raimondi, round the corner of Fitzcarrald's house and along the pavement towards the town hall. Three of them lurching in a flip-floppy walk.

"Tell you what," says the captain.

"What?" asks Gabriel.

"Let's go to the Teletroca."

"The Teletroca?"

The mate's face creases in a gargoyle grin. He snuffles his approval and elbows Gabriel in the side. Gabriel looks at him. On his pock-marked cheeks, he seems to be wearing make-up.

"Don't you like girls, señor? Or is it boys you like?"

"No," hiccups Gabriel. "I like girls." The statement is bent with tiredness. To his companions it acknowledges arousal.

"Sometimes," says the captain, "the only thing that keeps me going are my balls."

"Echo!" says his mate.

"He can get through two or three a night," the captain tells Gabriel. "It builds up, when you've been on the river."

"To the Teletroca, then," says Gabriel.

"To the Teletroca," the others roar.

They begin crossing the road as a car turns the corner. It yelps to a halt in front of them. Capitán Velarde leans out of his window. "Hey, there! Sh-sh-sh-shift it," he screams, raising his Ray-Bans because he cannot see, then realizing the blackout has put dark glasses over the whole town. Still chanting, the figures move from the road onto the central square.

Furiously, Velarde thrusts his car into gear. His mind is on a million things as he drives out to the municipal electricity station near the airport. His promotion, his shares in Electro-Peru, the news that his wife wants to leave him for a young man she met at a party to celebrate the publication of Jaime Regan's *Hacia la Tierra Sin Mal*. It will be an hour before something triggers the image of the face frozen in his Datsun's headlight, the face of a man who has dogged his steps since more or less the moment he put on a policeman's badge, a man he had imagined to be lying safely in the ground at San Bartolo.

In the square, the captain, the captain's mate and Gabriel walk past the statue of Admiral Grau. They are propelled by the full moon at their backs. They are hauled by their shadows. They walk by without noticing the singer, the drinker or the local historian.

Gabriel trips on the verge, causing a flutter of feathers and a scratching of feet from the pigeons on the calamina roof of the Club de Leones. The others steady him and head off down Calle Nauta.

"It's him," observes Don Wenceslau. "The Chino."

"I would say," adds Don Leopoldo after a certain passage of time, "he has been drinking."

"I would say," says Don Wenceslau, "he has every good reason. What do you think García?"

At first there is no reply to the drinker's question. Then the bench creaks. Don García stands up. He appears to smell the air, but he is preparing to sing. He begins cautiously, forcing the breath from his larynx in a voice that rises steadily and smoothly until the words he sings vibrate in all the cavities of the square, causing the birds on the roof to take flight and his two companions to marvel at the beauty of a sound which suggests to Don Wenceslau that while he might have a cebiche ache, their friend in the trilby has a nest of nightingales in his belly.

"And what is that?" asks Don Leopoldo.

"That," responds the singer, on completing the Mad Scene from *Lucia di Lammermoor*, "is what singing's all about."

"Down here," says the captain. "I'm sure it's down here."

They have reached a track leading from the main road to the river. People pass them from behind. Others emerge from the night. The track's descent is marked by candles in Carnation milk tins. The only other light is from the airport tower, lassoing the stars in dizzy sweeps.

Without power, the dead street lamps are perches for vultures. Every now and then, a bird opens a frayed parasol and floats down towards a rubbish dump. Gabriel smells the sweet refuse. He remembers the place where they dropped Don Miguel, by the waters of Sachachorro.

The captain is mumbling. "Yes, yes. Now I know. Past those trees." They follow him, into the shirtless crowd.

Suddenly, a figure materializes in front of Gabriel. The captain's mate licks his lip.

"Gabriel!"

Dimly, in the flicker of a candle, behind the black wildcat smudges on her face, Gabriel recognizes Edith. He swears. He lifts his hand but she rushes to him.

"Gabriel, come now and we might be able . . . "

"Don't touch me."

"Gabriel . . . "

"You lied." His words cut the air. "You never told me about the mission. You knew all along. Where is she? Hija de puta, where is she?"

"Gabriel, I don't know, believe me. I don't know. But you don't realize. Bonifacio is looking for you. I have instructions . . . "

"How is he dressed this time? Flower-seller? Ballet-dancer? Circus clown?"

"Gabriel, if you come . . . "

He slaps her across the face. The blow throws her back into the night.

"Go to hell. I'm going with my friends . . . " He grabs hold of the captain's mate, into whose rouged face the light reflected from the candles inserts eyes of different colours.

Clapping an arm about the necks of the two men, Gabriel urges them on. The captain's mate winks a farewell in Edith's direction, perhaps mistaking her camouflage for make-up. He flings out a hand.

"The Teletroca!"

It's a well-known fact that only the airport in Belén has a generator – and the Teletroca. They see its light through the trees, flashing from a neon mermaid on the roof. Above her green scales a blue sign glows with the letters TELETROCA. Below, a writhing red line promises The Best Fuck in the Amazon.

The courtyard is a melée of men coming and going. They bounce back along the track on motorbikes. They stroll down to the river. Others sit at benches drinking soup and joking. A woman fans the pot with her skirt. A boy offers cigarettes and sweets from an open briefcase.

By the entrance, an old woman sits at a formica table. For 5 intis she gives out a pink ticket of admission. Between two rooty fingers her other hand riffles through a box and issues contraband Sultan condoms.

"New girls tonight," Cleopatra Zumate tells each customer joyfully. "New girls from Nauta."

In the queue, the captain rubs his hands. He cannot wait to see them. The girls of the Teletroca are famous from Requena to Belén.

"Put a candle in a girl from Brazil," he whispers to Gabriel, "it comes out molten. Put it in a girl from the Teletroca" – his semitic eyes glitter – "it comes out lit."

They pass into a room pulsing with music. When his eyes are used to the low light, Gabriel makes out a bar, some cane chairs along the wall and a short corridor leading into another courtyard. The only source of illumination is a large television on the bar. Five European girls, dressed up as nurses, fellate a bearded doctor on a surgical couch.

"Playing the cornet," giggles the captain. He orders three beers from the barman. "Hey, this is my friend," he tells the man. "He plays the human flute." The barman nods. He lifts the lid on a fridge and produces the bottles.

The captain drinks. He beams tipsily at the television set. Gabriel finishes his bottle. Then he drains the bottle ordered for the captain's mate. The man has vanished.

"Look!" The captain doesn't turn his head. "Pucha . . ." he swears. He cannot believe his eyes. Gabriel tries to look but he is dazzled by the light. Instead, he focuses on the men who stand with arms crossed staring at the screen.

Some of them are old, like Don Tonsurans and the man he speaks to who wears a grey hat and a red handkerchief. Others he recognizes from school: Alberto, who has become a hydrologist. Abel Fonseca who works in the film business. The manager of the plywood factory, José da Silva. Gonzalo Mego, the administrator of the Club de Leones. Dr Lache, the bigamist.

On their faces, like underwater patterns on sand, are the reflections of whatever makes the captain gasp.

Gabriel orders another beer. As he waits for it, his eyes stray to a movement on the green wall behind the fridge, below a rack of Gigi toilet paper. He looks at a small frog. It rests its panting belly on the acrylic O of Dora, one of several names painted in stencilled letters. With another hop it lands on Carmen. With another, on Gloria.

"Angels," he tells the barman. "Lovely angels."

"You should see the girls when they look at this," says the captain. He juts his chin at the screen. "They get really excited, I tell you."

"Where are the girls?" asks Gabriel. He squeezes his palm. It still contains his Sultan.

The captain nods his head at the corridor. "Let's go inspect the merchandise."

The courtyard is a red glow. A cone of multi-coloured light projects the same television scenes onto a wall. In the centre of the wall is a basin, above it painted the words "I fuck. And you?"

There are twelve rooms on either side. In two of them a girl leans with hand on hip against the doorframe. The remaining doors are closed.

The captain leaves Gabriel's side. He stands in the middle of the film, looking at one of the two open doors.

"An open door tempts a saint," he says. As he moves towards it, a penis the size of a paddle ejaculates on his back.

At the end, on the right, a door opens. A man walks to the basin. Gabriel recognizes the captain's mate. A figure takes up her position at the low entrance of the room he has vacated.

Lazily she scratches one leg with another.

Gabriel stumbles towards her. He feels a hand between his legs. He looks up.

It is her.

Chapter 28

THE STORIES DIFFER about what happened that night.

After mulching on it, Don Leopoldo has come down on the side of Capitán Velarde. It is only luck that made him visit the Club de Leones on the very afternoon that Velarde's report is suppressed. "In the interests of the municipality and the Roman Catholic Church," sneers the policeman.

Until Don Leopoldo turned up with that bag of his, which he somehow manages to trip over every time, the policeman could find no one to lend an ear.

"Hey, Leopoldo, come here. You interested in that crazy business? Two brandies, Gonzalo. No one else gives a whore's kiss for what happened. You know what Barrantes said about Elena Silves? He said hers was the love of a bad woman. I mean, shit!"

If Velarde is to be believed, shortly after 9.45 p.m. – the time given by Cleopatra Zumate at the door – a man and a woman forced their way into the Teletroca. They were dressed from head to toe in black. At the time, Señora Zumate passed them off as security police.

"I thought they were looking for the terrorists who blew up the power-station. Either that, Capitán, or they had come to clean their pistols – like you boys do on a Friday night. I didn't know what the woman wanted. It didn't cross my mind they were terrucos."

The two of them scanned the faces at the bar, then walked into the courtyard. According to one of Señora Zumate's girls – one of the vaunted new girls from Nauta – a client was pressing his face against a door by the basin. The door was closed. The girl thought she heard crying on the other side and what could have been the sound of a head knocking against the doorframe.

The man in black approached the client from behind. He put an arm round his neck and jerked him away. The client seemed very groggy, so groggy that he could hardly walk as he was pulled from the courtyard.

The other person, the woman, took his place at the door. She said something through it. A few minutes later the door opened and a girl emerged, wearing a shirt and a pair of trousers. She was weeping hysterically.

Despite the low red light from the bulb above the room, despite the shifting beams from the projector, painting her in the colours of the spectrum, the girl from Nauta recognized the person who had joined them on the journey down river.

"Describe her," said Velarde.

"She was a woman . . . " began the girl.

"Of course she was a woman," said the policeman. "What do you think this is, the Club de Leones?"

But a much older woman.

"She was also a gringa."

The girl saw nothing else. She was watching the two of them disappear into the television room, when her vision was blocked by a man with a toothpick in his teeth and one eye different from the other.

She laughed. "He fucked like a tunchi."

Five weeks later, two bodies were discovered twenty kilometres down stream from Belén, tied together at the wrist and ankle and eaten by fishes. Both had red scarves tied about their skulls. Both scarves contained a powder-burned hole. The bodies were described by Dr Lache, the elderly pathologist, as being "in their late thirties/early forties."

Don Leopoldo's belief that these are the bodies of Gabriel Rondón Lung and Elena Colina Silves is shared by Don Wenceslau. Where Don Wenceslau parts company with Capitán Velarde's version is in the timing of their death.

According to an article Vásquez showed him in *El Oriente*, they were found five weeks later – but they had only been in the river two weeks.

"That leaves three weeks, right?"

"Two weeks and five days."

"Two weeks and five days. But that was the time they had to themselves."

"Why on earth, Wenceslau, would they have had time to themselves?"

"Until it was decided what to do with them." That was why they had died with Pía Zumate's smile on their faces.

Don Leopoldo says there has never been any mention of a smile.

"Yes, there has," says Don Wenceslau. "It was there in Vásquez's paper."

Don Leopoldo cannot conceal the contempt that forms on his lips.

"Journalism," he spits.

Don Wenceslau disregards him. In the end it all comes down to Edith. (He bets a day without masato that her breasts are stunted – so she might shoot arrows, like the Amazon she evidently was. "Only the right breast was stunted," Don Leopoldo points out.)

Obviously, it was Edith who spared them initially. But in the end it had been she who recommended their execution.

"She couldn't live with the knowledge of their happiness," he says dramatically. His voice imitates Don García. He inspects Don García to see if the singer recognizes this, but he doesn't. In the shape of Elena Silves' life Don García sees something worthy of an opera by Donizetti or Verdi. His version of that night differs from the others in one crucial aspect.

Don García believes the lovers are still alive.

But to begin with, he wishes to exonerate Elena from what he interprets as disapproval on the part of at least one of his companions on the bench. His chromatic mind can easily picture how she came to arrive at Señora Zumate's establishment by the river.

He sees the expression on Elena's face when the rivereño mentions the prison massacre. He watches the man produce from his dirty jacket a copy of *El Oriente* with the details of those killed by the military. He feels the fuse inside her go when she sees the name of Gabriel Rondón Lung. He sees it all.

She walks through the stiff grass of Father Maby's lawn and into the carob trees. She doesn't know where she is walking. For one hour, for two hours, for three hours she walks. She goes deeper still into the jungle. She has lost all motive except to walk. The trees rip her clothes. They tear at her face, her hair, her hands which take on the colour and texture and smell of the branches. Towards evening she enters a Devil's Farm, a clearing made by a poisonous tree, full of dead leaves like a park she once visited in Lima. She sits among them. A wind comes up and the leaves rise slowly as if they are snowflakes in the paperweight shaken by her father when he lies on the bed of his sick wife, not knowing what to do. They rise against her where she sits, each leaf a jigsaw piece of memory; and she thinks of her father and mother, who read Kipling to each other and never quarrelled about anything except the properties of hair oil, and her aunt who was always talking of the day she would live in Obidos, in a house with blue and gold stripes on its outer wall to ward off flies and witches who might think they had flown too close to Heaven, and Madre Ana who smelt of Vaseline and Nivea and who could never pass the reproduction of Saint Bernadette without admiring herself in the glass, and pigeons flying from a bell tower, and the lines of a song, and Gabriel whom she had last seen on the cold concrete floor of Hipólito's hut, his face austere with desire. And these fragments swirl against her and about her, rising in a vortex until they become indistinguishable from the vultures who have begun to wheel and eddy on the evening air, waiting to see if she is dead, like the leaves. She closes her eyes.

She sleeps, she doesn't know how long. One morning she reaches a river. On the bank she finds a raft. She takes the raft to what is Dos de Mayo. The current is strong. It carries her past the village. It carries her into the Amazon. A small boat with a thatched roof, like a floating hut, approaches from upstream. It brims with cheerful Indian girls. They have come from the jungle near Nauta, recruited by the man who sits at the engine. They wave. They smile. They reach out their hands and flick water at her. When Elena doesn't respond, they call to the man. The long boat turns, making a wave like a scythe. The girls stretch out to the raft. They hold it. They lift her aboard. She allows them to do this without struggling. She lets them surround her. She lets them embrace her. After three years in the jungle, she knows their ways. Only this time she has no instructions, no comfort, no hope to give them.

No longer sustained by the God she deserted or by the promise of finding again the man she loved, she now wants their simplicity for herself.

In the late afternoon, the noise of the engine dies down. The boat slides onto the bank. The girls step ashore. The man points to a path and they begin walking into the trees. He sees Elena standing back. Go on, he tells her. Go on, you'll lose them. She sets off after them in a trance. Soon they arrive at a building with a large courtyard and a wire mermaid on its roof.

Someone takes off the remnants of her wet, muddy cushma. She is given a bath. Then a new dress. Then shown to a room.

When the man with the strange coloured eyes fills her doorway, she is clean and ready. Like someone quenched with absinthe, thinks Don García, not that he has ever tasted the wormwood spirit.

But it is the sighting of a Venezuelan engineer six months after that night in the Teletroca which convinces Don García the two lovers are alive and reunited.

On a tributary of the Putumayo, a day's journey from the village where he was constructing a new school, the engineer, Firmino Rojas, came upon a group of Indians engaged in clearing the forest.

Recognizing a minga – the custom of gathering neighbours into a work party – Rojas was surprised to see the foundations of an unusually sophisticated building. Curiosity combined with a professional admiration caused the engineer to stand up in his boat.

Directing the Indians was a tall man without a shirt. On his thin chest he had a series of scars. Beside a large bonfire, on which the felled trees were burning, he was talking to someone.

At first the distortions created by the veil of hot air made it difficult for the engineer to see this other person. As the boat moved on he recognized a woman. The woman was white. When the man said something, pointing at the trees, she threw back her head and laughed. When she laughed, it was with her whole body. She was very beautiful.

Neither of them noticed the Venezuelan.

"A romantic extravaganza," says Don Leopoldo.

"Could have been anyone," says Don Wenceslau.

Don García thinks otherwise. For Don García everything ends in song.

In his mission in the jungle, Father Paul Maby hears nothing of this. Along with his flock, he continues to lament the absence of Elena, instinctively looking up whenever a wind moves the carob trees. Somewhere in his secret heart he hopes that Gabriel will find her, but he doubts it. He writes several letters to Eucario Barrantes urging him to make representations to the appropriate authorities. (In passing, he informs Barrantes of strange men who warn that if his Indians show their faces on a certain stretch of water they will be shot. Of late, his Indians have stopped eating fish. Too many bodies, they say, have been found in the river, and they have never been cannibals.)

As expected, Father Maby receives no reply.

At night he often has dreams of being thrust down a dark well by a toothless Virgin Mary who admonishes him with a shake of the egret feathers on her trousered head – sometimes for betraying the secrets of the confessional, sometimes for not trying harder.

In a hotel room somewhere in the country, Presidente Ezequiel continues to scratch the silver dollars proliferating on his arm. The happenings in a jungle town are of little moment to him now the revolution is at hand.

Against the gathering rhythms of early Sinatra, he contents himself with the knowledge that on a given evening his people are able to black out the capital cities of every department in the land, leaving only his bonfired name to vie with the stars and the moon.

In the blackout, Don Leopoldo is dreaming of Cochrane, the gringo, the scientist's son, the firework-maker known up and down the coast as El Diablo, the dashing peer who beat Drake's drum and slipped one midnight with a "Viva el rey" into the Callao fog.

He hears small boats grating the side of Spanish frigates and warm wind in the rigging.

He sees the sky explode with fantastic rockets that zig-zag crazily in all directions, and in all colours, because they have been filled by royalist prisoners with rags and sand and birdshit.

And he smiles at the sight of Spain's great flagship slipping cable into the agitated night, its liberator on deck, his face elated in the saltpetre blaze.

As he dreams the lights come on again in the square.

He finds himself in painful contiguity with Don Wenceslau, scratching his crotch.

"Have patience, fleas, the night is long," says the drinker. He looks at his watch. "You still going to this film, García? If so, I might join you."

He stretches out his arms. He yawns. He examines his feet and the two red shoes shining there.

He gives out a cry.

"I'm sure it wasn't intended," says Don García. "You can tell him tomorrow."

"Just look at that," says Don Wenceslau, leaping from the bench. He is sulphurous with anger.

"Just look," he says.

Don Leopoldo gathers up his bag. He ignores Don Wenceslau, whose feet squirm in their crimson brogues. He ignores Don García, the man who believes Caruso sang in a chicken yard. His mind is on the man opposite, sailing forever in his legendary iron-clad.

He sees the horizon in his eyes, the vertebrae of smoke from six enemy funnels, one of them the *Cochrane*'s. Watching the lamps glint on the face of Admiral Grau, who died outnumbered and outgunned but who has never been more alive, he fancies that he sees Peru's sole hope rise again to give his orders.

A NOTE ON THE TYPE

The text of this book was set in Sabon, a type face designed by Jan Tschichold (1902–1974), the well-known German typographer. Because it was designed in Frankfurt, Sabon was named for the famous Frankfurt type founder Jacques Sabon, who died in 1580 while manager of the Egenolff foundry. Based loosely on the original designs of Claude Garamond (c. 1480–1561), Sabon is unique in that it was explicitly designed for hot-metal composition on both the Monotype and Linotype machines as well as for film composition.

READ MORE IN PENGUIN

In every corner of the world, on every subject under the sun, Penguin represents quality and variety – the very best in publishing today.

For complete information about books available from Penguin – including Puffins, Penguin Classics and Arkana – and how to order them, write to us at the appropriate address below. Please note that for copyright reasons the selection of books varies from country to country.

In the United Kingdom: Please write to *Dept. JC, Penguin Books Ltd, FREEPOST, West Drayton, Middlesex UB7 OBR*

If you have any difficulty in obtaining a title, please send your order with the correct money, plus ten per cent for postage and packaging, to *PO Box No. 11, West Drayton, Middlesex UB7 OBR*

In the United States: Please write to *Penguin USA Inc., 375 Hudson Street, New York, NY 10014*

In Canada: Please write to *Penguin Books Canada Ltd, 10 Alcorn Avenue, Suite 300, Toronto, Ontario M4V 3B2*

In Australia: Please write to *Penguin Books Australia Ltd, 487 Maroondah Highway, Ringwood, Victoria 3134*

In New Zealand: Please write to *Penguin Books (NZ) Ltd, 182–190 Wairau Road, Private Bag, Takapuna, Auckland 9*

In India: Please write to *Penguin Books India Pvt Ltd, 706 Eros Apartments, 56 Nehru Place, New Delhi 110 019*

In the Netherlands: Please write to *Penguin Books Netherlands B.V., Keizersgracht 231 NL–1016 DV Amsterdam*

In Germany: Please write to *Penguin Books Deutschland GmbH, Friedrichstrasse 10–12, W–6000 Frankfurt/Main 1*

In Spain: Please write to *Penguin Books S. A., C. San Bernardo 117–6° E–28015 Madrid*

In Italy: Please write to *Penguin Italia s.r.l., Via Felice Casati 20, I–20124 Milano*

In France: Please write to *Penguin France S. A., 17 rue Lejeune, F–31000 Toulouse*

In Japan: Please write to *Penguin Books Japan, Ishikiribashi Building, 2–5–4, Suido, Tokyo 112*

In Greece: Please write to *Penguin Hellas Ltd, Dimocritou 3, GR–106 71 Athens*

In South Africa: Please write to *Longman Penguin Southern Africa (Pty) Ltd, Private Bag X08, Bertsham 2013*

A CHOICE OF PENGUIN FICTION

The Captain and the Enemy   Graham Greene

The Captain always maintained that he won Jim from his father at a game of backgammon … 'It is good to find the best living writer … still in such first-rate form' – Francis King in the *Spectator*

The Book and the Brotherhood   Iris Murdoch

'Why should we go on supporting a book which we detest?' Rose Curtland asks. 'The brotherhood of Western intellectuals versus the book of history,' Jenkin Riderhood suggests. 'A thoroughly gripping, stimulating and challenging fiction' – *The Times*

The Image and Other Stories   Isaac Bashevis Singer

'These touching, humorous, beautifully executed stories are the work of a true artist' – *Daily Telegraph*. 'Singer's robust new collection of tales shows a wise teacher at his best' – *Mail on Sunday*

The Enigma of Arrival   V. S. Naipaul

'For sheer abundance of talent, there can hardly be a writer alive who surpasses V. S. Naipaul. Whatever we want in a novelist is to be found in his books' – Irving Howe in *The New York Times Book Review*

Earthly Powers   Anthony Burgess

Anthony Burgess's masterpiece: an enthralling, epic narrative spanning six decades and spotlighting some of the most vivid events and characters of our time. 'Enormous imagination and vitality … a huge book in every way' – Bernard Levin in the *Sunday Times*

A CHOICE OF PENGUIN FICTION

A Theft Saul Bellow

Subtle and tense, the tale of the passionate Clara Velde and her stolen ring. 'The warmth, the kindness, the tenderness of *A Theft* overpower criticism' – *Sunday Telegraph*

Incline Our Hearts A. N. Wilson

'An account of an eccentric childhood so moving, so private and personal, and so intensely funny that it bears inescapable comparison with that greatest of childhood novels, *David Copperfield*' – *Daily Telegraph*

Three Continents Ruth Prawer Jhabvala

Last-of-line scions of a prominent American family, spoilt, blindly idealistic and extremely rich, Harriet and her twin brother Michael seem set to prove perfect fodder for the charismatic Rawul of Dhoka and his sinister Sixth World Movement. 'A writer of world class' – *Sunday Times*

The New Confessions William Boyd

The outrageous, hilarious autobiography of John James Todd, a Scotsman born in 1899 and one of the great self-appointed (and failed) geniuses of the twentieth century. 'Brilliant ... a Citizen Kane of a novel' – *Daily Telegraph*

Maia Richard Adams

The heroic romance of love and war in an ancient empire from one of our greatest storytellers. 'Enormous and powerful' – *Sunday Times*

A CHOICE OF PENGUIN FICTION

A Far Cry From Kensington   Muriel Spark

'Pure delight' – Claire Tomalin in the *Independent*. 'A 1950s Kensington of shabby-genteel bedsitters, espresso bars and A-line dresses ... irradiated with sudden glows of lyricism she can so beautifully effect' – Peter Kemp in the *Sunday Times*

Love in the Time of Cholera   Gabriel García Márquez

The Number One international bestseller. 'Admirers of *One Hundred Years of Solitude* may find it hard to believe that García Márquez can have written an ever better novel. But that's what he's done' – *Newsweek*

Lolita   Vladimir Nabokov

Shot through with Nabokov's mercurial wit, quicksilver prose and intoxicating sensuality, *Lolita* is one of the world's greatest love stories. 'A great book' – Dorothy Parker

My Secret History   Paul Theroux

'André Parent saunters into the book, aged fifteen ... a creature of naked and unquenchable ego, greedy for sex, money, experience, *another life* ... read it warily; read it twice, and more; it is darker and deeper than it looks' – *Observer*. 'On his best form since *The Mosquito Coast*' – *Time Out*

Decline and Fall   Evelyn Waugh

A comic yet curiously touching account of an innocent plunged into the sham, brittle world of high society. Evelyn Waugh's first novel brought him immediate public acclaim and remains a classic of its kind.

FOR THE BEST IN PAPERBACKS, LOOK FOR THE 🐧

A CHOICE OF PENGUIN FICTION

The House of Stairs   Barbara Vine

'A masterly and hypnotic synthesis of past, present and terrifying future ... both compelling and disturbing' – *Sunday Times*. 'Not only ... a quietly smouldering suspense novel but also ... an accurately atmospheric portrayal of London in the heady '60s. Literally unputdownable' – *Time Out*

Other Women   Lisa Alther

From the bestselling author of *Kinflicks* comes this compelling novel of today's woman – and a heroine with whom millions of women will identify.

The Old Jest   Jennifer Johnston

Late summer near Dublin, 1920. Even before she meets the mysterious fugitive on the beach, eighteen-year-old Nancy has begun to sense that the old charmed life of the Anglo-Irish ascendancy simply cannot go on forever ... 'Subtle, moving and distinguished' – *Observer*

Your Lover Just Called   John Updike

Stories of Joan and Richard Maple – a couple multiplied by love and divided by lovers. Here is a portrait of a modern American marriage in all its mundane moments as only John Updike could draw it.

To Have and to Hold   Deborah Moggach

Attractive, radical and fecund, Viv has been lucky with life. In return, she is generous with her time and with her love: she can afford to be. And now Viv is giving her sister Ann – sterile, less glamorous, apparently conventional – the best present she can think of: a baby.

A CHOICE OF PENGUIN FICTION

The High Road   Edna O'Brien

Her long-awaited new novel of a lyrical love between two women. 'Contemporary and sophisticated ... *The High Road* is all that I wanted it to be ... the same emotional sensitivity, especially in the arena of sexual passion. The same authority of characterization' – *Guardian*

The Philosopher's Pupil   Iris Murdoch

'We are back, of course, with great delight, in the land of Iris Murdoch, which is like no other but Prospero's' – *Sunday Telegraph*. 'The most daring and original of all her novels' – A. N. Wilson

Paradise Postponed   John Mortimer

'Hats off to John Mortimer. He's done it again' – *Spectator*. Why does Simeon Simcox, the CND-marching Rector of Rapstone Fanner, leave his fortune not to his two sons but to an odious Tory Minister? A rumbustious, hilarious novel from the creator of Rumpole.

The Anatomy Lesson   Philip Roth

The famous forty-year-old writer Nathan Zuckerman decides to give it all up and become a doctor – and a pornographer – instead. 'The finest, boldest and funniest piece of fiction that Philip Roth has yet produced' – *Spectator*

Gabriel's Lament   Paul Bailey

'The best novel yet by one of the most careful fiction craftsmen of his generation' – *Guardian*. 'A magnificent novel, moving, eccentric and unforgettable. He has a rare feeling for language and an understanding of character which few can rival' – *Daily Telegraph*

FOR THE BEST IN PAPERBACKS, LOOK FOR THE 🐧

A CHOICE OF PENGUIN FICTION

The Woman in Black   Susan Hill

Young Arthur Kipps had no suspicion that Eel Marsh House guarded the memories of a pitiful secret – nor did he understand that the black-robed woman who inhabited its shuttered rooms exacted a terrible revenge. 'Authentically chilling' – *Sunday Times*

A Handful of Dust   Evelyn Waugh

From a decaying country estate to the decadent savagery of '30s London society, and finally to a living hell in the Brazilian jungle ... With cold comedy and lacerating irony, Waugh's masterpiece traces the break-up of a marriage.

Animal Farm   George Orwell

'The creatures outside looked from pig to man, and from man to pig, and from pig to man again; but already it was impossible to say which was which.' Orwell's fable of a revolution that went wrong has become the classic satire of the twentieth century.

The Old Devils   Kingsley Amis

This Booker Prize-winning novel about Alun Weaver's and his wife's return to their Celtic roots is 'vintage Kingsley Amis, 50 per cent pure alcohol with splashes of sad savagery' – *The Times*. 'Crackling with marvellous Taff comedy ... this is probably Mr Amis's best book since *Lucky Jim*' – *Guardian*

Him with His Foot in His Mouth   Saul Bellow

A collection of first-class short stories. 'If there is a better living writer of fiction, I'd very much like to know who he or she is' – *The Times*